AMERICAN CRIME STORY

After Prison Comes Vengeance

SIMON WELLINGTON

AMERICAN CRIME STORY

TABLE OF CONTENTS

PART I

CHAPTER ONE

I think the guy was actually surprised when I gave him the 'Fuck off' stare. Either that or he just didn't get it. He wasn't bumming a cigarette from me either way. When I realized he was still in front of me I said, "Buy your own smokes, asshole," with enough menace in my voice to make him tuck his tail and move off to where a few other smokers had gathered behind the bus.

As I watched him try to mooch from them, I took a last drag off my own cigarette, butted it out with my boot, and re-boarded the Montana-bound bus.

Montana. A place to lose myself. A place where there would be time and space to do some thinking.

I'd needed that space for a long time, but there'd always been one more job. And then another, and then one more... It sometimes seemed that there would be no end, but finally, after two years of it, I knew I had to take the time to gather my thoughts or I'd start making mistakes. And if I made mistakes, I'd soon be out of time permanently.

I caught a stare from the long-hair outside my window. Someone had taken pity on him and given him a smoke. I stared back, raised my eyebrows up and down like I was looking for some lovin', and then blew him a kiss. That, especially coming from a face as scarred-up as mine, made him lose interest in the staring contest, and he backed away quickly. I hoped he knew enough to stay clear of me. I was wound up tighter than the top string on a guitar and I knew that it wouldn't take much to set me off.

The driver got on and shut the doors up front, and we rolled out of whatever town it was we'd stopped in. Granola-boy put on his headphones and was soon zoned out into his own private world. I stared off into the meandering hills and let my thoughts come and go, and pretty soon I was in *my* own private world.

A week ago, after a couple of months cleaning up some loose ends up and down the west coast, I'd arrived in Seattle thinking that I'd be able to settle there. With a great music scene, and all those coffee shops, it had seemed like a good place to relax and cool down before my tensions tore me apart; but it hadn't taken long to realize that a 'scene' was exactly what I didn't need. What I needed was peace, and I knew far too much about the dark side of life to get that in any big city.

California was the place I knew best, and there are some pretty remote and quiet places in California, but there were also too many memories for me to ever be comfortable there again. So, I decided to try Montana. I'd never been there, but I'd read and heard a lot about it. It was sparsely populated. Shit, even the big cities were little. And it had a reputation as the kind of place where people were willing to leave you alone as long as you left them alone. Which was exactly what I now knew I wanted—and the sooner, the better. Travelling by bus had sounded like a relaxing way to go, but twelve hours into the trip my butt was starting to get numb and I was wishing I'd flown.

But flying means leaving a trail, and aside from a numb ass this wasn't too bad. Kind of peaceful actually.

I stared off into the empty valleys and rivers, but gradually focused on my own reflection in the window glass. Whatever I was on the inside, the reflection showed a fit and strong-looking man in his mid-thirties. A man who might have been good looking if his face wasn't so banged-up and scarred.

And inside? Well, I had more than my fair share of scars there too, but maybe if I found a quiet place somewhere in the Montana wilderness, I could start the healing process. Find out who Todd Black really was and figure out what he should do next.

As I stared off again into the countryside, I imagined that Ponyboy Curtis, my favorite fictional character, was walking along the side of the road. I could see him outside the window, just like he looked in the movie, **The Outsiders**. The story had moved me, and I related to it better than any other. There was so much of my life that was similar to his story—he was a young teenager trying to live up to what he thought his older brother had wanted him to be. I didn't have an older brother, but I was pretty confused about what the world wanted from me, just like him. And both of us lost our parents when we were young. His were killed in a car accident, mine by home invaders. Whoever had intruded had found my mother and father at home. Dad had been executed with a bullet to the back of his head. My mother had been a good-looking woman. They took their time with her and enjoyed themselves. When they were satisfied with her, and with their haul, she died too.

That left my sister and me to fend for ourselves. I was only nine, but my sister was already thirteen, and would have looked after me had she had the chance. Sometimes I think we could have made it if only ...

Yeah, right. If only ...

We were close and all I can say is that I miss her terribly. Fucking nightmare man, my whole fucking life is a fucking nightmare.

I looked over at the granola head. He was fast asleep with his music still playing. Didn't look like *he* had any demons. Lucky little prick. What the fuck could anybody know about my demons? My demons and what they made me do? Nobody could have a fucking clue.

I don't remember falling asleep, but I woke up, along with everybody else, when the hypnotic motion of the bus ceased. Another rest stop. I grabbed my jean jacket and got off the bus, stretched, and lit a smoke, then watched as the other passengers came out and milled around. There were a couple of old ladies, probably going to visit their grandchildren. Granola-boy kept his eyes fixed on his Walkman as he passed by me, then struck up a conversation with three middle-aged couples. Women with stupid permed hair and men with ties. *Ties* for Christ's sake. Who'd want to wear a tie on a fucking bus ride? Last off was a pair of human hippos who headed straight for the café and started pigging out on pastries.

My eyes took me back to Granola-boy. Pale skin, hair halfway down to his asshole, and a purple acid-wash shirt made him look pretty grungy. And seeing him bumming a cigarette from one of the women he was talking to didn't help change my opinion of him. He wasn't actually a boy, although he sure acted like one. Probably in his late twenties, I figured. What a waste of life.

I guess what bothers me about people like him, people who just float along through life, is that they don't appreciate what they have. I wondered what my life would have been like if things hadn't happened as they did; if I'd had even half the chances that this kid had.

I still remember May 5, 1974, like it was yesterday. The principal of the elementary school I went to came into my classroom and called the teacher out into the hall. A couple of minutes later she came back and took me to his office. I wondered what I had done wrong and what my dad would think when he found out.

But when we got to the office, I saw that my sister Susan was there too, and a whole bunch of adults, all looking serious and not saying anything, and I realized that whatever was going on, it wasn't something I'd done in the schoolyard.

The principal said that the two men, who I remember were wearing pretty much identical blue suits, were from the police, and that the lady was a social worker. I didn't know what a social worker was, and all I remember about her from that meeting was that she had a really fake smile. It took them a while to spit out what was going on. At first, they talked about an "accident", then about what relatives we had, and finally, in the most roundabout way possible, they let it slip that our parents were dead.

I didn't have much of a reaction at first. In my mind, it was only temporary, and mom and dad would surely return soon. My sister, on the other hand, took the news as any normal thirteen-year-old girl would. She went hysterical.

We had only been in the United States for ten months at that point. I don't remember why it was we left Australia. Maybe my parents figured they'd have a better life in America. Wrong fucking guess that was. My grandparents were all dead by then, and we didn't have any other living relatives back at home that I knew of, and none in America either. They asked us a lot of questions about that, but there just wasn't anybody.

I don't think Susan heard much of anything during her crying and shaking. I hadn't seen her so upset before and I think her hysteria was more frightening for me than the news that my parents were dead. I was just totally numb, and I don't think I felt anything that day at all. I wanted my parents and couldn't really accept that they weren't going to be coming back.

To this day, I dream about my childhood in Australia, and wonder what would have become of me if my parents hadn't decided to move. Most of my memories center around nice people, and endless sand beaches and warm ocean. Probably no more accurate than anybody else's childhood memories, but they're all I've got.

We had just moved into a new house two months earlier. We'd rented a place for the first few months until Mom and Dad found their perfect home. A cozy place in a safe district, close to where they worked and near a good school. Safe district my ass. But looking back now, twenty-five years down the road, I can tell you that no district in the United States, or Australia, or any other country for that matter, is really safe.

The principal and the social worker decided that school wasn't an option for the next little while in our lives, and we weren't allowed to go back to our home either. We each had to tell the social worker what we needed for the next couple of days and she would go and get it for us. This upset me but there wasn't much I could do about it. I understand now that seeing the bloody mess that those psychos had left behind would have been a terrible thing for us, but at the time, with my life being taken away from me, I just wanted to go home.

Mrs. Pridy, the social worker, left us with the principal and the police, and returned in an hour with a bag of clothes for each of us. We had both asked for some of our favorite books and toys, but she just smiled her plastic smile and said that we shouldn't worry, that she was going to take us to a nice new home where there would be other books and toys, and that in a few days, when the police were finished in our old house, she could go back and get some other things for us.

The house she took us to was a long way away. It took over an hour to get there, and on the way, she explained about foster care, making it sound like the best thing in the world, like something we should be thankful for. It wasn't the last time she'd lie to me. When we got there, we were both pretty out of it, and I don't remember a whole lot about that night, just that the McLeods—the family she took us to—only had one extra room, and Susan and I fell asleep crying in each other's arms.

So, we were on our own. We didn't have any living relatives that we knew of in the United States. Nor were we aware of any others back in Australia except for my mother's sister and we had no idea where she was. She was always marrying men and moving in with them, then looking for someone new when they divorced her. She had been married five times that my mom knew of, but they hadn't kept in touch for years, so who knew what number she was up to now, or where she might be living. So, because Mrs. Pridy couldn't place us with any living relatives, we had no choice but to enter the foster care system. I remembered trying to explain that my sister could look after the both of us, but Mrs. Pridy wouldn't have any of it.

11

In the morning we went downstairs and joined everyone for breakfast. We were still pretty messed up about losing our parents, but at least we had each other. The McLeod family seemed nice, and, for the first time since the day before, we started to take some interest in life. Then the bomb dropped. Mrs. McLeod said something like "Now Susan, when you're finished breakfast, you go and wash up and get your things so that you'll be ready when Mrs. Pridy comes to get you."

At first we thought that she meant that Susan would be going to school after all, or maybe to see a counselor, but what they told us was that I would be staying there, with the McLeods, and that Susan would be taken to live with another family. We pleaded with them to let us both stay, but to no avail. The decision wasn't theirs to make, it was the call of the Social Services department, and a few minutes later Mrs. Pridy showed up.

We pleaded with her too, but it didn't help. Social Services had decided to place us in separate homes, and we might as well make the best of it, she said. We tried to plead more, but she just gave us a bunch of shit about how it was very bad for brothers and sisters to remain together in the same foster home and that it was in our own best interests that we were being separated. We both cried even harder because we were being taken away from the only other person left in our lives. Where was the sense in that? No one answered me then and no one has been able to answer since. I thought then, and I still believe it now, that that was the cruelest possible thing that could be done to children in a situation like ours.

When I started to get angry Mrs. Pridy got angry too and told Susan to hurry up and get her clothes. We clung to each other desperately, and when they separated us it became a bawling and screaming match. Both of us were being as loud and as vicious as we could be. Mr. McLeod picked me up and carried me to his son's room and ensured that I would stay there by closing the door and standing in front of it. I howled and threw myself at him, but he was far too big for a nine-year-old to budge. He didn't hit me or hurt me, he just made sure I couldn't get past him. All I could do was flail away at him as Susan called out for me.

I saw my sister three months later at a scheduled visit in the presence of the social worker. She had changed dramatically. She hardly spoke, and mostly sat curled in a ball on her chair. For a while she didn't seem to recognize me, and when she did, tears rolled down her face. She seemed distant and alone. She looked skinny and unkempt, her hair was all matted, and her clothes were dirty. We didn't speak much but mostly just looked at each other, then sat together in the chair hugging. I think we both wondered if this was all a dream or if it really was us together again.

It ended all too soon, and once again we had to be forcibly detached from one another. The next day, when I told my foster mom how Susan had looked, and asked when I could visit her again, she got really upset. Not at me, more like she was sad and angry about something she couldn't do anything about. She told me that the social worker felt that the visit had done more harm than good, and that we would have to wait quite a while.

I couldn't understand what was going on. In my nine-year-old mind it was obvious that Susan had been sad to see me go, so how could anyone say that we shouldn't see each other? I missed her, and she missed me. We desperately needed each other. Why couldn't the Pridy woman understand that?

My own life gradually got a little better. I still missed my parents terribly and wished that I was back in Sydney where I had friends and where my parents would still be alive, and my sister would be okay. It hurt me to think of Susan being so miserable, but the McLeods were decent people who did the best they could to make a new life for the lost little boy they had taken in. Three months later though, when they finally let Susan and me have another visit, it was obvious that her life had only gotten worse.

She was even skinnier, so thin that I could see her cheekbones through her skin. The energetic older sister that I used to know had completely disappeared, and the girl before me hardly looked at me. It was as if she had completely given up on life. The sound of my voice brought tears to her face and I thought at first that I had hurt her in some way, but then she clung to me and I knew that it wasn't me that was hurting her.

She didn't talk, just made little mumbling noises, and hung onto me like she was a preschooler and I was her teddy bear. When the visit ended, she pretty much went crazy. She was obviously terrified of going wherever they wanted to take her. She screamed and screamed. Twenty years later I still have nightmares about those screams.

The next time I saw Susan was at the official hearing where we were declared wards of the state. She was anorexic. I didn't know that word back then, but it was obvious that she was deathly ill. Just a skeleton with clothes on.

The judge made the official decision to declare us wards of the state of California. I didn't know exactly what that meant, and in fact I didn't really pay much attention. I couldn't take my eyes off Susan. She was in her own world through the entire hearing and rarely answered any of the few questions that the judge asked her. Just sat slumped in her chair with her head down, staring at the floor.

When it was over and we were all getting our coats on, Susan finally raised her head. She looked at me—we locked eyes and our souls intertwined. I felt love and I know she did as well. I saw a smile on her face as she looked in my direction on her way out of the courtroom. It was the last time I saw her alive.

A week later the social worker showed up at the house. It came fast and abruptly. My sister had killed herself for "reasons that we can only speculate about."

I don't remember anything more of that day. My next memory is of waking up in the hospital the next day morning with bandaged arms, legs and head. Apparently, I had run across the room and crashed through a window, gashing myself deeply on the broken pieces of glass. I was fortunate that we'd been on the first floor, otherwise I might have killed myself.

Fortunate? There were certainly times in the next ten years when I wished I *had* been killed…

CHAPTER TWO

The bus hit a rough patch in the road, and I was jarred back into the present. Better to be looking at the view outside the bus window than the view inside my head. Even though my last meeting with Mrs. Mia Pridy hadn't been as bad as all the others; not for me anyway. She was one of the first I tracked down after I got out of prison—one of the first ones to die. I shook my head in disgust as I remembered the records I'd copied from hospitals, clinics, and Social Services offices. Records that showed beyond any doubt that she knew what was happening to Susan. Knew that she was being abused by her stepfather.

Abused. Shit. "Abuse" doesn't even *begin* to cover what that animal did to her. And Pridy knew. She fucking knew. Three doctors and two hospitals had notified her office of what was going on, and she just ignored it. "Too many cases to help them all," she whined when she realized what I was going to do to her. "Not my fault."

"It was just the way the system…"

System my ass. It was Pridy's willingness to let a little girl live in Hell that had killed my sister, and even though I couldn't go back in time and change anything, I eventually made her pay.

After my sister's death, I just dried up inside. I wanted to be with my parents and my sister again, and I gradually shut the rest of the world out. The McLeods were good people who obviously cared about their own son and the two foster kids that they were looking after, but they weren't my parents. They gave me healthy food, decent clothing, and as much love as they could, but it wasn't enough. How could it have been?

I had cut myself up pretty badly jumping through the window. It took a few months to heal and left me with some spectacular scars, but my body did heal. It was my soul that didn't do so well. I felt totally alone. I felt left out and forgotten about. I felt like no one really cared about my existence, about whether I lived or died.

I also felt anger and resentment, and I took those feelings out on whoever was closest to me. I feel sorrow now that I couldn't accept what the McLeods had to offer, that I put them through so much misery, but after the emotional shit-kicking I'd taken, I didn't really have a lot of control. I lived in two states: total withdrawal and total rage. Nothing in between.

I stayed in hospital for a few days, and then at my foster home for a few weeks. The McLeods kept a watchful eye over me and they tried to help. Mrs. McLeod often tried to start conversations, but I just wasn't much interested. I no longer trusted this world, so I created my own, and spent as much of my time there as I could.

And if home was bad, school was worse. I'd always liked school in Australia, and my first school in America hadn't been too bad. I didn't know anybody, and I guess I had a funny accent which made it hard for the kids to understand me, but I was starting to get along okay when my parents were murdered. My teacher at the school I was transferred to when I moved to the foster home had a really fat ass and a mustache. Her name was Mrs. Williams and she loved to chastise kids in front of the entire class. We all had to stand up and say, "good morning Mrs. Williams," every single day when she walked into our classroom.

I was one of her favorite people to pick on, apparently because my accent made her believe that I thought myself better than the others. What a load of shitballs. Far from being better than anyone else, I was treated like dirt by the other kids, and pretty much accepted it. Recess and lunch hour were times of torment for me. The teasing started with a few kids, then more, and soon I was everybody's favorite punching bag. At that age it was mostly pushing and slapping and there wasn't much blood spilled, but it certainly was a steppingstone for what I was to become later in my life.

The principal, a man named Sumner, was my first personal encounter with an abuser. He coached the basketball team, and even though the gym was in a separate wing, you could hear him all over the school, screaming out, "Press, press," or yelling at the players for not doing what he wanted. He also hit kids behind closed doors. He was a big man: six-two, and maybe two-hundred pounds, and the kids he was knocking around were elementary schoolers. Eight-and ten-year-olds. He was a total prick, a grown man who got his rocks off beating little kids. Killing that fucker had been a right pleasure.

I first came to his attention about two months after I started at his school. This was before my sister died, and I was just beginning to come out of the shell I had gone into after the death of my parents. I was playing soccer on the playground with a bunch of kids. Since I was the new kid, and they were mostly older than me anyway, they put me in goal, where before long I stopped a missile of a shot with my groin. I was curled up on the ground, gasping for air and trying not to puke, when the kid that had nailed me started laughing and teasing me about faking it to get attention.

His name was Ian something or other. I didn't really know him, or much about him, except that he was captain of the basketball team and Sumner's pet.

I eventually managed to stand up, and while he was still laughing at me, I gave him a full-power shot to the gonads to see if he wanted to attract some attention too. He dropped to the ground trying to breathe, and I stumbled over to where I could lean against the wall to try to recover. I figured we were even, and was just starting to smile about it when I picked up fast movement coming towards me and the next thing I knew Mr. Sumner had slammed me back against the wall, then grabbed me by the throat and lifted me off my feet.

Years later, in prison, I came to know the kind of glare that came into his eyes then. His pupils dilated and the whites of his eyes grew huge. He was totally focused on me and his grip tightened on my throat as he began smashing my body against the wall. He looked down towards Ian who was still curled up on the ground, gurgling and sucking in air, then pinned me against the wall and screamed something like, "You wanna try that shit with me?"

I like to think that if he hadn't been choking me, I'd have tried to say 'yes.'

The next day, about mid-afternoon, I was called down to his office. My social worker was there, and Mrs. McLeod, my foster mother. Sumner had had enough time with them to paint a disturbing picture of me as a boy who was constantly violent and uncontrollable. Not only had he convinced them that I had attacked a smaller boy and would have crippled him had not he, Sumner, come to the rescue, but also that this was only the latest in a string of unacceptable outbursts.

I was completely unable to respond. I was frightened that if I said anything, he would beat me again, in fact I was so terrified that I couldn't even shake my head to deny him. I just sat, speechless, staring at the floor, as he said that, as of that day, I was expelled from his school.

I know now what he was doing, of course. He knew he had gone too far, attacking me on school grounds where other children could see what he had done, but he also knew that if he started the big lie and got rid of me right away he'd never have to worry about it. But on that day, I didn't understand, and could only tuck my tail and take it, like a dog being whipped.

* * *

The bus rolled on, daylight turned to darkness, and eventually I fell into an uneasy sleep.

During the first two years following my release, as I lived out the plans I had made while doing my time, I had slept fairly well—something I hadn't done from the day my parents died—but over the course of the last six months or so I'd begun having trouble at night again. Restlessness, anxiety, sweats, nightmares… So letting the motion of the bus take my mind off my past and lull me to sleep was a welcome relief, and I was more than a little pissed off when the granola-head two rows back woke me up by turning on his music. Me and most of the other passengers unlucky enough to be seated near him.

Music is important. Every man should listen to some form of music, but 5 a.m. on a Greyhound is what headphones were invented for, and this dickhead was using a ghetto blaster. Maybe he figured it was the middle of the night and no one would notice if he didn't turn it up too loud. Maybe he didn't care. And maybe he didn't care if the smoke from the cigarette he'd just lit bothered anyone.

The other passengers were mumbling to each other and kind of glaring at him, but most of them were meek-looking grayheads, so it looked like it was going to be my job to let him know what his place in the world really was.

I walked back to his row and dropped into the empty seat beside him. "Put out the smoke and turn off the jukebox."

Maybe he figured that because there were so many people around there was no way anything bad could happen to him. Maybe he was just stupid. Whichever, he gave me his best 'fuck you' stare and started to take a big drag off the butt.

Wrong thing to do. I had the cigarette in one hand and his hair in the other before he could inhale. I pulled him around and yanked him down so that he was face up with his head in my lap. He couldn't move because I had his hair, and he couldn't talk or yell because all the wind had gone out of him when my knee nailed him in the back on his way down. I brought the cigarette slowly toward his eye, stopping when it was close enough that he could feel the heat.

"Any more bullshit from you, and I butt the next one out in your face. You understand that, fuckhead?"

I spoke quietly so no one else could hear, and the way I was leaning over him no one could see what was going on either. "Now I'm going to let you go, and you're going to sit up, and you're going to keep your mouth shut for the rest of this trip. If you say one word to anybody, or do anything, anything at all to mess this ride up for any of the other passengers, the next time we stop I'll take you out behind the station and I'll break every single one of your fingers. You understand that?"

I eased off on his hair enough to let him nod.

"Fine. Now sit up and be a good boy." I handed him back the cigarette. "Butt this out, turn off the sound, and don't do anything to make me notice you again."

It was still night outside, and now that the music had stopped, I drifted back into a light sleep.

By early evening we had reached Kellogg, Idaho, where we had a full hour stopover. I was first off, and, as I had at every other stop, I lit up a smoke and didn't stray too far from the bus while the driver had the luggage compartment open for those who weren't going any further. What I really wanted to do was open my suitcases and make sure everything was okay, but I resisted the urge and just hung around, smoked, and enjoyed the sunshine and the fresh air.

It was a small town, no pollution, hardly any noise, clean air, mountains on the horizon, and a gentle breeze. The sun was still warm, and the cool evening air felt good against my face. I could feel myself beginning to unwind.

When the driver shut the luggage compartment and headed into the café, I turned onto the street and walked a few blocks to the edge of town, where I found a big rock not far off the road, facing the setting sun. I sat down and leaned back against it and looked up at the forested hills around me and felt alive for the first time in two decades. I had made the right decision to leave the city and my old life behind.

I let the sun work on me and drifted back to the years that followed my expulsion from Jefferson Elementary School. They'd been hard years. Hard for me, hard for everyone else whose life intersected with mine. By my eleventh birthday I had been in four different foster homes and expelled from two more schools. I became destructive with my anger. I didn't feel safe or comfortable being in a clean room, so I would always trash it. I slept on the floor in a corner with my back against a wall, or underneath the bed, wrapped up in a nest of blankets, and I always placed something—thumbtacks when I could get them, crumpled newspapers when I couldn't—on the floor inside the door to announce the arrival of any intruder.

Some of my foster families would try to clean up my room, although they usually gave up after a while, but most of them didn't really give much of a shit what I did as long as I stayed out of their hair and they got their checks on time.

In school we were sometimes asked to draw pictures or paintings of things we saw inside our heads or how we felt on a given day. I think I freaked the shit out of my teachers because I drew pictures of decapitated people, of forests being bombarded with rainstorms of falling blood, of cars running over old ladies. Just my personal Kodak Moments. They'd send me to the school counselors, and sometimes to shrinks they brought in, but none of those so-called experts ever told me how to make any sense out of my family's deaths or how to bring them back.

For the first few months following Susan's death I was pretty much numb to my surroundings and to the people around me, both those few who tried to help, and the many who didn't. Eventually though, I woke up to the fact that my classmates considered me the freak of the year, and as soon as I responded, the torment began. For a while I took the teasing at recess and lunch and the pushing and shoving after school, but gradually the pushing grew into punching, and the punching into more serious stuff. I was in my own world most of the time but getting shitkicked hurt just as much there as it did back on planet earth, so eventually I began to fight back. Before long, it seemed like I was in a fight almost every day, and in a few months, I had established a reputation of sorts for being handy with my fists and shoes.

I wish the old story that establishing a reputation for toughness would keep others from picking fights was true, but the reality was that the more I defended myself, the more kids came out of the woodwork to fight me in order to prove how tough *they* were. Word got around to neighboring schools, and by the time I was in eighth grade it seemed that I was working my way up a list of opponents that would never end.

What these kids didn't understand was that I had an edge they could never have. I wanted to die. Everything that I loved had been taken away from me. No one else cared if I lived or died, so I didn't give a fuck either. Fighting offered the possibility of release, and as long as the release was violent and bloody, I didn't care if I lost.

Frightened mothers soon began to complain to principals at both the new schools that I was sent to. Their children were bruised and bloodied, I had done the bruising, therefore the blame must be mine. What no one seemed to care about was that these kids came looking for me. I probably got in more fights at school than anyone else in the whole country, but I don't think I ever tried to start one. Maybe I'd start swinging without much provocation, but I didn't actually go looking for fights.

At least the principals at the next couple of schools weren't as bad as Sumner had been. They both tried to help me themselves, and to get counseling for me, and it wasn't their fault that it didn't work. For me, with everything in my life gone, what was the point of talking about it? After what had happened, I trusted no one and I certainly wasn't going to talk about my feelings with some dickhead counselor at school.

The foster homes were a lot worse than the schools. The McLeods had been caring people, and had genuinely tried to help me, but I hadn't been ready for help, and when I began threatening the other kids who lived there with my fists, the social services people moved me out at the McLeods' request.

Other foster homes appeared nice and the people appeared helpful in front of the social worker, but as soon as they had me on my own, things would quickly go to shit. The food I got in prison never tasted like much, but at least it was semi-nutritious. In most of the homes I lived in the foster kids considered themselves lucky anytime canned ravioli was on sale at the supermarket. We were fed a diet of mostly Kraft dinner and instant soup. Same with clothes. We were supposed to get new clothes every once in a while. Nothing special, but the families got a clothing allowance and if we needed a raincoat, we were supposed to be able to get it. Instead we usually got ratty stuff from second-hand stores and the foster families pocketed the difference.

I was never sexually abused like my sister had been, but I was certainly smacked around, pushed, and beaten on a regular basis, and locked in my room for long periods of time without access to the bathroom. I shat in the coffee can that I kept my marbles in if I had the absolute need and cleaned it out when I was released from my confinement.

This became the normal pattern of living for me, and when the bad stuff happened, I simply zoned out into my private magic world.

My average stay in a foster home was four to six months. If things got too bad, I would grab a weapon and threaten people. This usually led to a beating, but the second or third time I'd do it, the family would call Social Services to get rid of me.

When I was about eleven, I started smoking. I bought the cigarettes from a group of kids at my school who sold all sorts of stuff for cash. If there was something you needed, and couldn't get or couldn't afford, you could just place an order with the recess boys, as I called them. They were happy to take the money and some of them were even younger than I was. At first, I didn't understand where they got the stuff they sold, or how they could sell it cheaper than a store could sell it, but eventually I figured it out. Can't say it bothered me very much one way or the other. After what had happened to my mother and my father and my sister, it was hard to worry very much about the recess boys ripping off the corner store for cigarettes or stealing a Walkman for me from the local mall.

Despite all the things I've done, I don't think that I'm a bad person, and I sometimes wonder what my life would have been like if Social Services actually did what it was set up to do. If there had been the money and the will back then to take proper care of orphans and children in trouble, then maybe I'd be a priest or a doctor today, instead of a serial murderer. But there wasn't enough money, and there wasn't the will. Americans like to think of themselves as civilized, caring people. But what they really care about is keeping themselves from feeling guilty, and the way they do that is to give money.

Not too much though. Just enough so that they can say that a few pennies of their tax money are going to help people in trouble, and then they're comfortable. But nobody wants to give very **much** money, and they sure as hell don't want to get involved themselves, so they elect governments that they know won't give too much away to welfare bums (Like me? Is a nine-year-old orphan a "welfare bum"?) and then they close their eyes.

End of story. They've done their part, and if a bunch of petty criminals want to sexually and physically abuse helpless kids in order to get paid for being foster parents, it's not their fault.

The visits to my social worker and to the counselors didn't help much either. I didn't trust people. I mean, given what had happened to me, how could I? And the people who were supposed to be helping me had their problems too. I didn't know anything about governments and budgets when I was a kid, but I know now that even those people who genuinely cared were in an impossible situation. They simply didn't have the budget to do their job properly. The average load for a social worker was around a hundred cases. Realistically, for me to have had a chance at any kind of sane life, I'd have needed a full-time social worker of my own, plus loving foster care, plus a lot of psychiatric help.

Needless to say, I didn't get it. What I got instead was a social worker who didn't care what happened to me, foster families who, with only two exceptions, treated me worse than a slave, and the odd visit with an overworked psychologist.

Did any of you out there lose any sleep while my sister was being raped? While I was being beaten and malnourished? While ten thousand other kids were being raped and beaten? Or did you sleep well, comforted by the knowledge that, through your tax dollars, you had done your best to help us?

I sure as hell lost sleep. My nights were plagued with nightmares of torment and death, carnage and rape. And once in a long, long time, a dream of open green meadows with tall grass growing wild. Just that. No deer, no people, no fluffy clouds. Just a grassy meadow like my mother used to tell me about from her childhood in New Zealand. I'm not a dream analyst, and I don't know what that dream meant, or even if it actually meant anything, but I'm pretty sure that if I hadn't had it once in a while, I'd have killed myself long before my sixteenth birthday.

Reading and writing, and all the other school subjects, didn't play much of a part in my life. I could print by the eighth grade, but I couldn't write. I had a terrible time reading, but as I got lonelier, I consoled myself with books and spent a lot of time with them in my room at whatever foster home I was living in. My literacy level hadn't changed much since my parents' death, so reading was a struggle, but I kept at it because I knew that books offered me another way to escape. I can't say that I became some kind of literary genius, or even a very good reader, but I did get better, and I sure enjoyed the way that reading could take me out of this world and into a different, better one.

I started hanging around a nearby 7-11 after school and in the evenings. I didn't pay much attention to my curfews and I knew there would be a price to pay when I got home, but there was always a price to pay for something in the homes, so I didn't really care. There were some other kids who hung out there, but I didn't really get close to any of them. Mostly it was a place off the school grounds where I could get in more serious fights, the kind that gave me a better chance to cover up one kind of pain with another.

Some of my opponents fought fair and others had their friends jump in to give me a real shitkicking, but I didn't care. Bring one or all, step right up and get your pound of flesh. *But if I don't die, then friend, you're gonna suffer!* That was my motto. My life's frustrations just oozed out of my fists and feet. I was only twelve at that time. Almost four years had passed since my parents and sister had died, and all I wanted was to die and join them— to feel no more pain—but it had to be at the hands of someone else.

I'm not sure why I didn't consider some more practical form of suicide. Maybe I didn't really want to die. Maybe in some twisted way I blamed myself for what had happened and wanted punishment. Maybe it was something about that weird dream of the meadow. How would I know? Maybe a shrink could figure it out, but I sure couldn't.

Even for those who want time to stop in the most final and permanent way, it continues to pass. I did not die at the hands of any of the neighborhood kids, and I was not prepared to take my own life, so eventually I found myself climbing the steps to the main door of Sutherland Junior High School. How did I get there? Simple: my last school had been so bad that I, along with several others, was simply passed so that the teachers would be rid of us. It was a kind of buck-passing, but I can understand that a teacher has only so much to give. A student must want to learn. You can't force him, and I was one of the many who just couldn't be bothered.

Things were different here. There were four times as many students, the tough kids were bigger and meaner, and the girls started growing tits. Sex was a common subject in the hallways and on the campus. And during lunch break and after school, somebody's ghetto blaster was always roaring.

I was more curious than scared, but I didn't go looking for fights for the first two months that I was there. I kept to myself and observed. Instead of going home right after school, I walked around and watched the school's teams play and practice.

The school had a soccer team, a football team, a rugby team, and a tennis team. Tennis was not only boring, but pointless. Who could get anything out of batting a ball back and forth across a net? Back and forth, back and forth. Boring. Basketball was sort of like tennis, but with hands instead of rackets. A lot of running back and forth without anything to make it interesting. Football was okay, there was some good action, but there were so many rules that it seemed like the players spent about ten times as much time standing around doing nothing as actually playing. The game that I liked to watch most was rugby. It was really cool. Like football without any rules. Fast and violent.

I fantasized about playing. I knew that I'd never do it; there was no way I'd even talk to anyone about it, let alone actually try out for a team, but it was definitely cool to be at least a little bit interested in something besides getting killed in a fight or disappearing into a book.

During lunch break I usually just sat in the hall with a book on my lap to make it look like I was reading, but what I was really doing most of the time was listening to the music that the older kids played on their ghetto blasters. I'd never paid any attention to music before, it just plain hadn't interested me, but punk rock had just started to become huge, and what I heard around the school caught my attention.

It was also the time of the mod revival. Some of the older kids dressed up in suits when they came to school. I didn't know anything about mod style, I just thought they were a bunch of schmucks looking for attention. I mean, who in their right mind would want to dress up in a fucking suit every day? What purpose did it serve? I didn't have any real problem with them, and even if they were sort of stupid-looking, I liked listening in on their music. But then one day they decided, I guess just for a joke, to stuff one of the new kids into his locker and lock him in.

They didn't actually hurt him; after all, the lockers were well ventilated, and the school custodian got the lock open soon enough, so I figured that it was just a stupid prank and not any of my business.

That changed during lunch hour a few days later when a group of them charged down at me as I stood in front of my open locker. It was pretty obvious what they had in mind, and when the first suit-head tried to grab me, I shut off and let fly, knocking him flat on his ass with a bloody nose. I got the next one with a boot in the nuts, and when he doubled over in pain, the seat of his pants ripped quite loudly. The crowd that had gathered round us started hooting when it became obvious that he had nothing on underneath those skintight trousers. Even some of the other mods started laughing and they gathered up the two wounded guys and walked away, leaving me alone again, feeling a bit like some kind of zoo animal being stared at by the crowd.

I resumed my reading position on the hallway floor and didn't say anything, and pretty soon everyone got bored and wandered off. I watched as one of the kids who hung out in the punk crowd shut his locker and headed for the lunchroom.

Shut it but didn't lock it. I waited for the halls to clear and then moved to his locker. I looked to my left and then to my right. All clear. I opened it up. The locker door had a lot of posters on it of bands like the Sex Pistols and the New York Dolls. There were books on the bottom floor and up on the top was a shoebox filled with copied tapes and a Walkman. I grabbed a handful of tapes, shut the door, locked it and was back at my own locker in ten seconds.

I had nothing to play the tapes on, and for some reason, stealing the Walkman hadn't seemed right, so I started saving some of my lunch money. Within a month I had enough to buy a cheap cassette player from the recess boys. That night, after I had totaled my room as per normal, so that I felt safe, I plugged a tape into the recorder. The sounds on the tape were loud and angry, which was kind of how I felt a lot of the time, so I listened to it over and over. The tape was a copy of a copy, with nothing written anywhere on it, but it was my introduction to music, and I loved it.

Music allowed me to drift into realms I'd never been to before. When the lights were off and the music was on my mind, I would get a kind of freedom, and I could float away.

From then on, I made it a habit to listen in on the conversations of the punks and the other kids who hung around with them. A lot of the time they talked about stuff that didn't interest me, but music seemed important to them, and they often talked about bands, or compared musical tastes, or what radio stations were best, or where to get good deals on records and tapes. Some of the people in their group weren't punks at all, but they were different from regular kids. I guess they were all different from the norm, so they stuck together.

One day, one of the non-punk kids brought in a tape that he was really excited about. He said it was "ska," and played it really loud till one of the teachers made him turn it down. It was way different than the punk rock that they usually played. I liked the punk because it was all about the anger and violence that I felt, but this new stuff wasn't like that. It sort of took hold of me and made me feel better about everything.

At first, I thought "Ska" was the name of the band, but it wasn't. It was the name of this kind of music, and the bands that played it were mostly from England, where it was just catching on. Over the next few days, as the older kids brought new tapes to school, I was introduced to The Specials, English Beat, Selector, plus some whose names I never found out. Instead of reinforcing my pain, the way punk did, ska took my pain away. The music made me come alive and I felt tingling sensations on my hands, on my feet, and one time, while taking a piss actually, I realized I was humming, something I hadn't done in four years, and it felt weird. I needed to get my hands on some of this stuff.

The next week I skipped a school day to check out music stores. After paying bus fare I didn't have much money, but back then security in music stores was pretty lame, and I didn't have any trouble picking up a few tapes. I spent that night locked in my room, safe from everyone and everything. I listened to the music and I felt a little bit of myself come back to life.

On that same night, I also thought of my sister and couldn't help but cry. I was still alone and that made me angry again, but at least now, there was music to help me through the anger.

I wasn't much of a student, and the foster home I was in at that time was pretty fucked but getting into junior high seemed to have changed my life around a bit, and for the better. No fights, so I wasn't quite as full of pain all the time, and the discovery that music could help me through the times when I was angry and miserable.

Sometimes I wonder what might have happened if I'd walked a different way when I went outside the next day. Would I have turned from the path I was on, would I have had a normal life? Or would the world have found another way to make sure I followed my fate?

CHAPTER THREE

Like I said, for the first couple of months I kept totally to myself. At lunch, I stayed in the hall near my locker and read, or pretended to read, and the closest I got to having anything to do with anyone was eavesdropping on some of the conversations that the punks and their friends had, and sometimes watching the sports teams practice after school. But the day after I listened to the new tapes in my room, I decided that I might as well check out what was happening outside at lunch, and I started walking around the school grounds. I wasn't really paying much attention to anything, just sort of walking here and there, when this group of black kids got in front of me and started pushing me around and asked what I was doing on their turf.

I had no idea that I'd entered gang turf, and I would actually have walked away if they'd let me, but they were primed to fight, and never gave me the chance.

I wish I could say I beat them all, or even made a good showing, but there were too many of them, and they did a number on me. In fact, I thought that it might finally be the end. We were in a kind of corner, behind the tennis courts, and it was only by chance that one of the teachers on yard duty happened to walk past before they could finish me off. He started yelling, and fortunately, or unfortunately, the guys stopped laying the boots to me and split, leaving the teacher with a bloody, swollen pulp called Todd Black. He called for some help and managed to get me to the school nurse's clinic. She checked me over thoroughly, iced my eyes and lips and then drove me home, because I was in too much pain to walk very well.

The next day my knees were so bad that I couldn't walk at all. They had done a great job, but I hadn't left this Hell, and from that point on, my life at junior high became a rerun of life in elementary school with the big difference that because I was now in the lowest grade, pretty well everyone was bigger than me, and the shitkickings I took were more severe.

It didn't help that the family I was with at that time was practically starving me. It was probably the raggedy clothing they gave me that first caught my teachers' eyes, but it wasn't long before the lack of decent nutrition in my diet caused my teeth to loosen and my hair to start falling out. I tried to use eyeliner on my sideburns and scalp to keep anyone from noticing, but I also became apathetic and unresponsive, and eventually some of the teachers did notice, and did something about it.

Social Services came down on the foster family, and I soon had better-fitting clothes on my back, and food with some real nutritional value. My hair grew back, I felt more energetic, and I started to put on weight. There had been no change of heart in my foster parents; they didn't give a shit one way or the other about me or any of the other three kids in their home, but they knew that if they didn't look good in the eyes of the Social Services Department there was a chance they'd lose the checks they got each month. It was either feed and clothe the kids a little better, or risk losing it all.

As I got to know the neighborhood I found places to hang out, and other places that I used as thinking spots; places I could go when I felt like ditching school, where I could fantasize about other realities, or just listen to music. Ska music was all about good fun, which was something I had pretty much forgotten about, and the music the punks called "oi" seemed to be entirely about anger and getting back at the systems that had caused everyone harm. Four years in foster care had taught me all I needed to know about how the system could fuck people over, and both ska and oi helped me deal with it even though they were about as opposite as two kinds of music could be. Maybe having a friend would have helped, but I still had no way of making friends with anyone. I could trust my music and I could trust myself. That was it.

My nightmares slowed down to only a couple each week, and so did the fights, but both became more intense, and ninth grade turned out to be as painful as eighth, seventh, and sixth. The cycle of violence that I thought I might have left behind started up all over again with the beating I took from the black gang and reached a climax one day in the week before school ended the next spring.

School was over for the day, and I was headed for the 7-11 when I heard the familiar sounds of a fight coming out of an alley. I hustled to the entrance and saw that it was someone getting a beating from four of those same black kids that did the number on me in the fall. A bald-headed kid that I had seen hanging out with some of the punks was getting badly thrashed and was pleading for it to stop. As far as I could tell he wasn't looking for a scrap like I always was, and in that moment, I saw Susan calling for my help when we had been separated from the McLeods' foster home.

The next thing I knew, I was in the alley swinging a piece of two-by-four that I had picked up on the way.

A good whack at the base of one of their heads followed by a home-run swing to another's middle thigh got their attention. One of the remaining two turned his head towards me just in time to lose teeth on a wood sandwich. The last one backed off before I could get to him, but he recognized me. I could tell by the look in his eyes. He backed away but pointed at me and shouted, "You're dead. You're fuckin' dead," as he helped one of his buddies up. The two of them ran off and the one I'd got in the leg started crawling. I was tempted to go to work on him and the one who was still down with the board, but the kid they had been beating was bleeding and only half-conscious and I was pretty sure he needed medical help. I pulled him out to the street and laid him down and tried to figure out what I should do. If I hung around, I figured the gang would be back, probably with reinforcements, to stomp both of us, but if I took off for help and left him alone…

Approaching sirens made up my mind for me. Someone must have seen the fight and called the police. They could protect him better than I could and get him to the hospital if that's what he needed, so I took off and was out of sight before they turned the last corner.

I thought it would be a good idea to ditch school for the next couple of days. I wasn't sure why those guys had done the number on the bald kid, but I knew they'd recognized me and that I'd better give them a chance to cool off before they saw me again. I didn't know much about racism at that time. There were blacks, whites, Asians, and Hispanics at the school, but since I never had anything to do with *any* of them, I didn't know about what went on between them. All I knew was that the punches and kicks hurt even more than they had in elementary school.

When I did go back to school a few days later, I entered the grounds with my guard up, but everything seemed okay. I passed lots of black kids, but none of them looked at me any different from normal, so I figured that the guys in the gang had decided to drop it. Or at least that it was just the gang that I had crossed, not everyone with black skin. I relaxed a bit and went inside and up to the second floor to my locker. I was sorting out the books for the day when a hand slapped my shoulder from behind, and there, when I turned around, was the kid I had saved. Stubble was growing through the scabs on his head, his eyes were well and truly blackened, but he was trying to smile through his stitched face.

He stared into my eyes and I felt contact with another human for the first time in five years. "Thanks a lot man," was all he said.

I nodded in acknowledgment, and he turned back to a group of his friends who had gathered behind us.

"This is the guy who helped me out."

They all looked at me for a minute or two and then one of them said, "You wasted all four of them? Just you?"

I just nodded again.

"Pretty fucking cool, man." He looked me up and down. "Especially considering they were all bigger than you." He stuck out his hand, and at first, I didn't know what he was doing but then I realized what was going on and reached out myself and shook it. "You probably saved Robert's life, man. You ever need anything, you just ask."

One by one they introduced themselves to me, and one of them told me that they'd put the word out to the prez of the gang that had stomped Robert that I was strictly off limits, so I didn't have to worry about retaliation from that quarter.

It was the first time I could remember having a conversation with somebody who didn't want something from me, and it felt weird. I didn't know what to say at first, but they were cool about it, and soon I relaxed a bit and was able to just talk to them without thinking about keeping my guard up. We talked about music, about which gangs controlled which areas, and about Robert's face. I was just starting to feel comfortable when the bell rang to signal the start of classes, but before they left, they told me where they usually hung out and said I should join them any time.

That night I actually went to the area where the vacant lot they told me about was, but hanging out with people was something I had never done, and, to be honest, I was more afraid of approaching them than I had been about wading into the fight. I watched them that night from places where I knew I couldn't be seen, like behind some dumpsters and from an empty building across the street.

They talked to me a bit at school in the next few days, and I hid out and watched them a couple more times at night. I knew from the start that these kids were not angels, far from it, but they were together, and looked relaxed which was more than I could say for myself. They had a small fire going, and were just generally hanging out, talking, drinking, smoking, listening to music, and enjoying themselves.

More than once I fantasized about coming out of hiding and joining them. Just thinking about it took away my depressing thoughts about the emptiness that waited for me back at the foster home, but I couldn't bring myself to do it. I watched how they danced and wondered what that would be like. Or what it would be like to look and dress the way they did. Some of them had Mohawks, some had spiked hair, some had no hair at all. Some wore leather jackets, while others wore jean jackets. Almost everyone had black boots on.

That week was the end of school, and with the start of the holidays, things got a lot worse at home. Having us around all the time was more than the foster people could handle, and physical abuse, or being locked in our rooms all day and night with exception of meals, became the norm.

I soon learned how to climb down the garden trellis from my second-story window, and one night I collected enough guts to go to the vacant lot after I stole a sub sandwich from a local deli. The kids that I knew from school recognized me as soon as I walked out of the shadows and into the firelight. They were surprised to see me but made me feel like they were glad I came. I stayed for hours, and eventually fell asleep under the stars. When I woke in the morning, I thought I'd probably get a lot of shit when I got back to my foster home, but I didn't care. Being welcomed by people who didn't want anything from me was worth whatever I'd have to go through from my foster Nazis.

For the rest of the summer, that lot became my second home. It was in a block of rundown buildings, mostly abandoned warehouses where some of the kids squatted. The kid I'd rescued from the shitkicking, Robert Mandrake, turned out to be a really cool guy, and became my first true friend. I know he felt that he owed me something for saving his ass, but the important part was that he actually *liked* me.

I spent most of my summer nights there. I didn't talk much, but everybody seemed to accept me, and even though I mostly hung out with Robert, I gradually got to know a few of the others. It was a mixed group. There were a few kids who seemed pretty ordinary, that you wouldn't give a second glance to if you met them on a street, probably kids who were trying a bit of rebellion against their families but who would wind up just like their parents in twenty years.

But a lot of them were pretty extreme. Kids who had real problems with their parents, or who, like me, didn't even have parents or families. Some hated the world and had the suicide scars to prove it, and over the course of the summer two actually did kill themselves. Some saw no point in home or school and had dropped out completely. Even the youngest of these, fourteen to fifteen years old, who lived on the streets, seemed older and wiser and more seasoned than the kids who had a roof over their heads. They set up squats in abandoned buildings and lived by stealing and panhandling. Or so I believed.

"See that Todd?"

Robert was sitting beside me on an old sofa we had moved from an abandoned building. He took a drag on his cigarette and pointed to a girl sitting with some other people around a small fire on the other side of the lot.

"The one with the blue hair?" I asked.

"Yeah. That's Elizabeth Forest."

He didn't speak again for about thirty seconds and then blew a greener out of his mouth, hitting an old coffee tin some five feet away.

"Nice shot!" I said.

"Lizzie's been on the street for a whole year now. She doesn't talk a lot but she's cool. Plus, she's got a pair of thirty-six Charlies that I'd just love to stuff my face into. Even wrote a song about them," he told me. "And, check out her butt next time you see her walking, she's got a heart-shaped ass beneath that skirt of hers."

"You think she's good looking?" I asked.

"Haven't you been listening Todd?"

"Yeah, sorry. Does she know you?"

"Yeah, some, we're sort of friends. We hang out a little. I'd love a chance with her though. You?"

"Jeez. I don't know. I don't know if she's my type or not."

"What's your type?" he asked.

"I don't know. Fuck, I'm only fourteen. Gimme a break."

"Yeah sure—sorry."

Robert flicked his cigarette butt into the fire, excused himself and walked over to where Lizzie was. She looked like she was happy to see him, and they were soon talking. I watched them for a time, then I got up, stretched and went back to my foster home. On the walk back I looked past the city glare and into the black sky. In my head I saw Susan, mom, and dad smiling at me. I climbed up the trellis into my bedroom, adjusted everything to my satisfaction, and was soon fast asleep. I dreamed about the meadow in New Zealand again that night, and about swimming in the warm ocean near Sydney like I had before we moved to America.

When school started again in the fall, the foster creeps weren't as miserable as they had been during the summer but living with them still wasn't much fun. I didn't mind being back at school, and I could still hang out at the lot when I felt like it or listen to my ska music when I needed to escape.

When I listened to Pauline Black, the singer in the band Selector, I was able to dream about where my sister was now. To stay even partly sane, I had to believe in something after this pitiful existence. She deserved at least that, and I drew comfort believing that she was okay.

I kept to myself most days at school, but sometimes I'd hang out with Robert and his friends. He would talk about Elizabeth, and how cool it would be to live out on your own. I wasn't so sure. Most of the foster homes I lived in were pretty horrible, and getting away from that definitely sounded attractive, but it didn't seem to me that squatting, or living on the street, would be any picnic either.

During the fall semester of my fourteenth year, I started growing a lot, but the new foster parents I'd been transferred to were even stingier than the last ones, and when it got to the point that my shirts and pants didn't fit any more, I did what I had to, to get the clothing and food that I needed; I stole it.

I started shoplifting out of necessity. Clothes from the shopping centers and food from grocery stores or 7-11s. But before long it led me to stealing things for money, just like the recess boys that I'd run into at the elementary school, the kids who could get you anything as long as you were willing to pay. Once I got into it, I charged 30% of the label price and I had plenty of customers.

Some of the older, tougher-looking kids who hung out at the lot shaved their heads. The others called them skinheads. Robert wasn't fully a part of their group even though he kept his head bald, but they let him hang around them, and he filled me in on them as much as he could.

One time I saw a thing on TV about skinheads beating up Jews and blacks, and I asked him where he stood on that.

"Well, there's different branches of skinheads," he said. "The guys here aren't into that white power shit."

"Yeah? So, what *are* they into?" I was curious, the skins that hung around the lot looked tough, but I'd never heard them talk about stomping Jews or anything.

"I don't think they've got a particular name. They're just kind of ordinary, regular, non-racist skins."

"What other kinds are there?"

"Well, there's the white power types that you heard about. They're the ones who are always in the news. Everybody believes that all skins are like them, but there are plenty that aren't. There's the SHARPs for example, which stands for SkinHeads Against Racial Prejudice."

"Any others?" I asked.

"Well, I don't know about all groups, but I've heard of Trojan skins. They ride scooters that they chop up and they also listen to ska and oi music. Pretty friendly for the most part." He paused to light a cigarette. "Then there's the satanics, who I think listen to speed metal and do a lot of steroids. Not too friendly, from what I've heard."

"But the guys that you hang with aren't in any group?"

"Not really. They're sort of like the independent skins, but the independents are mostly older and sort of sure about what they believe in. The guys here are mostly not much older than us, and they want to belong to something while they try to find out who they are." Robert laughed. "But their clothes intimidate people, so they have something extra over you and me and people don't go looking to fight them too much."

"But they've fought lots, haven't they?" I asked. "I mean, they sure *look* tough."

"I think some of them have," replied Robert. "I really don't know them that well, but I know they're mostly young like us and most of them are still looking for something."

"Like what?" I wasn't sure what he meant.

"I don't know." Robert hesitated. "What do we all want? We want to belong to something or somebody. Or at least I do. Don't you?"

"I have questions, sure," I answered. "My main one is about people. Why the fuck do people do the things that they do?"

"What are you talking about?" asked Robert.

"Nothing," I mumbled. "Forget it."

A breaking bottle caught my attention and I looked to see who'd thrown it against the wall. It was one of the younger skins, obviously drunk on something and looking for trouble. He noticed me watching him and gave me the eye, so I turned back to Robert, then got thinking about whether I should go look for some food and didn't realize he'd come over and started talking to me until Robert nudged my leg with his knee.

"What the fuck were you starin' at, fucker?"

I didn't answer, but stared straight past him, not making eye contact. He hacked up a greener and let fly, hitting the wall right beside me.

"You got a problem?" He stared right at me. "Who the fuck are you anyway?"

The kid obviously wanted a go at me, so I didn't wait, but accepted his challenge my way, by driving my hand up against his nuts. He doubled over, letting out a huge whoofing sound, and I stood up and gave him a shot in the face with my knee. He landed on his back, blood spurting and gurgling out of his mouth and nose.

I knew he wouldn't give me any more trouble, so I looked around to see what else was coming my way, wondering if these skins were of the "fight one and you fight all" kind. A bunch of them started coming toward me, but I'd been in more than enough fights to know when someone's got aggression on his mind, and these guys didn't. They stopped and looked down at the guy on the ground, then at me.

"Stupid prick had it coming for a long time," said one of them. "You probably did us all a favor."

As they dragged him away, I wondered if he was like me. Some poor bugger with too much pain in his life, looking for a way to end it.

I wasn't happy about fighting on the lot. It was a sort of safe place where kids could go and not have to worry about that sort of thing, but I knew if I hadn't decked him, it would be me that they were dragging off to the hospital. I think Robert must have sensed what was going through my mind.

"Not your fault Todd. Everybody here knew he was looking for a fight, and no one's gonna get on your case about it. If it hadn't been you, it would have been someone else."

I nodded and walked away, wondering why it was that here, among a bunch of delinquents, runaways, and throwaways, I was treated fairly, but everywhere else I was pond scum.

After that night some of the older skins started sitting with me sometimes and made it clear that I was accepted and that they understood that I hadn't been trying to disturb the truce at the lot. I didn't feel too comfortable talking to them, but I didn't mind being around them, and I mostly just listened.

When they found out, I think from Robert's friend Elizabeth, that I stole things for money, almost all of them ordered Levi jackets and Fred Perry shirts. Those items were not things that were easy to steal, and on a few occasions, I was spotted in the act. I could usually tell when someone saw me, and I always had an escape route planned before I started, so I always managed to get away, but finally I got caught, restrained, and handed over to the police.

I was processed and released but the whole thing had been quite the scare. I damn near shit myself when the cops put the cuffs on me and put me in their car. When I went to court, I told the judge that I had to steal clothing because my foster parents wouldn't buy any for me. Which was actually true, and I think the judge bought it because he let me off with a warning and a stint of Community Service working at a local animal shelter after school.

From that day forward, my prices went up to 50% of retail, and pretty soon I was making enough to better my lifestyle. Things that I had always wanted—music, food, clothing for cold weather—I was now able to buy for myself. Sure, I could have pinched those things, but I felt like I had earned them through my hard work stealing, and laying cash down for them brought me real satisfaction.

I had started puberty by then, and I was growing quickly. I was no giant, but I was big enough that by the time I was fourteen, the foster families couldn't physically intimidate me the way they could when I was small. The funny thing is, that this actually worked to their advantage, because once they stopped hassling me, I stopped hassling them. As long as there was food on the table at meals, and I could come and go as I pleased, I bothered nobody.

CHAPTER FOUR

A change in the motion of the bus brought me back to the present. It was fully dark outside, and even with the light of the moon I couldn't tell much, but I think that we must have come to a place where the highway was under repair. We'd slowed down a bit, and the road beneath the wheels felt a little rougher than normal. Not much, but enough to bring me to full alert. None of the other passengers were stirring, but then they hadn't had seven years in foster homes and fifteen years in prison to make them as sensitive to that sort of thing as I was.

I checked my watch. Another few hours would bring me to Missoula. I didn't really know much about it, but from the maps I had looked at it seemed to be a good place to start unwinding. A small city surrounded by mountains and wild country. Big enough to have anything I was likely to need, but small enough to be free of the urban pressures that I wanted to get away from. And if it turned out not to be suitable, well, I'd go exploring and find some place that was.

The moonlight cast a silver color over the surrounding landscape, making the forests and mountains look like some kind of magic kingdom where anything was possible. The bus was dark and everyone else seemed to be fast asleep. I got up, took a shit in the can, and came back to my seat. The road was smooth again, and the hum of tires and steady growl of the engine eased me back into the past as I stared off into the moonlit forests.

* * *

Ninth grade had been my best year since the death of my family. Looking back on it, I know I was still pretty messed up, but compared to what had gone before, it was a step toward sanity. I think the key change was that I had a friend, and knew a few people who, if they weren't exactly friends, were at least comfortable to hang out with.

I got into fewer fights at school that year. I was only suspended twice and managed to pass almost all my courses. The school counselors, the social service psychologists, and the social workers themselves, all thought that I had finally straightened myself out, and I'm sure they all patted themselves on the back figuring it was them that had done it.

Bullshit. The fighting at school had dropped off because the kids that hung out at the lot made me welcome, not because the counselors knew what they were doing. And what the counselors and social workers **didn't** know was that my thievery had risen to an all-time high. They only knew of the one arrest and figured that moving me to a new foster home had fixed everything.

And then there was drinking. Kids at the lot, mainly the older skinheads, had access to alcohol, and I had my first drink with them and Robert. Beer was weird in the extreme. I liked it well enough, but drinking it made me piss all the time. Robert often joked that you didn't buy beer, you just rented it for an hour and then returned it to nature.

It was okay to get drunk, but I had a lot of trouble stopping at a point where I could just get a good buzz on and enjoy it. I always drank too much, and porcelain worship became a common thing for me. I kept on thinking that if I did it often enough, I'd eventually build up a tolerance, but the alcohol beat me every time and I soon stopped out of pain. Dry heaving or puking up bile hurt so much that eventually something clicked in my mind and spoke out to me, "This is stupid Todd—do you really get enjoyment out of this?"

The answer was no, and except for the odd beer I pretty much stopped drinking. I don't know why I could stop when other people couldn't. Maybe it was because I could never be moderate about anything. Like the anger, or the fighting, drinking seemed to be something I had to do to the very limit, and I guess I was just lucky that it made me so sick that I had to stop.

Most of the kids there, guys and girls, weren't so lucky, and continued to do battle with the alcohol dragon. A very powerful beast! If you consumed enough, it planted a seed in your stomach. If you kept feeding it, that seed grew, and in the end, it turned into a monster that consumed you.

One of the people who battled with the dragon was Robert. He often tried to impress Elizabeth by showing that he could consume large quantities of alcohol, but it actually had the opposite effect. Every time he drank heavily, she would get up and move to another campfire and talk with other people. As far as I could tell she really liked Robert, and didn't have any other boyfriend, but it was obvious to me that heavy-duty drinking was not the way to win her over. I often tried to explain to Robert, but as cool as he was about most things, he had trouble understanding this one, and often wondered why she wasn't responding to his advances.

"How much do you know about her?" I asked.

"I guess not that much, really." He replied.

"Do you even know where she lives?"

"Nope."

"How long have you known her for?"

"I dunno. About a couple of months longer than I've known you," he said.

"You seem to both get along alright," I added.

"Yeah, it's pretty cool between us, but I'd like more, you know?"

"Then don't drink so much."

"You think it's that?"

"I *know* it is."

He was startled by the certainty of my answer. "What makes you so sure? When did you become a fucking psychologist?"

I was no expert on human relationships, but on the other hand, as someone who spent most of his time watching, rather than getting involved, I think I knew more than you might expect, and I tried to convince him that maybe there were other ways to approach her than with a bottle.

"Oh yeah? *You* don't drink much, and I haven't noticed her coming on to you."

"She doesn't want me, she wants you. Just give yourself a chance and you'll see."

The next summer brought my fifteenth birthday. The other guys my age seemed to be constantly thinking and talking about getting their dicks wet for the first time, and talking about which girls had the biggest tits, or who might have the tightest, wettest cunt. But in all honesty, I didn't really find much interest in any of it. I just didn't think that much about girls. My daydreaming and my actual dreams were mostly about either finding some kind of peaceful happiness, or about total destruction and death. Not much in between.

My fifteenth year also brought me an expulsion from school, which kind of bummed me out. I got caught stealing leather high-school jackets from lockers by one of the hall monitors. Action was quick and the fact that my behavior had been improving didn't cut any ice with the principal. I might not have been getting in as much trouble lately, but I was still a regular enough visitor to his office that he was happy for the excuse to get rid of me. He wasn't a total prick the way some of my other principals and teachers had been, so I don't blame him too much, but on the other hand, I had been doing a bit better in school, and I was starting to make some friends, and I wish he'd given me another chance.

My new school was Carson Graham Junior High. And because it was too far from the home I was in at that time, I also got transferred to a new foster home.

I was sorry to leave Sutherland school. The teachers weren't bad, I'd made some friends, and I'd even started doing okay in my courses. The new school sucked big time. The teacher in my home-room class was a complete asshole who loved to intimidate the younger girls. I recognized all the signs of an abuser right away because so many years of getting kicked around by foster parents had given me great radar.

In fact, it was only a little while later that I caught him getting a blowjob from a student behind his desk after school. I'd come back because I'd left a book on my desk and got suspicious when I could hear his moans and groans through the crack where the door was a bit ajar. I tested the doorknob, and sure enough, it was locked, but he hadn't closed the door all the way. I opened the door as quietly as I could and looked inside. He was in his chair with his pants down and his legs apart, and one of the girls in the class was on her knees in front of him. He didn't see me watching, so I backed out quietly, and filed the scene into my memory in case I needed to pull it out later as a bargaining chip.

The foster home was just the opposite. It was the first place I'd been put since I left the McLeods that wasn't like a corner of Hell. My new foster parents, Mr. and Mrs. Fysh, were two of the nicest people I ever met, certainly the finest who ever took care of me, and I am still eternally grateful for all that they tried to do for me.

They let me settle in for a couple of days, being nice to me but mostly leaving me undisturbed, which I appreciated. On the evening of the third, while I was in my room getting ready to go to bed, Mrs. Fysh knocked on the door and asked if she could come in.

This was unusual. Normally, the foster creeps just barged right in, and I was taken by surprise by this politeness. Mrs. Fysh was about sixty. She was a bit on the short side, maybe five-four, but she seemed to be in pretty good health even though she didn't look like she weighed all that much.

I had been preparing the floor with her sheets and pillows but she didn't say anything about that, just sat on the edge of the bed and said that she'd like to talk with me for a few minutes if I didn't mind.

No one had ever asked whether I minded that they talked to me, and all I could say was, "Um, sure, okay."

She welcomed me again to her household and told me a little about herself. She was a nurse, just retired from working in a psychiatric hospital. She said her husband, who had been a bank manager, was also retired, but now volunteered his time during the day at a center that offered advice to people who were trying to start their own businesses as a way out of poverty.

This was a real change for me. I was used to people who didn't talk to me except to yell at me, and who were mostly borderline criminals who were exploiting kids for money. I wanted to say something about that but thought that maybe I'd better hold off until I was sure she really was what she seemed.

She went on to tell me about their only son, Edwin, who had enlisted in the army and was now twenty-three years old and serving as a Combat Engineer. She told me some of the stories he'd told her about how he put bridges up and took them apart, worked with explosives, and cleared minefields. It sounded pretty exciting to me, and I asked her if he had to have a university education to do that.

"No, he went to high school, and joined the army as soon as he finished twelfth grade and got all his training there. He wasn't such a great student in school, but he said that in the army he enjoyed the training so much that it seemed to make learning fun, and he worked very hard."

That made sense to me. Most of what I did in school was so boring that it was hard to put any effort into it, but the odd time when I took a course that I liked, I didn't mind working hard.

"But it wasn't all fun and games for him, and he says it still isn't. Sometimes they go up north and train with the Canadian Army in the winter. He says it's so cold that … " she blushed, "oh, I guess I can say it. He says it gets so cold that your pee freezes before it hits the ground."

She blushed some more, and I wondered what she would think if she heard the way most of my foster mothers had talked to me.

But then she got serious and changed the subject.

"Todd, I know you've been through an awful lot, but we need to talk about a few things if it's okay with you."

I nodded.

"First of all, this is your room. It has a lock on the door, and we're going to give you the key." She handed me a brass key and I looked at it like it was a piece of rock from Mars. They were actually offering me some privacy. I could hardly believe it.

"Nobody will come into this room unless you wish it. My husband and I are getting on, and can't force you to do anything that you don't want to do. We won't order you around, but I am going to request that you respect some basic rules. I'll explain them to you now, and if you have any concerns, feel free to say so. Better you should get everything straight now than have trouble later because you don't speak up."

I nodded again.

"Good. Now, the first thing is that if you want your room to be in this form, that's okay with me; I think I understand why, and I think you'll probably get over it, but in the meantime it's okay. But … " she paused so that I would be sure to pay attention to what was coming, "but, I want you to fold your sheets neatly and put them on the bed before you go to school in the morning, and you are responsible for washing them, and your clothes, at least once a week. I'll show you how to use the washer and dryer if you need me to."

That didn't seem too unreasonable, so I said okay.

"Next, about meals. I serve breakfast at 7 a.m. and supper at 6 p.m. You're responsible for being at the table on time. Do you have a watch and an alarm?"

"Um, I've got a watch, but not an alarm."

"That's fine, we've got an extra one that you can have. Now, your lunch; you'll buy that each day at the school cafeteria with money I give to you. If you'd rather have sandwiches from here that's fine too, but you'll have to make them yourself. Is that okay with you?"

I nodded again.

"Good. Now here's the part you may not like. We lock our doors and go to bed at ten o'clock. For the first while that you're here, we're going to insist that you be home before that time. If things work out between you and us, then in a month or so we'll give you a house key of your own and you can stay out a little later sometimes, but until then, you must be home by ten. Do you understand that?"

I was used to coming and going pretty much as I pleased, so this was not going to be easy to deal with. They were obviously good people, and I didn't want to piss them off, but a ten o'clock curfew wasn't something I was looking forward to. I think she sensed my feelings.

"Todd, if you have some special event that you want to go to, and you tell us in advance, then we will arrange for you to get in after ten, and on Friday and Saturday nights, eleven is okay, but in general, ten o'clock is closing time for the first month, and you must respect that."

What could I say? I was too far from the lot to go there every night anyway, and I didn't know anything about this new neighborhood yet, so maybe being home at ten most nights wouldn't be too bad. Especially if home was going to be a pleasant place.

"Okay Mrs. Fysh, that sounds alright with me. I'll do my best."

It was the first time that I had been treated as a person, as something other than a piece of meat used to get monthly checks from the government. I hardly knew this woman, but I really did want to try not to do anything that would hurt her.

"The last thing I need to say, Todd, is that we like to hear about your activities and your friends, and while we encourage you to get out of this house and have some fun, we also want you to know that you are welcome to bring your friends here."

She crossed the room to the door and opened it, but before she left she looked me in the eyes and said, "If ever you need to talk to someone, about anything, my husband and I are here for you. We'll do our best to help in any way we can, and to leave you to yourself when you prefer that."

As she walked out, she looked back. "And please respect our privacy too. Each person's room is their own. Please don't go into anyone else's room, and we won't go into yours, okay?" I nodded.

"And Todd, I'm an old lady now, and my husband's even older, but our son is a combat soldier, and if you ever steal from us, he'll be down here on the next plane ... " she blushed again, "to kick your ass all the way into next week, do you understand?"

"Yes Ma'am, that's fair."

I could tell that the last bit had been hard for her to say, but she didn't have to worry, I had no intention of being kicked out of this great home and placed in another shithouse again. I shut off the light in my room and wrapped up in my blankets on the floor. I wondered if she was right about my being able to sleep in the bed eventually. Maybe I'd try it sometime, but not yet.

The first day I went to school, I knew that there would be a welcoming conversation with the principal in the morning, and then at lunch a probing by the schoolyard bulldogs. It had been the same thing at each school that I had ever gone to, but this school had a tougher reputation than the last, so my guard was up.

As I had expected, the principal welcomed me and warned me at the same time, then showed me to my homeroom and introduced me to the teacher that I later caught with his pants down. The violence didn't come for a couple of weeks, but when it did come, it was more than I bargained for.

I had bought lunch in the cafeteria but taken it outside and found a place where I could eat it sitting in the sun, leaning against a wall. I was about halfway finished when I saw the would-be tough guys coming. There were two of them, one was stocky and the other was almost fat, and they both had a lot more weight on their bones than I had.

They probably thought they'd be able to surprise me, but I stood up while they were still about twenty feet away, and stared them down, which stopped them for a moment. But they started moving again, picking up speed and starting to yell. Knowing what was going to happen if I stayed still, I charged at them. I made like I was going to jump into the air and try for a kick like some kind of Kung Fu Charlie, but instead stayed on the ground and stomped the fat one on the instep, which dropped him to the ground instantly and stopped his buddy in his tracks.

I had a quick second to look around. No yard-duty teachers in sight, so I was on my own.

The stocky kid backed off a bit to reevaluate the situation, and when he took another step back, I thought that he might call it quits. But instead he bent and picked up a discarded bottle and smashed it on the pavement, leaving him holding the broken top, a formidable weapon.

"You think you're tough?" he screamed at me, then charged, yelling, "Eat glass fuckhead!" The stocky shoulders gave him speed and power, and if I hadn't been wearing a heavy jacket, I might not be telling this story. I was moving, and the jacket caught the broken bottle as he struck, but even so I could feel it stabbing into my chest and dragging down my side.

A sharp pain filled my entire body, followed by an intense burning sensation. He knew that he had cut me, and backed off, not entirely sure what his next move should be.

By this time the fat one had gotten back onto his feet. I saw him move out of the corner of my eye and saw behind him a group of kids gathering to watch.

I backed up against the wall and was looking desperately around me for anything I could use as a weapon of my own, when a rock took me square in the temple. I lost my surroundings to a flash of pain.

"C'mon newboy, wha'cha got for us now?" The fat one shouted.

"Maybe he's got some more blood to give us." The other one said.

Blood? I reached under my jacket and felt the wetness soaking my shirt over my lower ribs. Pulled out my hand to see it covered in blood.

The world was moving, spinning around. I felt nauseous and sick at the same time. I looked down at my feet and saw the blood pooling on the ground.

I felt my legs giving up underneath me.

I knew that as soon as I was down, they'd move in for the kill, and I fought to stay on my feet, but couldn't. As I started to sag, I saw the stocky one coming in. I could see through his body language that he was going to finish the job with his shoes.

Kick the shit out of me and leave me to bleed to death? Wasn't that what I'd always wanted? Maybe a year ago I would have simply given up, accepted death, but something had changed, and even though I didn't think I had a chance, I tried to protect myself.

His leg came at me in slow motion and I threw my arms up to trap it between my arm and my body, then used it to help myself stand up again. I didn't have any plan any more than a cornered animal has a plan. I was just fighting to postpone the inevitable, and what happened next was pure chance.

"Gimme my fucking leg back you stupid cocksucker!" He screamed out as he slashed at me with the bottle. I backed away from the slash, lost my balance, and trying to regain it, I fell forward, putting my foot out to catch myself as I did. But my foot caught him just below the knee, and with his other leg in my grasp, the knee bent backward to full lock, and then gave with a loud and sickening crunch.

His mouth opened up like a black hole, but there was so much pain in that kid that he couldn't make a sound. Only fall to the ground and writhe in agony.

That's all I remember. Without his leg to hold on to, I collapsed on the ground beside him, and passed out.

If no one had been around, maybe fatty would have finished the job his partner started. I found out later that he tried, that he'd picked up the broken bottle and was about to stab me when a couple of teachers arrived and pulled him off me.

I woke up in the hospital, where I spent the next two days under observation. The broken bottle had sliced me from just below my sternum almost to the top of my left hipbone, and the blood had really poured out. The blood loss, combined with a mild concussion from the rock I took on the temple, left me weak and confused. They kept me in hospital till they were sure that I didn't have any permanent damage, then sent me home to Mrs. Fysh, who put me in bed and kept me there for almost a week. It was nice to be taken care of like that, and I felt safe and comfortable for the first time since the death of my parents.

Enough kids had seen the fight to make it clear to the principal that I was an innocent victim, picked on for no reason other than that I was a new guy with a reputation; a way for fatty and his friend to make their marks. They were both expelled, and nobody came down on me which was another first, and the week I spent in bed gave me time to think about something.

That fight had been the closest I had come to reaching my long-standing goal of leaving this world, and yet, at the end, when it looked like my time had come, I had fought against it as hard as I could. Why? Didn't I still want to die? The opportunity had been handed to me, and I hadn't accepted. I had survived, and now I didn't know if I was the luckiest man in the world or the most cursed.

After a couple of weeks of stiffness and headaches, I began to feel better and, late on a Saturday afternoon, I decided that I could probably handle the walk to the lot. It was almost forty-five minutes from where I now lived, but the wound was healing pretty well, and I thought that if it started hurting, I could just turn around and come home.

The news of my first weapon fight had spread, and I was treated like a celebrity, which I wasn't sure I liked. It was cool to have some respect, but I wasn't comfortable with people I didn't know getting into my face. I saw Robert talking with Elizabeth in front of a small fire, and made my way over to them.

"Hey, look who's here! You been hiding from us these last three weeks?" he asked. "Where've you been?"

"Healing." I lifted my shirt, showing the long gash, still stitched up.

"Holy shit! That must have hurt."

"Sure didn't tickle!" I responded. "What have you been up to?"

"Not much, hanging out here, going to school, you know. How's the new school?"

"Well, it's different." I pointed to my side, where he had seen the wound. "That's where I got this. And the day before that I caught my teacher getting a blowjob from one of the girls in the class."

"You got cut up *at school?*" Robert sounded shocked. "We heard you'd been in a heavy-duty fight, and got cut, but I figured that meant you'd show up with a few scabs, not a fucking knife wound from hell. And, fuck me, at school? How could something like that happen at school?"

I told them about the two guys who thought they'd be able to score points by kicking the new kid around, and how it had got ugly through no intention of mine. When I got to the part about seeing the big puddle of blood around my feet, Elizabeth stood up.

"Oh my God. You almost died, didn't you?" She looked upset. "This is just too ugly. I'm really glad you're okay Todd, but if I listen to any more of this I'll get sick or pass out or something." She walked away to join some kids around another fire.

"You were lucky to get out of that," Robert said genuinely.

"Yeah, lucky or cursed," I replied.

"What do you mean by that?"

"Aw, nothing." Robert was as good a friend as I ever had, but I wasn't ready to go into that story with him. I switched back to the fight and told him about how I'd accidentally broken the guy's knee, and how the teachers had arrived just in time to keep the fat kid from killing me. "I guess I *was* lucky. Anyway, it's good to be back with you guys. How are things going with you and Elizabeth?"

"I don't know for sure, but things are definitely looking good. I still don't know a whole lot about her, but I sure like her, and I'm pretty sure she likes me." He exhaled cigarette smoke and played with the burning sticks in the fire in front of us. "I've never had the nerve to ask her out. I mean to a movie or something. Shit, I don't even know where she lives, or what she does when she's not here."

"Well, why don't we find out a little more about her?"

"What do you mean?"

"How about next week, if I'm healed up more, we follow her from the lot one night, and find out where she lives. Then, we can skip school one day and hang out near her place and see what happens."

"You mean spy on her?"

"Sure. Why not?"

Robert didn't look too sure about the idea.

"Look, it's not as if we're going to be doing something that'd hurt her. I mean, we both like her, and it's just for fun."

He thought about it for a minute, then said, "Okay. I'm in." He lit another cigarette and then added, "but if she sees us, we don't try to hide, or run away or anything, right? We explain right away that we're not stalking her, and that it was your idea, not mine, okay?"

"Sure, now shut up cuz she's coming back over here."

When she got to our fire and was sure that we weren't still talking about blood and gore, she sat down beside Robert again. They started talking about the usual stuff and I sat back and stared into the fire. Nine o'clock came and went, and I knew that I wasn't going to make the ten o'clock curfew at the Fysh house. I didn't want them to worry about me, so I went to a gas station a couple of blocks away, where I knew there was a pay phone. I told Mr. Fysh that I was feeling better, and that I'd be staying at a friend's place that night, but would be home the next morning so that I would have plenty of time for the studying and homework that the teachers had given me to do while I recuperated.

I knew I'd probably wind up sleeping at the lot, or in one of the empty buildings nearby, and I didn't like lying to the Fyshs', but it was sort of a white lie, and wouldn't do any harm. They'd be really upset if they knew where I was spending the night, but I knew that I'd be okay, and I didn't want them to worry about me.

They'd been badly shaken by the stabbing, Mrs. Fysh especially. At first she had feared for my life, then she worried that I was going back to my old ways, but I had explained everything to her exactly as it had happened, and although they were still worried that someone else might try me out when I went back to school, they knew that at least I was doing my best to stay out of trouble.

She was a cool lady. I knew that she would be able to tell if I lied, so I was glad that I could be honest with her about what had happened. I didn't want to blow it with her and her husband. They were the first people in a long time who treated me like a human being, and I liked being around them. I even came out of my room sometimes to help with the work around the house—washing dishes, or sweeping the floor, or whatever; and I'd sure as shit never done that in any of the other foster homes.

I went back to school on Monday, and things there were okay. My home-room teacher was still an asshole, but at least nobody looked like they wanted revenge for what had happened. That didn't mean I could let my guard down, because I knew that sooner or later somebody would decide that he was ready to make his reputation by taking on the tough kid that could break your leg even after you sliced him up, but I hoped it wouldn't be for a while, because I was still recovering from that slicing.

On Friday evening I walked to the lot again, where Robert was waiting with some news for me. Elizabeth had told him that one of her friends was interested in me. Her name was Bernie O'Conner, which didn't mean anything to me at first, but when he pointed her out to me, standing at a fire with Elizabeth, I remembered seeing her around, maybe talking to her now and then.

I hadn't thought much about girls up till then. I talked to them, same as to guys, but that was all. That night though, looking at her and knowing that she'd been curious about me, something in me came alive. I think it was my dick.

Robert and I walked over, which wasn't easy, because my knob was trying to burst out of my jeans, and I had to adjust myself every few steps. The girls pretended not to notice, but they must have seen me, and I think they were giggling a bit. I tried to be casual, like talking to her was nothing special, but I caught her glancing down at the bulge in my pants, so being casual was anything but easy.

She was about my age, or maybe a year older. Long, straight, red-blonde hair. Pixie face. Sweet looking, but definitely with what Robert would have called 36 Charlies.

I have no idea what we talked about, or whether I even made any sense. I felt totally brainless and was lucky to remember about phoning home to tell my foster parents that I was going to stay over with Robert again. Eventually Bernie left with Elizabeth, and as soon as they were out of hearing Robert said, "Tonight's the night, right?"

I was still feeling all weird and had no idea what he was talking about. "Huh?"

"We can follow them. Find out where they live."

We gave them a couple of blocks head start and then headed out behind them, trying to look inconspicuous. At least my hard-on had finally subsided and I could walk. We stayed back as far as we could, and then raced to catch up whenever they turned a corner out of sight. They headed for a nearby industrial area that had a lot of ongoing demolition. Big dump trucks, bulldozers, and excavators were parked everywhere, but the girls didn't pay them any attention. They were talking and laughing, probably about what had been trying to get out of my pants and behaving as if this was a well-lit residential street instead of a dark and deserted construction zone.

They turned into a narrow lane between a semi-demolished building and one which looked abandoned but wasn't being demolished. We got to the lane entrance just in time to see them climb up a fire-escape ladder and into a third-story window in the second building. They closed the window behind them, but soon we saw candlelight glimmering in a window a little further back down the lane.

"I guess that's what they call home."

Robert didn't reply at first, but then said, "Well, it's as cheap as you can get ain't it?"

"Yeah, I guess so."

"If they're using candles, they probably don't have electricity, and I bet they don't have water either." He sounded like he thought that was the way to live.

I tried to imagine what it would be like to live in a place where there was no water. How the fuck would you deal with that? Carry it up from the nearest gas station in a bucket? "That would suck, big time. You still think squatting is cool?"

"Shit, I don't know, Elizabeth always looks clean. She must be able to get a bath or shower somewhere. It can't be that bad." Robert obviously thought it was cool that the girl he had the hots for lived in an abandoned building, but it sure didn't seem like anything I'd want to do.

Three days later, we both skipped school and met at the lot a little before noon. We went to the nearest 7-11 where Robert distracted the cashiers and I lifted some subs. We munched as we walked toward the squat. With all the demolition going on it was a different area during the day. Noisy and dusty and ugly.

When we reached their building, we suddenly didn't know what to do. It was just one more empty-looking building, in a district that was full of them. We stood around for a while behind a broken fence across the street, but nothing was happening. We could hear the noise of a crew working inside the neighboring building, but there wasn't much happening on the street except for the occasional dump truck rumbling by.

"I'm going in."

"You're what?" Robert replied.

"Watching nothing happen is fucking boring!" I said. "We're not going to learn anything standing around out here."

I stepped out from behind the fence. "If you move into that doorway a little further down, I'll be able to see you from the lane. Just wave if it looks like somebody is coming." I crossed the street and entered the lane. Nothing special, just another alley full of garbage in another run-down neighborhood. Someone had wired the bottom section of the fire escape ladder to a broken chunk of cement to keep it down, and I guess either the police hadn't noticed or didn't care.

Robert gave me a thumbs-up, which I took to mean the coast was clear, so I started up the ladder. The paint was all chipped and the rails were badly rusted, but it seemed solid enough. When I reached the third floor, I checked the window we'd seen the girls step through. It gave me a view into a dark, empty hallway. I tested it, and it opened easily. Exciting shit this spying. I looked back to Robert and got another thumbs-up, so I pulled the window wide open and stepped in.

What now? There was enough light coming into the hall for me to see that there was half a dozen or so doors on each side, and the light we'd seen probably came from either the closest one or the one after that. I stepped along and listened at the first door.

Nothing.

But now that my heart wasn't beating quite so fast, I thought I could hear something from further along, and I could definitely smell cigarette smoke, so as quietly as I could I moved to the next door and stuck my ear against it.

"...your turn to go for water or mine?"

Elizabeth's voice. Not very loud, but I could hear it if I listened carefully. "Uh, mine, I think. I'll go in a few minutes, okay?"

And Bernie! *Awwwriiiight*!

"Sure, no hurry. I'll go buy some more smokes and maybe some coffee while you get the water. You want anything else?"

"Maybe a sandwich. Nothing too expensive though. If we don't spend too much we won't have to work again till next week."

Work? Maybe I'd get to hear where they panhandled.

"That'd be just fine with me. I'm going to visit my brother this weekend, and I'll probably stay there Sunday night, so why don't I just meet you at the corner on Monday afternoon?"

At the corner? I willed Bernie to give me a clue. "Sure. How 'bout four o'clock?"

Elizabeth didn't say anything for a minute. Then, "Yeah, I guess. I shouldn't have any trouble making it to Fourth and Valemont by four."

Fourth and Valemont? Fourth wasn't far from the lot, but where the fuck was Valemont? Maybe Robert would know. They didn't say anything more for a minute and I wondered if they were getting ready to leave, if I should retreat to the fire escape, but then Bernie spoke.

"What about Friday night? Don't you want to go down to the lot on Friday?"

"Bet your ass I do. I'm not going to my brother's till Saturday."

"Bet it's not *my* ass you're thinking about. I've seen how you watch Robert when he's walking the other way."

I could hear laughter.

"Well, do you blame me? Robert has got the hardest looking butt I've ever seen."

"And you just can't wait to get your fingernails into it, can you?"

Whew! This was getting steamy, and I could feel my newfound friend rising to attention in my pants.

"And I suppose I'm the only one thinking that way? You telling me you aren't thinking about Todd every once in a while?"

More laughter.

"He is definitely the mystery man. Hardly ever talks, but when he does, he always has something interesting to say. Not like most of the assholes we hang out with there."

"Well, we'll see what happens Friday. Too bad they're both in school and can't get out much during the week. It'd be cool to see them more often."

Jesus Christ! Much more of this and I'd have to whip it out and jerk it off right there. "You just about finished that smoke?"

I heard a chair scrape and footsteps in the room. "Yeah, just about. Let's go."

Mission accomplished. Time for me to disappear.

"'Nice hard ass?' She actually *said* that?" Robert was practically slobbering with excitement.

"Oh yeah. She's had her eye on it for quite a while." He actually gurgled with pleasure when I said that.

"What about you? Did they say anything about you?"

"Bernie calls me the mystery man."

"She wanna get you in between her legs?"

"She didn't actually say that, but I'll sure let her, if she wants."

We chewed up our cheeseburgers and headed back toward the lot. Robert was on cloud nine, and I wasn't far from it, but then I remembered about the other part of their conversation.

"Robert, get your hand outta your pocket and off your dick, I got a question for you."

"What?"

"You know where Valemont Street is?"

"Sure. What's on Valemont?"

"Somebody who wants your nice hard ass, that's what."

He didn't get it at first. "Lizzie lives on Valemont? You mean that place they were at was Bernie's?"

"No. I think they both live in the squat, but they panhandle at Fourth and Valemont. They're gonna go there Monday afternoon, so I think we should find out where it is and be there ahead of time."

"You mean do the James Bond thing again?"

On Friday night I became a man. We met at the lot, as usual, but this time, without anybody really suggesting it, the four of us sat on our own. Robert had a bottle of Smirnoff vodka, and we took turns drinking from it, straight up. I only had a couple of sips, and the others didn't have that much either, because before long we'd started making out and pretty much forgotten the bottle.

It was a new experience for me, but I guess it's one of those things that you don't really need to go to school to learn. Kissing came naturally, and when Bernie started giving me some wet tongue action my hand found its way under her shirt as if it had done it a hundred times before. I'd been aroused right from the beginning, but when I felt those tits my hard-on nearly ripped through my jeans.

Elizabeth and Robert must have reached the same point, because the girls pulled away almost at the same time. I thought maybe they were going to tell us to cool down or something, but instead they asked if we'd like to go to the beach where there weren't so many people. I didn't have a clue about any beach, but Bernie could have invited me to a public rat-fuck and I'd have gone along happily.

They led us through the streets for about half an hour, with plenty of stops for kissing and feels, and eventually we came to a section of the beach where there were a lot of old piers. It was a warm night and there were people walking on the sand, but the girls led us off to the right, under a pier where we had to pretty much crawl to get through, and onto a section of beach that was hidden from the world.

Elizabeth dropped the shoulder bag she'd been carrying and threw herself around Robert. I started to reach for Bernie, but she took my hand and led me under the next pier to our own private area.

I'd like to say that I was a tough guy, who could make love to any girl and not think twice about it, but to tell the truth, I was nervous as hell and, well, just followed Bernie's lead.

She pulled a blanket out of her bag and laid it out over the sand, then pulled me down onto it with her. My lips were dry, my dick throbbing to be released.

She guided my mouth to hers and we were soon entwined in passionate kissing. I had no idea kissing could be that great, and it seemed to happen so naturally. I felt her breasts. They were **huge**. I felt her ass as she felt mine. I undid her pants and explored. She had no panties on underneath, and just a small Mohawk of pubic hair. My hand found its way to her pussy. She moaned as I pushed in two fingers, and that moaning turned me on even more.

I played with her pussy until she was wet with anticipation, and she caressed my cock through my jeans. It was begging to be released from its cage, and just when I thought I couldn't take any more, she rolled me onto my back and undid my pants. When Dicky D was out, she put him in her mouth and moved up and down the shaft, circling her tongue around the head. Licking and sucking. What incredible sensations!

She pulled my jeans all the way off, and then stood over me and peeled off her own pants, then pulled her sweater off over her head. Staring up into her pussy as she stood over me, I was rock hard, and the seconds that passed as she slowly lowered herself onto me were the longest ones of my life. She tortured me by rubbing herself up and down my shaft, making little squeals of excitement as she did.

Just as I was sure I was going to come that very second, she lifted off and told me to close my eyes. I did as she told me, and though I couldn't see the moonlight glinting off those gorgeous tits, I could still imagine them above me as I felt her slide forward. She was careful not to put too much weight on my still-healing scar, just touched her pussy delicately against it, then slid further forward until she was right over me, rubbing her soaking wet pussy all around my face.

I didn't know what to do at first, but when I smelled her essence, I just about went crazy with desire. With my eyes still shut I grabbed her hips and pulled her to my mouth. She tasted wonderful. I tongued her as hard as I could, and she arched her back and moaned.

After a few minutes of squirming on my face, she lifted, moved back, and jammed herself down onto my dick as hard as she could.

She was warm and wet. And tight. It felt so incredibly good. She leaned forward and rocked herself up and down my shaft while I grabbed her tits and squeezed them and sucked them.

Somehow, she could tell whenever I was about to come, and she'd slow down and just squirm so that she was getting the pleasure without pushing me over the edge, until finally her squeals of pleasure started getting louder and she squirmed faster and faster until suddenly she stopped moving and tensed up completely. Her back was arched, her hands were grasping my shoulders, and she had gone totally motionless. Then her whole body shuddered, and she let out a huge gasping breath.

After a minute of gathering her wits, she looked down at me and said, "your turn." She started riding me up and down as hard as she could and within a minute, I was shooting my cum deep inside of her.

It was *glorious*.

Spent for a time, we just lay on the blanket and cuddled. I'd thought about sex a lot in the last few days, but this was beyond my wildest imagining, and I started to drift into a coma from the sheer ecstasy of it all. I have no idea how much time passed that way, but the next thing I remember is Bernie poking me and pointing through the timbers of the pier to where we could see the bucking shapes of Robert and Elizabeth doing it doggie style.

"Want to go for a ride Todd?"

Dicky D woke up immediately. "Ohhhhhh yeah."

She positioned herself in front of me, and soon my balls were slapping into her ass. Her pussy was tight and wet, her ass round and soft, her breasts magnificent. What a hot creature. She moaned and reached back, grabbing my ass cheeks, pulling me into her harder and faster. Pretty soon we were both snorting and moaning until I couldn't hold back any longer and sent another load deep into her pussy. I collapsed over her back for a minute, then rolled her over, put my face into those giant tits and collapsed where I lay, with sweat beading all over our bodies.

We made it one more time before we finally packed up to leave. She joked about my cum dripping down her legs, and wiped it off with the blanket. We called out to Robert and Elizabeth and soon the four of us were walking back to the lot together with the girls laughing because Robert and I had such huge shit-eating grins on our faces. But we didn't care. We were happy as any fifteen-year-olds anywhere and felt like the world was ours for the taking.

If only we'd known.

As we got closer to the lot, I realized that I didn't feel like going back to the crowd tonight. This girl was having a powerful effect on me, and I wanted to be by myself for a little while so I could savor the feeling. I was afraid that if I tried to explain myself I'd wind up saying something silly though, and I also felt that even though Bernie had enjoyed the workout on the beach as much as I had, that she probably didn't think of me as much more than a sex partner. But before I could think of a way to excuse myself, Robert spoke up suggesting that we should all meet at the lot late the next afternoon. I said I'd be there for sure, but Elizabeth told us that she had made plans to visit her brother for the rest of the weekend. We pretended we didn't already know and turned to Bernie.

She took my hand and said, right out loud so that Elizabeth and Robert could hear her, "I think I might be falling in love." She kissed me. "My body is telling me that I should see you tomorrow Todd, but I think I'd better take a few days to myself to think things over."

Whooeeeee! It was all I could do to stop myself from turning cartwheels in the street.

Without having to discuss it, we all knew it was time to go our separate ways, so we had some final kisses, agreed to meet at the lot next Friday, and said good-bye. Robert and I watched the girls head off in the direction of their squat, then we turned and started the other way.

We walked and talked quietly for a few minutes, then just walked. At one point, Robert yelled, "*pussy*!" into the lonely night, but other than that we didn't talk much more, and soon parted, heading home in different directions. Boys no more.

CHAPTER FIVE

It was past midnight when I got home, but I'd been getting on so well with Mr. and Mrs. Fysh that they'd already given me a key, so I was able to let myself in and not worry about having to sleep at the lot.

It was a strange weekend. I stayed home with the Fyshs, helped with some chores, did quite a lot of studying, but mostly just sat quietly in my room, trying to understand my feelings.

Six years ago, I'd been condemned to Hell. I was only nine at the time and didn't understand any of it. All I understood was suffering, and for five years suffering is what I'd done. I'd become good at it. I'd reached the point where I accepted that suffering was going to be my life until somebody released me with boots or a knife or a gun. But now I was confused. The last year had been different. I'd made a friend. A couple of teachers had found a way to give me an interest in something other than death. Mr. and Mrs. Fysh treated me with love and respect, not as a piece of human garbage.

And now Bernie.

The sex had been fantastic, but I tried to push that to one side and think just about Bernie the person, not Bernie the wild fuck. I didn't know her all that well, but there was something about her that I liked. She was quiet, like me, and the more I thought about it, the more I realized that I wanted her as a friend. Big tits were fine, more than fine, but I also liked her laughing eyes and her quiet ways.

Thinking about her made me feel warm inside. It was not something I was used to, but I liked it. I wanted more of it.

I wanted to live.

On Monday I followed the directions Robert had given me to get to Fourth and Valemont. It was about halfway between our schools, so it was easy for us to get there well ahead of the time the girls were planning to meet. There was a McDonald's right on the corner, so we ordered burgers and ate them as we cruised the area, trying to figure out the best spot to do our spying from.

It was run down, like the area where the girls lived, but busier. Lots of traffic passing on the streets, and plenty of people walking home from work.

"They didn't say exactly where they'd meet, did they?" Robert was trying to look in every direction at once.

"No. Just 'Fourth and Valemont.'"

"So how the fuck are we supposed to..."

He stopped as we both got it at the same time. "The McDonald's."

"Yeah, of course." I looked around more carefully. "Look, across the street. That gas station went out of business years ago. If we duck in behind the garage part, we can see the entrance to the Macdonald's and they'll never spot us."

I checked my watch. "Quarter to. We better get over there in case one of them shows up early."

Bernie arrived first, and as soon as I saw her, I got that warm feeling all over again. Not to mention a hard-on. Elizabeth was a few minutes late, and we sat around, smoking and talking, waiting for them to finish whatever food they'd ordered, and show their faces again.

We didn't have long to wait. Less than ten minutes after Elizabeth went in, they came out together, and walked up the street directly opposite us. About fifty feet further along, they turned in beside an old three-story apartment building with boarded-up windows, and from where we were hiding, we could see them go in through a side door.

"What the fuck?" We looked at each other. "Have they got another squat?"

"I don't know. When I overheard them talking that day, they sounded like they definitely lived in that place and only came over here to panhandle." I thought about it. "I guess I never actually heard them say the word 'panhandle' though, so maybe they've got some kind of work they do in there."

"Like what?" Robert was as confused as I was.

"How would I know?" We eased out onto the street and looked down past the building they'd gone into. No clues there. "I guess I could go in, just like I did in the other place and have a listen at the different doors." I grabbed his arm. "Let's get back out of sight, and give them a few minutes to get settled into whatever it is they're doing, and then I'll sneak in."

We lit up, but before two minutes had passed the side door opened. "Jesus fucking Christ!" Robert saw them first, and I turned to look.

"Fuck me!"

Short skirts, high heels, jackets open over low-cut blouses, lipstick. "Man, oh man, do they ever look good."

"Oh yeah, I'm getting a boner out to here."

We laughed, then got serious. "They must work in a restaurant or something." said Robert. "Or maybe ushers at a movie theater," was my guess.

"But they're not going anywhere."

It was true. They stood on the sidewalk together for a minute, then Bernie walked to the front entrance of the building they'd come out of, and moved into the recessed doorway, pretty much disappearing in the shadow, while Elizabeth stayed where she was, just kind of hanging out on the sidewalk, looking gorgeous. We looked at each other, baffled.

Cut us some slack here. We were fifteen years old, and although we thought we were pretty cool, hanging out at the lot and all, we really didn't have much of a clue about what went on in the real world, and although you might think it was pretty obvious what they were doing, we had no idea.

"She's just standing there."

"And what's Bernie doing? I don't think she went inside."

We peered into the shadowed entranceway and I finally realized that she was sitting on a milk crate, reading a book.

We didn't have to wait long for something to happen. A car pulled to the curb where Elizabeth was standing, and the driver leaned over to talk to her. She pointed to a driveway a few feet along and the car turned in and parked. A middle-aged guy in a suit got out, and he and Elizabeth walked along the side of the building and in through the door she and Bernie had used earlier. Bernie came out of the entranceway, checked out the car, then went back to her book.

Robert and I scratched our heads, still not getting it.

Fifteen minutes later the guy came out, with Elizabeth a few feet behind him. As soon as he drove off, Bernie came out to the sidewalk too, and she and Elizabeth changed places, Elizabeth going into the shadows of the building's front entrance, Bernie hanging out beside the street for about ten minutes until the same thing happened. This time it was a younger guy in a pickup truck, dressed like a construction worker.

Same deal. They go inside, Elizabeth comes out and takes a good look at the truck, and then, in about fifteen minutes, Bernie and the guy come out, he drives off, and Elizabeth takes up position on the street with Bernie in the shadows.

When the next guy stopped, I finally got it. He'd come up on foot, but the same thing happened. He spoke to Elizabeth for a minute and they disappeared inside.

My guts started to churn, and I felt like I was going to throw up. "Jesus Christ Robert, they're **hookers.** Fucking hookers, man. We lost it to a pair of fucking **hookers.**"

"Oh, fuck me dead." Robert looked as stunned as I felt. "Did you wrap yours?" I asked

"No."

"Me neither."

"Fuck!"

"Your dick hurt?" he asked.

"No."

"Mine neither."

"Think we got something? How long has it been—three days? We'd know within a few days, wouldn't we? Oh, fuck me!"

Robert lit another smoke and sat down against the wall of the garage, looking ill. "They fuck for money. They give blowjobs to whoever has the cash." I said.

"Then what were we?" Robert asked.

"Charity?"

"Fuck you, Todd!"

"Well, what then?"

"I don't know. What's happening up there?"

I looked over toward the boarded-up apartment. "Nothing. It's getting kind of dark, but I think Bernie's still sitting in the doorway." I realized that they were taking turns so that they could act as backup to each other. Whoever was outside would check out the car, probably remembering the make and model and license number so that if anything happened, they could... Could what? Go to the police and say, 'This guy I was fucking wouldn't pay me?' Who were they kidding?

I sat down beside Robert and lit a smoke myself. I thought I knew something about how miserable life could be, but I wondered what sort of life Elizabeth and Bernie had had that would make selling themselves on the street seem like a better alternative. I said as much to Robert.

"I don't know, man, I just don't know." He looked like he was going to cry, and I didn't feel far from it myself. How could I fall for a hooker?

But who was I to talk? Liar. Streetfighter. Thief. Maybe Bernie was like me. Maybe she was doing this because she had to. What I *did* know for sure was that she was nice to me, which almost no one else was, so maybe I should judge her for that, not for what she did to buy her food.

We talked for a few minutes, trying to come to terms with what we had discovered, not really knowing what to think. Finally, I stood up and forced myself to take another look. "Nothing happening. She's still inside."

Robert wasn't very happy. "It's been twenty-five minutes. What's she doing, giving him a blowjob *and* fucking him? Maybe taking it in the ass too? Giving him a real world tour."

"I don't know." I felt sorry for him, having to think about what his girlfriend was doing with some stranger. "Hey, wait a minute, Bernie's coming out of the doorway."

Robert stood up beside me, and we watched as Bernie came out to the sidewalk and kind of stood around as if she wasn't sure what to do.

"Something isn't right," I said.

"What do you mean?"

"She's been in there over half an hour now. And look, Bernie's pacing."

"Maybe she's worried about not getting her share." Robert was pretty bitter.

"No way. Look at her. She's acting really weird." She was walking toward the side door, nervously, as if she wasn't sure what she should do. Finally, she opened it, and eased in, then almost instantly came running back out and around to her hiding place in the front.

A minute later the man who had gone in with Elizabeth came out too. It was almost dark, but we could see that he was a fairly big guy, maybe thirty-five or forty, dressed neatly, but not in a suit. He walked out to the sidewalk, stretched and yawned, then sauntered back the way he'd come.

As soon as he was past the door, Bernie rushed around the side and ran in, out of our sight. But not out of our hearing. Even over the traffic noise we heard her scream.

"What the fuck?" For a second the sound paralyzed us, then I was running across the street, dodging cars and screaming, "Robert! Come on. **Now**!"

Robert was right behind me as I slammed open the door and raced down the hallway to the room where we could hear Bernie whimpering.

She was kneeling beside Elizabeth, her hands over her mouth, tears smearing her makeup.

She didn't question our presence but grabbed onto me as Robert jumped into the room. He let out a low moan.

Elizabeth's naked body was covered with blood, one of her arms was bent at an impossible angle, her face was almost unrecognizable, and there was a scarf or bandana tied around her throat.

She was dead, I was sure of it.

Robert knelt and touched her and started crying loudly. Then leaped to his feet and screamed, "The bastard's gonna pay for this. He's fucking dead already!" He ran from the room at full speed and I was about to follow when Bernie grabbed my arm and pointed. Elizabeth's fingers were moving. She wasn't dead.

I grabbed the bandana that was tied around her throat and worked frantically at the knot, jumping to my feet as soon as it was undone.

"Get help Bernie!" I took her shoulders and spoke slowly, so she'd understand. "There's a pay phone across the street, call 911 and get an ambulance. I'm going after Robert."

She looked at me trying to say something with her eyes.

"You can't do anything for her yourself Bernie, you've got to leave her here and go to the telephone. I have to go after Robert, or he may wind up dead too."

She nodded, knelt beside Elizabeth, kissed her, and said that she was going for help. We ran out of the building. I pointed to the pay phone near where Robert and I had hidden, and took off in the direction that the maniac had gone, hoping that I'd spot Robert before he got himself murdered.

I ran up one street and down another, not knowing where I should be going, but looking into every alley and side street. I was about to give up and go back to see what I could do to help Elizabeth when I heard shouting and crashing from an alley just ahead.

I rocketed around the corner in time to see two dark figures thrashing on the ground, but before I could get there the bigger one threw a couple of hard punches then stood up and delivered the sprawled figure a real shot with his boot.

I recognized the pain sounds as Robert's, but he wasn't struggling any more, just moaning on the ground. The man stepped back and reached for something in the small of his back. I knew what was coming. It was like a slow-motion nightmare. I knew that he was drawing a gun and I knew there was nothing I could do. I couldn't get to them in time to tackle him, and if I screamed to distract him, he'd simply shoot me first and then Robert. I reached blindly into the trash spilling from a garbage can that they had knocked over, felt something hard and threw it before even knowing what it was.

It was an empty wine bottle, and it smacked him in the side of the face just as he was bringing the gun up. He hadn't seen it coming, and it did its job, taking him by surprise so that he dropped the gun as he reached for his head.

I dived for the gun, but even before I got to it, Robert had staggered to his feet and crashed into the guy. They toppled over into a stairwell leading down from the lane, and I heard a loud grunt, then silence.

I picked up the gun. I'd never used one, didn't know if I was supposed to undo some kind of safety, or do something to get it ready to fire, but I pointed it at the stairwell and went forward slowly.

It was a short flight of stairs, leading to the basement of whatever building we were behind. There were no lights in the alley, but the moon was bright enough that I could see Robert standing, looking dazed, and the man lying at his feet, not moving. The door at the foot of the stairs was either missing or open, and through it I could just make out a jumble of wood and scrap that meant renovation.

As I climbed down the stairs, I saw what had happened. The work crew had ripped out a lot of the old cement down there, probably to widen the entrance, and the john had landed on his back on a piece of rebar. It had gone right through him, and was poking out of his chest, wet with dark blood in the moonlight.

"Robert, you okay?" I was gasping from all the running and could hardly talk.

"I'm hurting." He was having some trouble standing, supporting himself leaning against the old doorframe. "I think I've got some broken ribs." I could hear the pain in his voice. "Is he..."

"Dead? Yeah, looks that way"

"Fucker deserved it."

"Who was he?" I asked.

"Fucking psycho murderer."

I could hear sirens now. The ambulance coming for Elizabeth, and cops too, no doubt. I bent down over the dead guy and started going through his pockets. Robert stayed leaning against the wall, sobbing.

"Take it easy Robert, Elizabeth's still alive."

"What?"

"Yeah man, she was unconscious, but she wasn't dead. Bernie called 911, and those sirens mean that she'll be in hospital soon. Fucker meant to kill her though, that's for fucking sure."

My hands hit leather in his inside pocket. I pulled out a small case, flipped it open and held it so I could see it in the moonlight.

"Oh, fuck me."

"What. What is it?"

"Robert, he's a fucking cop! You were getting your ass kicked by a fucking *cop*! A cop that just fucked Elizabeth and tried to kill her!" I screamed.

"Let me see," Robert put his hand out for the badge. I threw it to him. There were now more sirens.

"They're coming Robert. We have to move."

"What?"

"Bernie will have told the cops that the guy went this way, they'll be searching this whole area, we have to fucking well get out of here."

I started up the steps, but he didn't follow. "Robert, snap out of it!"

He was staring at the dead cop's body.

"We have to go man. We killed a cop, if we get caught here, we're dead meat."

Running must have been hell with his broken ribs, but he ran anyway. Nobody spotted us, and before long we were a mile away. It wasn't until the next day that I realized I had put the gun down when I searched the guy's body.

PART II

CHAPTER SIX

It was still dark when the bus arrived in Missoula at 6:30. Grateful that the ride was over, I stashed my suitcases in a locker in the bus depot and went for a walk.

An hour later the blood was flowing again in my legs and butt, and the cool morning air made me realize that I hadn't eaten in fourteen hours. There was no shortage of restaurants, but I wanted real food, so I walked a little longer till I found a workingman's café that looked like my kind of place. Not the kind of yuppie hangout where the espresso drink menu would be longer than the food menu, and not a grease pit where the food would remind me of what I'd had to eat in prison.

There was coffee in my cup and a menu in front of me thirty seconds after I sat down.

"Do you want some time to look at the menu, or do you know what you want?" The waitress was a middle-aged woman who looked like she actually enjoyed her job.

"Do you have a special?" I asked.

"Eggs Benedict for $4.95."

"Sounds good." It *did* sound good. And the place smelled good too. "And a side of hashbrowns if you can do that. And maybe make it three eggs instead of two."

"No problem." She topped up my coffee and headed down the line of tables, refilling cups and talking to most of the customers like she knew them.

It was good to sit and think of nothing. The little city of Missoula had seemed clean and fresh as the sun rose on it during my walk, and for the first time in fifteen years there was no worry about whether I'd be around to see the sun rise again twenty-four hours from now. The only thing weighing on my mind was whether my breakfast would taste as good as I hoped.

"More coffee?" The waitress was back with my breakfast.

"Sure, that'd be great."

She put my breakfast down in front of me and went for the coffee pot.

"Is there someplace around here where I can get a paper?" I asked as she poured.

"If you want to buy one, there's a box just around the corner. If you just want one to read while you eat, we've got a few here. I'll bring one over if you want. National or local?"

What planet had I landed on that people were friendly and helpful? She brought the local paper and I started reading as I dug into breakfast. The local news made zero sense. Maybe if I stayed here for a while, made a home for myself, I'd eventually start caring about politics, or the environment, or even what was going on in some other country, but none of it meant anything to me that day. I turned to the Classifieds and started looking for a room for a few days while I looked for a more permanent place to rent.

A hotel would have been easiest, but I was sick of hotels and motels. The same room over and over and over again. No matter what they did to make them fancy, hotels always reminded me of prison, so I had taken to looking for bed & breakfast places. They weren't always great, but at least they were human. This time though there weren't any advertised, so it looked like a hotel for at least one night. Unless...

"Excuse me ma'am." I flagged down the waitress.

"Ready for the bill?"

"I am." She refilled my coffee cup and started to go. "And maybe you can help me with something else." She seemed to know everybody who came into the place and looked like she'd been around this town for a long time.

"And what might that be?"

"I'd like to stay in town for a couple of days, and I'm looking for a bed and breakfast, but there's none in the paper. You know where I might find one?"

She looked at me for a minute like she wasn't sure she wanted to answer. Finally, she said, "What brings you to Missoula?"

I thought about telling her to go fuck herself—seven years of abuse in foster homes, and fifteen years of hell in Folsom haven't made me comfortable with people who ask me questions—but I bit my tongue. She'd been pretty polite to me, and if she was going to recommend me to someone who had a bed and breakfast place, she had a right to ask a couple of questions.

"I don't honestly know. I've been working way too hard and I need a holiday. Montana sounded like a good place to relax for a while, and Missoula is where I stopped."

She thought about that, then said "Well, the Deborcier's, Anna and Will Deborcier, run a B&B and since this ain't exactly tourist season they probably have space." She looked me up and down again. "They have the Hardware on Third. You drop in there and introduce yourself and they'd probably put you up. Anna's a good cook, and they keep a clean place."

I found my way to Third Street, and an hour later I carried my two suitcases from a taxi into the "Mountain View B&B" with three days paid in advance. Half an hour after that, with the bus ride showered out of my hair, I sat down on the couch planning to kick back for a minute or two before going for another walk around town. But pretty soon I'd stretched out full length and was drifting again, back to the last months of freedom before I moved into Hell.

* * *

Robert and I managed to get away from the death scene without being spotted, although a couple of times we had to duck out of sight as police cars screamed by, and half an hour later, we stopped a hundred yards or so from the lot, and just stood there, looking down the block.

Robert was the first to speak what was in both our minds. "I don't know if I wanna go there right now Todd. I don't think I could talk to anybody right now."

"Me neither."

We'd come to the lot without thinking about it. Robert's parents weren't too bad, and Mr. and Mrs. Fysh were good to me, but that vacant lot had become the center of our lives, and when trouble landed on us we'd automatically headed for it.

"I think I should just go home." Robert was so scared he was almost shaking. "You saved my life back there, man. That psycho was going to shoot me dead, and there wasn't a fuckin' thing I could do about it." He coughed, then hugged his broken ribs in pain. "That's two I owe you, but right now I just can't handle anything besides getting to bed."

I figured he probably should get home. I wanted to go home myself, but what about Bernie? There was nothing we could do for Elizabeth, but Bernie was probably going to need some help.

"You go, man. I'm gonna wait here for a bit. Bernie is going to be totally fucked up by this and I think I should wait here for her."

So, I waited. I waited in one of the abandoned buildings that had a view of the lot. Then I went to her squat and waited there for a while. Then back to the lot.

But I never saw her again.

We got the news the next day that Elizabeth had been found dead in the apartment where we'd left her. They didn't know her name. Just an unidentified teenage prostitute who was beaten to death by, get this, "probably the same psychopathic killer who brutally murdered LAPD Detective Rick Hatcher by impaling him on a yard-long piece of steel reinforcing rod."

My best guess is that when Bernie got back from calling 911 she found Liz dead and just decided to disappear. I hope that wherever she went things worked out okay for her. She meant a lot to me. Not just for the sex, but for seeing something worthwhile in me and giving me a chance as a person.

I didn't go back to the lot for almost a month. I didn't feel like seeing anyone or anything that would remind me of what had happened that night, and since I'd reopened the wound in my chest with all the running, I needed some down time to heal anyway. I kept in touch with Robert though. He was having a harder time of it than I was—not surprising, considering that it was his girlfriend that had been murdered, and him who had actually killed the cop—and he wound up spending a lot of time over at the Fyshs' house.

We let a month go by, then another. Right from the beginning nobody really gave a shit about Elizabeth. One more dead runaway isn't something the TV news gets excited about, and even the cop murder got old pretty soon. We figured that with Bernie gone there was no way anybody could connect us to anything, and eventually we both felt well enough, and safe enough, to go back to the lot.

It was too weird. Everybody wanted to talk to us about Elizabeth, and even though it was something that neither of us wanted to ever think about again, we couldn't risk telling people to fuck off about it. We made up a story about how we'd tried to do a break-in that night and got the shit kicked out of us by a couple of security guards, and that we hadn't heard about Lizzie till a few days later. As far as I could tell, everybody there bought it, and after a couple more weeks, life started to settle back down to normal.

It didn't last very long. The cops barged in and took me down at school one day, and if my life had seemed rough before, it was nothing to what I had to live through from then on.

I never really knew what hit me. I had a lawyer of course, some loser the government paid, but he might as well have been working for the prosecutor for all the good he did me. He told me that the only reason they hadn't nailed me sooner was that they couldn't identify Elizabeth. It was a couple of months before her brother reported her missing, but once he did, it wasn't long before they traced her to the lot, and that led them to Robert and me. My prints were on the cop's badge and gun, and that was enough for a society that needed someone to blame for the murder of a police officer.

Police officer my ass. The guy was a rapist and a sadistic killer, and all we were guilty of was trying to keep him from killing Robert. But nobody wanted to know about that. The only witness who could have helped us was Bernie, and since she had disappeared, they just assumed we'd murdered her too.

Robert got off lucky. He was only fifteen and had a good family and no record. They gave him three years in a juvie tank, which probably wasn't a lot of fun, but compared to what happened to me it was like a three-year paid vacation in Hawaii.

I was a sixteen-year-old juvenile delinquent with no family, and a record of violence from the time I was nine. It was a no-brainer for the judge and jury. In their eyes I was guilty from the second I was escorted into the courtroom, and the only question they had to ask themselves was whether to hang me or shoot me. In the end, because I was only sixteen, they decided to dump me into prison and lose the key.

It happened fast. It was over in a month from the time they pulled me in, and I was almost completely numb through the whole thing. The hardest part was feeling that I'd somehow betrayed Mrs. Fysh. She sat through all of it, and the look in her eyes was worse than anything the judge or the prosecutor said. But what could I do? I tried to tell my story, tried to explain what had happened, but nobody listened. This was long before Rodney King got booted around, and back then nobody even **wanted** to listen to a story about a bent cop.

The prosecutor's story was simple and easy: A brave detective tried to apprehend a couple of crazed punks who had raped and murdered a young girl, but they turned on him and he died in the line of duty.

My story was long and involved and hardly believable: Even though the girls were our friends, we'd spied on them to find out where they worked. Then we'd spied on them *at* work. Then we'd run after a psycho cop who'd butchered one of them for no reason. And finally, we'd 'accidentally' killed him in self-defense.

"Guilty," said the jury.

"Life in prison," said the judge.

Bang! went the gavel, and I was on my way to Hell.

CHAPTER SEVEN

I spent a few more weeks in the city jail waiting to be transported to prison, and now that I wasn't going to be seen by the jury anymore, the cops that had me in custody didn't have to hold back. When I finally left, I had broken ribs and was pissing blood, and throughout it all they kept telling me that compared to what was going to happen to me in the big house, this was easy street.

They'd take turns smacking me around, saying things like, "Soon as I find out where they're sendin' you, you know what I'm gonna do?"

Half the time I'd be too busy spitting blood to answer.

"I'm gonna phone ahead and let them know they got a cop-killer coming." In would go the boot. Or a fist.

"And I'm gonna tell them to have a special reception, just for you." Wham.

"They are gonna round up the biggest, meanest, blackest motherfuckers they got, guys with cocks a foot long and big around as your arm and tell them that you are there for the sole purpose of keeping them happy."

Wham, wham, wham.

"When those niggers finish with you, your asshole is gonna be so big and loose, you could drive a car into it."

Half the time I believed them and was so shit-scared I couldn't think of anything other than praying for death. The other half I figured they were the same as all the other lying jerkwads that had hurt me, and I couldn't wait to get to prison where I'd be safe. Whichever way it turned out, I'd had the shit kicked out of me before, and dealt with that part of it the way I always did, by retreating inside.

"C'mon shithead, time to ride the chain." Two guards, banging on the cell, waking me up out of my private world. "Turn round and gimme your hands."

Why was I being cuffed? What did they mean by 'ride the chain'? By that time, I knew better than to ask questions, and all I could think of was that it was some new way for them to torture me, but it turned out to be my ride from their jail to Folsom Prison. Chained to a dozen men, all bigger than me, and most of them black, and marched to a bus. Then eight fucking hours chained to a ring on my seat on that bus while an endless line of flat fucking desert hills and nameless towns rolled by.

Nobody talked to me that whole ride. A couple of them talked to each other, but mostly we all just stared out the window, taking a last look at the free world, while the guards smoked and joked in the front of the bus.

"Okay ladies, listen up." When the bus finally stopped, we'd been uncuffed and led into a large, ugly room and lined up. We'd stood there for a while, with the guards watching us, and then a huge man in a different uniform from the bus guards came into the room and started yelling at us.

"My name is Sergeant Wood, but you and all the other fuckheads in here call me 'Sir'. While you're in here, you're mine. You understand that?" He looked up and down the line. "I *own* you, and when I say 'jump' you better be three feet off the floor before I finish saying it."

He walked forward till he was face-to-face with the biggest guy in the line and yelled "jump!"

"Huh?"

Next thing we knew the big guy was lying on the floor holding his gut and Wood was sliding a baton back into his belt.

"You all starting to get the picture?" he asked. "Do what you're told and stay out of trouble and we won't need to talk further. Give me or any of the other Corrections Officers any grief and you'll be doing most of your time on your knees, suckin' dick!"

He walked down the line, giving each of us the once over, then came back and stood in front of me.

"Well precious, what's your name?" he asked.

"Todd Black"

Wham!

I didn't even see his hand move, but my ears were ringing so hard I barely heard him, "What did you say?"

"Todd Black, sir."

"That's better." He looked me up and down. "You're cute, Black. We like cute boys in here. We'll be sure to take real good care of you."

He stared at me a little longer and I started to shake with fear, which I think is what he wanted, because he suddenly stepped back and yelled "Atkinson! McDonald! Feller!"

Three guards I hadn't noticed when we came in stepped away from the wall.

"Check 'em over and clean 'em up. You guys," he looked at the guards that had been with us on the bus, "go get your papers signed and head home." He turned back to the three prison guards. "Process 'em and find temporary homes for them. I'll look over the paperwork tomorrow and figure out assignments." He gave us all one last glare and left the room.

"Right, pussies. *Strip*!" One of the new guards screamed. "Clothes off and fold 'em neatly behind you."

We took off our clothes and placed them behind us.

"Now do as I say!" he shouted. "Fold your ears and show the guard in front of you." I did.

"Run your hands through your hair vigorously." I did.

"Stick out your tongue, lift it up." I did.

"Lift up your arms." I did.

"Lift up your balls." I did.

"Now virgins, hands on the wall, bend over and smile!"

What? The promises the police had made about having me raped sprang into my mind. Was that what was going to happen? Were they going to rape us? Right here? Everyone else was facing the wall and bent over but I was too scared to move.

"You got a problem, precious?" the guard in front of me was pulling on a pair of plastic gloves.

"Sir?"

His reply was a baton into my gut, making me bend over. His gloved finger went up my ass. "She's all clean!" he shouted out, and started down the line, fingering one asshole after another.

The sensation of him shoving his finger up my ass was horrible. I couldn't get it out of my mind. What the fuck had he done it for? Why were they fingering our assholes?

"Lift up your feet."

None of this was making sense. Lift my feet? Why did they want to look at my feet? I started to lift one foot, but stopped when the guard that was halfway down the line of bare butts called out, "Hoho! Someone's brought us a present." He was pulling something out of the asshole of one of the black guys.

A condom. A condom stuffed with something and knotted off at the end. I just about puked.

He held it up in his gloved hand, dangling it in the air for everyone to see, then dropped it on the floor and moved on down the line, checking the remaining holes. When he was done, he walked back behind the guy he'd pulled the condom out of and said, "What's your name?"

"Richards, sir." It was hardly more than a mumble. Sounded to me like the guy knew what was coming.

"Richards, you maintain the position. The rest of you, stand up and move over to the far wall."

Once we were all over there he said, "The first thing you scumbags gotta learn is that you don't do **nothin** in here without we say so. You unnerstand? Nothin! From the second you get up in the morning, till the second you fall asleep at night, you are **ours**." He roared out the last word and pointed to his chest.

"And **this** is what happens when you forget that." He turned around and booted Richards, the bent-over guy, in the balls.

Richards collapsed on the floor making little whining sounds, then went rigid and didn't move, but the guards didn't even look at him. It was like he was just some kind of dirt on the floor that someone would get around to sweeping up later.

"Awright, move along. Into the shower room."

We were showered with a big hose and forced to soap up and shampoo while they watched. As I was trying to dry myself off with the tiny towel they gave me, one of the guards pinched my ass and said, "He's gonna break some hearts in here with this."

I froze, and he laughed when he saw my fear. "Hey, it's not me you gotta worry about, what I like to fuck, you ain't got." He turned to the other guard. "But he ain't gonna lack for attention inside."

The other one was checking something off on a clipboard and didn't even look up. "Little fuck killed a cop. Who gives a shit what happens to him?"

"No shit? Killed a cop, huh? Does Wood know about that?"

"Not yet."

The one who had pinched me looked at me again, a weird, empty look like I was already dead.

Once we were dry, they doused us with some kind of powder, and sent us on to another room to get our prison clothes and basic toiletries, and finally back into the main room to wait. The guy they'd booted was gone, and so was the condom. I heard later on the grapevine that he recovered, but that his nuts were ruptured so bad the doc had to cut them out, but at that time I didn't have a clue, I figured he was probably dead, and that I'd probably wind up dead soon too.

"Okay shitheads. Time to go meet your new friends and neighbors."

As we were paraded into the cellblock, carrying our little piles of clothes and possessions, a cry went up and down the tiers of cells.

"Fish! *New fish*!

They banged on their bars. They yelled and screamed. They catcalled and pointed fingers.

Especially at me.

"Hey, look! We got ourselves a baby."

"Yeehaw! A virgin."

"C'mon baby, give me some of that virgin booty!"

"Girlfriend, you'll be mine!"

"Hey sweetcheeks, I got a present for you. It's big and hard and it'll fit perfect up your lily-white ass!"

They blew kisses at me. Some of them bent over and patted their asses. The catcalls kept on coming until it was my turn to be assigned a cell.

"Guard, when does the bidding start at for the baby?"

"Heeey baby, need a man?"

"I got something for ya precious!"

"Oh *yeah* baby. We're gonna have lots of fun. Let's party!"

"Look at that cute little ass!"

It went on and on. The guards never said a word and I was so terrified I could hardly walk. "Black." The guard that was leading us checked his clipboard and stopped in front of a second-tier cell that looked empty. "Sir?"

"In here, 241-B."

I went in. I turned around and stood on the red line inside the cell, like they'd told us to—stand on the line and don't move till every one of us was assigned to a cell.

It didn't take long. Couldn't have been more than about five more minutes, but it felt like five days. These prisoners who'd been yelling at me were big. Most of them looked twice my size. And most of them were black. The schools I'd gone to had had a fair number of black kids, but they'd mostly hung out with themselves. Blacks with blacks. Whites with whites. Chicanos with Chicanos. But these were full-grown men. Huge black guys yelling out that they could hardly wait to fuck my 'lily-white ass.'

"*Level three—close*!" I heard the shout from somewhere above. Followed by "*close two*!" And "*close one*!"

The cell doors all clanged shut and I turned around to look at my new home. Two bunks. One toilet. No privacy here. And someone lying on the top bunk, looking at me with cold gray eyes.

I tried to return his stare, but I couldn't. I put my stuff on the bottom bunk and was about to sit down when he said, in a voice that had no emotion at all, "That's my bunk, punk."

"But you're in the top one."

"That's mine too." He sat up, lit a cigarette and continued to stare at me through the smoke. His bare arms were pale white and heavily tattooed.

"Where do I sleep?"

"Don't care. This is my house, not yours."

"I *have* to stay here. They *put* me in here."

"You won't be here long sonny boy. They'll be bidding on your ass anytime now."

"What?" I asked.

"You'll see. Now get your shit off my bed."

"*No*," I replied.

He jumped down, and the next thing I knew I was lying on the floor clutching my gut. I hadn't even seen him move, and he'd nailed me with the hardest shot I'd ever taken. He leaned down, grabbed the front of my shirt and lifted me up.

"You're trouble fuckboy, and I don't need trouble." He tossed me so that my head banged against the back wall of the cell and I fell, half sitting, onto the shitter. He hopped back up onto the top bunk and picked up the smoke he'd left on the metal frame. "You'll be gone tomorrow, so just don't bother me tonight."

"But where do I sleep?"

"Where you are now." He flicked his butt at me and turned over. Five minutes after that the lights went out.

I didn't sleep the entire night. At first there was chatter coming from all around me. And over the chatter, I could hear the muffled screams of someone else who was also being mistreated. I wondered how badly. And even after things quieted down, I couldn't sleep sitting on the toilet. Every once in a while, I'd get up and pace around the cell as quietly as I could, hoping that I didn't wake up the guy in the bed. I finally found some pajamas in the pile he'd pushed off the bed and changed into them, then fell into a sort of doze sitting on the floor beside the shitter, with my back to the wall.

At 6:00 a.m. the lights came on, and I could hear the prison coming to life around me. My cellmate got off the bunk and looked at me for a minute, as if debating whether to do another number on me. He was older than I'd realized the night before. Forty-something at least, going bald. Not exactly fat, but with a bit of a pot belly. Sort of like a medium-sized bear.

"Get away from the can."

I got up as fast as I could and moved away while he took a long piss. The sound of it made me realize that I badly needed a piss myself, but I was scared that he'd smack me around again for using 'his' toilet, and decided to hold it until I could find a toilet somewhere else. In a bathroom with a door and a lock—no such thing in that prison, but I didn't know it then.

"Stand ready behind the red line! Floor Two, stand ready!" a guard shouted.

"Move your ass kid, get out of my way," my cellmate growled.

He moved to the front of the cell and stood dead center, leaving no room for me, so I stood behind him and hoped that the guards wouldn't jump on me for not standing on the line.

Our doors clanged open.

"Shower time ladies!" screamed another guard.

I followed my tormentor out of the cell and joined the line of pajama-clad men heading for the showers, amid the yelling and prodding of the guards.

"Disrobe ladies, drop your socks, grab those cocks! In ya go."

I felt like a dwarf. These guys were huge, and a lot of them were heavily muscled.

Into the showers we went. There were twice as many people as showerheads, and I wasn't sure where I should stand. Most of the men were two to a showerhead, taking turns under the spray, but I was afraid that if I tried to share with somebody, I'd get the same treatment I got last night.

The room was filling with steam, and I was just standing there, unsure of what to do, when a big hand grabbed me and pushed me into the spray of a shower. "I'm finished kid, get yourself clean." The body that went with the hand was huge and black, but the voice wasn't unfriendly. Not friendly either. Just neutral.

As soon as the guy that had given me his shower was gone, the catcalls started. "So, who wants the new kitten?"

I turned fast, but couldn't tell who had spoken. "Kitty? How 'bout some pussy?"

Laughter.

Someone touched me. I whirled. The man under the shower behind mine said, "Such a cute little kitty. You need a home, kitty?"

"Fuck off! I don't need a home. Leave me be."

"Oooh! I'm so scared. You gonna scratch me, kitty?"

He started soaping up his nuts, massaging his dick in front of me. "You like what you see? Think you can take it all?" he mocked.

The others laughed, and fear began overwhelming me. I shut off the shower and moved to leave but my shower buddy got in my way.

"Leavin' already kitten? Yer breakin my heart." Then he finally stepped out of the way, but as I moved past him, he grabbed my ass and gave it a squeeze.

"Nice. Real nice," he leered, and blew me a kiss.

Back in the changing room I got my pajamas back on as fast as I could, then waited till everyone else was done and we all marched back to our cells to get on our day clothes and wait for breakfast call.

Moving along the meal line was okay. Plenty of people stared at the new face, but nobody said anything to me. Eventually, food was thrown on my plate. It was unrecognizable goo.

"What's this?" I asked the food server.

He looked me over. "Food or lube, take your pick. It'll do for either end."

I took the slop, found space at a table, and sat down. The food tasted about the way it looked, but I'd only managed one mouthful when a voice behind me said, "You're in my place, fish." I turned to see a three-hundred-pound ape staring at me.

"I'm sorry, I didn't..."

He dropped a gigantic hand on my shoulder and heaved me backwards off the bench, onto the floor.

"But I..."

My tray landed beside me, upside down, and I reacted as I always did when pushed too far, by jumping up and taking a wild swing at him. He didn't move or even try to block my punch, just let my small fist bounce off his giant body, then backhanded me so hard that I wound up on the floor again, about ten feet away.

The inmates at the nearby tables looked at me lying there, but nobody said anything, or moved out of his seat. The big guy leaned over me and said, "Find your own fuckin' table." Then walked back to where I'd been, sat down without looking back at me and started shoveling food into his mouth.

A guard walked over as I was standing up, and I wondered how he would handle the gorilla.

I soon found out.

"What's goin on here?"

Before I could say anything, the big guy looked over his shoulder and said, with his mouth full of food, "Little cunt tried to take my place."

The screw took a good look at me. "You're Black, aren't you?"

"That's right. That guy knocked..."

"Shut up."

"What?" I couldn't believe this.

"I said shut the fuck up."

"But that fat ass..." I didn't finish.

"Look shit-for-brains, you're messing with me—yes?" His hand dropped to his baton.

"No sir."

"Then shut your fucking cake-hole and clean up this mess. You have a problem with that?"

"No sir."

"You better not. They told us about you, Black. You worthless fuckin' little cop-killer, you better understand that nobody gives a shit whether you live or die in here—especially me. Got it?"

I nodded. I couldn't have spoken if I'd wanted to.

"Well, don't just fuckin' stand there. Go get a mop and clean this shit off the floor." He pointed to the guys serving the food and walked off. I went over to them and asked for a mop, then cleaned up the mess as best I could. When I was done, I got another tray of slop and found a place at a table that was mostly empty.

In prison, you work. I got laundry.

One of the screws escorted me and several other new fish, to the laundry plant, and told the inmate that ran the place to "…put this little prick on one of the presses."

Two minutes of instruction and I started pressing an endless pile of shirts. The work was noisy, hot, and hard. I didn't understand the instructions and didn't have a clue what I was doing. In the first half hour I didn't get one shirt done right, and came close to scalding myself a few times, until an old guy who was folding and packing clothes showed me what to do. I got it eventually, but the presses produced a huge amount of heat and steam and had no safety features that I could see.

The heat of the press dehydrated me something fierce, and when we were escorted to the cafeteria at noon, I must have drunk a gallon of water. But at least no one beat on me. This time around I didn't look at anyone. I ignored comments. When I got my food, I moved to the same table I'd found at the end of breakfast and inhaled the shit on my tray and kept my eyes down. The food was all mush except for a lump of mystery meat that had been thrown in the middle of it. Still, it went down as fast as I could scoop it up.

After lunch it was back to the laundry and the endless pile of shirts. The heat was almost unbearable. There were a couple of water breaks, but I was soaked with sweat within minutes of starting, and lost way more water than I could get back in.

We finished up in the laundry at 5:00 p.m. My clothes were soaked with sweat and steam and I felt exhausted. It was all I could do to guzzle a load of water and stumble back along behind the others to the yard, where I found a bench and sat down and zoned out.

Supper call was at six—different slop, same taste. This time I sat at a table with some of the laundry workers, which turned out to be the right thing to do. They didn't talk to me, but I watched as a couple of the other new fish from the laundry tried to sit at other tables and were promptly told to fuck off. It had been obvious in the morning that running a press was the worst job in the laundry, and now I could see that laundry was the worst job in the prison. Laundry workers were segregated because of their stinking, sweaty clothes and bodies, and I was singled out among the laundry workers because the guards had put the word out that I was shit.

There wasn't much I could do about it, and I'd had enough experience as the world's punching bag to know that trying to suck up to people and explain that I didn't deserve the treatment I was getting was the worst thing I could do. I figured that eventually things would sort themselves out and I'd learn to cope. Either that or I'd soon be dead.

After supper we were escorted back to our cellblock. The cell doors were all open. People sat on stairs, leaned over railings on the floors above, talking and smoking, smoking and talking. Not much else that they could do. Nobody had told me that I had been transferred to a new cell, so I went back to 241-B, hoping that my cellmate had gotten used to the idea of having company.

He wasn't there, so I took a good look around. He'd made the place as nice as he could, but fuck, it was a prison cell, and there's just not a whole lot you can do that would make it into anything else. There was a chair, an ugly plastic thing, and he had pictures up on the walls, mostly military, but also some drawings that looked like they'd been done by a little kid. On the bookshelf there were a bunch of books on weight training and martial arts—which maybe explained how he'd tossed me around so easily—and a framed picture of a young girl who looked to be maybe twelve or thirteen.

She reminded me of my sister, and all the hopelessness that I'd managed to push away in the last couple of years came crashing down onto me like a tidal wave of wet sand. It was more than I could take, and I fell onto the bottom bunk, and buried my face in the pillow, crying like I hadn't done since I was ten or eleven.

"What the fuck do you think you're doing? Get the fuck off my bed!" Hands grabbed my shoulders and heaved me off the bed, spinning me around and pinning me up against the wall.

He brought his face an inch away from mine, pissed off and looking like he wanted to kill me.

I hung there, helpless and crying, thinking of the time the school principal had lifted me against a wall and slapped me around, and of the misery that I lived through for years afterward.

If he had thought that what he was doing right then was what was making me cry, he probably wouldn't have stopped. Maybe he would have killed me. But I think he could tell that I'd been deep in tears before he'd come into the cell, and something changed in him.

He eased up his grip a little, and said, "So you're still here eh, stinkchild? Well, I don't suppose that's your fault." He pushed me roughly into the chair and stood looming over me, still glaring, but at least not looking like he was about to kick the shit out of me. "I got nothing against you personally kid, but this is *my* house and you are *not* wanted in it. I don't want you sleeping in my beds. I don't want you shitting in my toilet, I don't even want you breathing my air, but there's not a fuck of a lot I can do about it right now, so until someone else claims you, we're both just gonna have to put up with it."

He pulled out a pouch of tobacco and started rolling a cigarette. I didn't say anything, just watched as he lit up.

"That's not gonna be very long I reckon, but until then you stay outta my hair and I'll leave you be." He sucked smoke. "You got that?"

"Yes sir." I was having trouble talking. "But where do I sleep? I can't sleep on the toilet." The tears started again. "I just can't. I tried last night, but I just couldn't."

"Yeah, and your fuckin' pacing around woke me up about fifty times." He thought about it for a while and finally said. "Okay, I don't want you stinkin' up my mattresses, but you can take the blankets off the bottom bunk and sleep on the floor. Just make sure that you fold 'em neatly and put 'em under the bed when you get up. You understand?"

"Yes sir." I didn't tell him that that's what I'd done for a lot of years, and that it wouldn't be a problem.

He walked up and down the length of the little room. "One day, two days, three days, you'll be out of here soon enough. Now wash yourself before you stink up my fucking house any worse." He watched me move to the metal sink and then jumped up to the top bunk.

As I washed up, I could see him in the mirror above the sink. The mirror was metal, and didn't show a clear reflection, but I could see he was reading a book. I didn't want to risk upsetting him again, but he seemed to have backed off from the desire to kick me around.

"What did you mean about someone claiming me? Is that how you get assigned to cells here?" I think I knew what the answer was, but I was desperate for it not to be so.

He didn't answer at first but stared at something I couldn't see in the mirror. Maybe his bookshelf. "I don't know what a kid has to do to wind up in a place like this, but whatever it was … "

I started to speak but he held up his hand to stop me. "I don't want to know. Whatever it was, it hasn't exactly made you flavor of the month with the COs. Up to a point, they try to keep things under control in here, but you are on their shit list, and nobody, from the Warden on down to the lowest badge on the totem pole, is going to do spit for you." He stared down at whatever it was he was looking at on the bookshelf again. "And bein' as you are a cute little piece of ass, you are going to get auctioned off to the highest bidder." He paused to pull out his tobacco. "And then traded around to pay for favors."

I went numb. I could feel the tears coming on again and there was nothing I could do to stop them. "But what can I do?" I wailed.

He looked down again, and this time I could see what he was looking at. It was the picture of the girl. Probably his daughter.

"There's only two things you can do kid." He lit a match and held it to his cigarette. "Stay outta the sight of anybody that wears a uniform," he blew smoke and stared at me without much expression on his face, "and learn to enjoy sucking dick."

With that he opened his book again, leaned back against his pillow, and tuned me out of his world.

At first all I could do was stand there. I couldn't move. Couldn't think. And when my first real thought settled in, it was that I might as well end everything right now. In the past, even in the darkest times, there'd always been the chance that things would get better. And in fact, things **had** gotten better. I'd had a friend. I'd had a girlfriend. I'd started doing okay in school. I'd wound up in a decent home …

But here there would be no escape. I was going to become a bumboy to a bunch of criminals and there was nothing I could do about it. Nowhere to run. Nowhere to hide. No one to turn to for help.

Well, there was **one** thing I could do. I walked out of the cell, across the walkway, and looked over the railing to the cement, two floors below. Looked like about twenty feet, not enough to be sure. There were two more levels above and if I went head-first from the top one, that would probably do it. I turned and headed for the stairs but had only taken two steps when the speakers came to life.

"Time for the count. Back to your mansions ladies."

If I'd been on Tier 3, I might have taken a chance and jumped anyway, but the way things went in my life, if I took a dive from here I'd land on a guard and hurt him just enough to really piss him off. So, I stepped back into the cell, far enough that when my cellmate stood on the red line, I'd be behind him, but when he got down off his bunk he motioned me up to the line and stood beside me. Ten minutes later, once they had reassured themselves that we were all still there, they locked us in for the night.

Comforted by the thought that tomorrow my problems would be over, I slept pretty well.

CHAPTER EIGHT

Morning was okay. The routine was fixed, and there was no way I could get up to Tier 4, but it was okay. I knew that there'd be no problem getting there during gate time in the evening, so I just went with the flow. Shower time featured the same catcalls and pinching as it had the day before, but I didn't get too worked up about it.

"Mmm, looks like we got some jailbait for breakfast."

"Hey, Babyface, you got any hair on that ass or is gonna be smooth and soft like my old lady's?"

"Bet it's tighter than your old lady's!"

"Gonna give me hips or lips tonight, baby?"

I let it roll off like the water from the shower, and the rest of the morning went by smoothly enough. Change, eat the breakfast slop, mail call, shuffle off to the laundry.

The pile of shirts was smaller this morning, and I wondered what we were supposed to do once everything was cleaned and pressed. Just after ten, I discovered that wasn't going to be a problem. A screw, driving some kind of mini tractor thing, showed up pulling three big bins on wheels with 'Block A' stenciled on them.

"Dump 'em, sort 'em, and clean 'em." He was a weaselly looking little guy with a face-full of pimples. He hung around, smoking and talking to the convict boss, while we pulled dirty clothes out of the carts and tossed them into the 'Block A, dirty' bins. Shirts, pants, T-shirts, pajamas, underwear, socks.

"Okay fish, back on your press." Along with the other new guys, I got back to frying my brains in front of the big press. Lift the lever. Put in the shirt. Pull down the lever. Whoosh! Lift the lever, adjust the shirt, pull down the lever …

When I saw the condom full of drugs pulled out of that guy's ass in the reception center, I should have realized that smuggling would be a big industry in the joint. And after the lecture I'd had from my cellmate the night before, I should have had the brains to realize that keeping my eyes pointed straight ahead was the only way to survive. But since I'd decided to take the high dive tonight anyway I wasn't worried too much, and when the convict boss and the screw, along with a couple of inmates that came in from the outside, rolled the bins to the back of the plant I saw them drop in a bunch of boxes and packages before they started loading the clean clothes from the Block A shelves.

"What the fuck are you doing, new fish?" It was a quiet voice from right behind my ear. I started to turn around and felt something sharp just under my ear.

I froze. "Nothing."

"What were you looking at, boy?" the voice asked.

"Nothing, man, just nothing. It's just so hot I have to look away from this press sometimes or I'll scald my eyeballs."

"What'd you rather have kid, scalded eyeballs or me pushin' this shank into your brain?" He pushed it enough so that it broke the skin. "You keep your eyes on your work from now on or you are gonna be a dead fish instead of a new fish." The pressure eased. "You on that?"

"Yeah."

I felt him move away, but I didn't turn around. I kept on working and didn't look up again till lunch. Fuck them all. Six more hours and I was taking the big dive out of here forever.

They came for me that afternoon. I was zoned into the work and with the noise of the laundry plant they could have driven up in a tank and I wouldn't have heard them. The first I knew of it was a raging pain in the back of my leg when the first boot landed. I toppled forward, out of control, reaching for something to steady myself and coming down on the press. The pain was intense, but before I could react the next kick took me in the other leg and the laundry press closed on my hands. Three hundred degrees of heat was like nothing I'd ever felt before.

I wrenched my hands free and screamed, but a blanket went over my head even as the scream came out of my mouth, and the next boot took me in the gut, ending any possibility of noise from me.

Another boot landed on my hip as I collapsed on the floor, and then a couple more in the back, below my ribcage and on either side of the spine. I was fully in the hurt locker by then, and not aware of anything but the pain.

They must have picked me up and carried me into the back room, because that's where I was eventually found, but it was so sudden, and so incredibly painful that I lost all idea of what was happening to me until they threw me down on a hard floor and started pulling my pants off. I thrashed and tried to stand but that just got me a boot in the side of the head.

I wanted to keep fighting, but my body was no longer under my control. Not that it would have mattered. There were four of them, all grown men about twice my size, and even if I had been able to struggle there was never a chance that I'd have been able to stop what was about to happen.

The shot to the head had completely disconnected me from control of my muscles. I was there, and I could feel the pain, but there wasn't much I could do. I tried to move, but my brain wasn't in charge of my body anymore. I've heard that some people have out of body experiences where they feel like they're floating above, watching themselves. Well, this wasn't anything like that. I was still in my body, face down on a cement floor with a blanket over my head. I couldn't see shit, but I could feel every bit of the pain.

Once my pants were gone, they forced me into a kneeling position. One got on his knees behind me. My heart was pounding so hard I thought it would burst. I was almost sick with the rushes of adrenaline. I started to shake and the pain suddenly exploded in my ass.

I was being raped.

"*Nooo*!" I screamed. He tore me as he entered. I tried to fight but they were ten times stronger than me. I tried to scream, but they pulled off the blanket and stuffed a stinking rag in my mouth.

Then the commentary started.

"You take it bitch. You do as we say from now on."

"Yeah baby, you like what I got. Huh bitch?"

"Look at that ass! Ain't that something? No hair at all."

One of them dropped an elbow onto my lower ribs. Another stomped on my head and kicked me in the ear and face. Teeth loosened and part of my ear tore away from the side of my head. My hands felt like they were on fire, like they were still in the press. And all the while, the animal that was riding me pumped in and out of my ass. I could only scream into the towel. I was helpless.

He blew his load, and another took his place. When that one finished, the third one started in. Then the fourth. And when I was no longer of any use to them, one of them stomped on my burned hands. I felt the flesh come off, but the pain didn't last long because at that point they got serious about laying the boots to me, and after the third or fourth shot to the head I passed out.

Consciousness came slowly, and for a long time I had no idea where or even who I was. I tried to move, and pain flooded in from every part of my body. I screamed, but nothing happened. My mouth! What was wrong with my mouth? It wouldn't move. I tried to bring up a hand to touch it, but my hand was wrapped in a huge mitten of gauze bandage and I couldn't feel anything with it. Except pain.

Seeing my bandaged hand brought my memory flooding back, and that was even worse than the pain.

Floating around incoherently on a sea of pain and evil memories kept me from thinking too much for a while, but gradually my mind started to clear and I tried to figure out where I was. The only two things I could be sure of were that I wasn't dead—no way I could be dead and still feel pain like this—and that I must be in a hospital. I could hardly move my head to look around, but I had been in hospital before, and I could see enough to know that that's where I was now.

Taking inventory on my body was tougher. About the only thing I could move was my right arm, and that hurt bad enough that I didn't really want to do it if I didn't have to. And I couldn't seem to think about anything for very long without getting carried back to Neverland on waves of pain.

But if I was in hospital, why weren't they giving me drugs for the pain? Maybe it was a prison hospital where they just let you suffer. On that happy thought I passed out again, and when I came to, I found out that I **had** been drugged. I knew that because my mind was clearer, and my pain was infinitely worse. It had been horrible before, but now it was so far beyond horrible, that horrible sounded good.

I screamed, but nothing happened.

Panic filled me once more. My jaw! What the fuck was wrong with my jaw? It hurt like it was broken in fifty places, but it wouldn't move. And the inside of my mouth… What the hell? Just as I realized that my jaw was wired shut, I heard footsteps, and then a nurse appeared in my limited field of view.

She said some kind words to me, did something to the drip-feed bag they had running into my arm and kept talking till the pain receded and I floated back to La-La Land.

When I woke up, she was still there, or there again, I had no way of knowing. I still didn't make much sense of what she was saying, but I figured out, when she pushed the plunger on the doodad that was attached to the line between my arm and the IV bag, that she was giving me more painkillers.

It took a few cycles in and out of unconsciousness, and several shift-changes of nurses before I could think straight enough to understand what I was being told. The one that finally found me aware enough to follow what she said was the same one I'd seen the first couple of times; a middle-aged woman who looked kind of like an extra-large version of Mrs. Fysh. Caring, but not ready to take much nonsense.

I was in a civilian hospital in Sacramento. I was strapped onto a bed, not because I was a convict who might escape, but because, for the first few days anyway, trying to get up might kill me. I had been beaten pretty close to death, and what they found when they got me into the ER was enough to fill a medical book.

Broken skull, with concussion—they put a drain in the back of my skull to relieve the pressure inside my head. Broken nose. Broken jaw. Multiple facial lacerations, including an ear that was almost torn off. Broken left collarbone. Broken left arm. Severely burned hands with terrible loss of skin on the backs. Eight broken ribs, one of which had punctured a lung, another of which had lacerated my right kidney, which had required major surgery to repair. And, the clincher for me, a severely torn-up asshole.

She didn't put the last part in quite those words, but that's what she meant. Four animals had gang-fucked me to the point that my asshole was torn up so badly that the doctors had to stitch it up.

"You're a very lucky guy Mister Black," she said.

Oh yeah. Right. Lucky Todd Black. All I could think of was the humiliation and pain of having them sliding their dicks into me. With my jaw wired shut I couldn't say anything, but she must have sensed my feelings.

"What I mean is that considering what you've been through, you're lucky to be alive."

Was I? Last night, or last week, or whenever it was, all I wanted was to take my own life *before* something like this happened. Was it lucky that they'd got to me before I could do that? That's not how I felt about it.

"I want to explain something to you. Can you understand what I am saying to you?" she asked.

I nodded.

"You've survived a brutal assault in the prison. Do you know who did this to you?" I tried to shake my head. I really didn't know.

"You were attacked, beaten, and raped Mr. Black." I hoped the other patients couldn't hear.

She touched my arm. "It's not your fault Mr. Black, you need to know that. Do you understand? It's not your fault." She looked into my eyes and for a few seconds we saw each other's soul. Tears streamed down my face.

She reached down like she wanted to hold my hand, then settled for resting her hand on my forearm again. It was hard to tell through my own tears, but it looked like she was crying too. Finally, she said "I'm going to go see a few other patients, but I'll be back in about half an hour to talk to you again and to give you medication for your pain if you need it."

If I needed it?

Once again, she read my mind. "I know you're going to need some, but it's powerful stuff and we're going to try to gradually taper you off it. So, each time we hope that you can try to go a little longer between doses. Do you think you can try to do that?"

I nodded again. Didn't make much difference to me.

"Good. Now if you need help before I get back there's a button here…" she pointed to where a big thing was attached to the blanket, "and you should be able to push it even with your bandages."

I nodded one more time. She patted my arm, stood up, and turned to walk out; but as she turned, I saw her wiping her eyes.

She *had* been crying.

Over the next few days a lot of doctors checked on various parts of me, but most of them didn't say much. It was the nurses that actually talked to me, and from them I learned that, medically at least, things looked good.

"Your kidneys are both going to be fine. You're still passing a lot of blood in your urine, but that's normal, and it'll stop after a while."

Blood in my urine? I hadn't taken a piss since I got here, so how would she know that? And how could I go this long without pissing?

I guess she was getting good at reading my expressions, because she said. "You were catheterized before your surgery, and the catheter is still in place." When I tipped my head in the way that meant "Huh?" she explained what a catheter was.

"And your head is doing just fine too, Mr. Black. They're going to take the drain out tomorrow."

No arguments from me about that one. The goddamn thing drove me crazy rubbing against the pillow.

"Your ribs are going to take a while. There's nothing much that anyone can do about them, but as long as you don't move around much for a couple of weeks, they'll take care of themselves."

Move around? Even after however long I'd been in here, the most I could do without passing out was move my feet and my right arm. They didn't have to worry about me doing any pole vaulting while they weren't looking.

"Your punctured lung sealed up right away; you were lucky on that one." Right. Good thing she reminded me, or I might have forgotten how lucky I was.

"Your anus was torn, and will be swollen for some time, but the doctors tell me that it is also going to heal nicely."

I wondered how it would feel when I finally had to take a shit. And what about food? I hadn't been hungry yet, but there was no way I could eat with my jaw wired. And why wasn't I hungry?

She didn't manage to read my mind this time. She shook her head and said, "They did some terrible things to you—poor thing." And sat patting my arm again.

I nodded, and then the tears started down my face. I was torn between wanting her to stay and comfort me and wanting to be alone. I didn't want this woman to look into my eyes and tell me I had been raped. I didn't want anybody to know—ever!

The next day I got my first food. If you can call mush sucked up through a straw food. I hadn't been hungry, but they told me that I had to start eating in order to help my body heal. By pointing to my mouth and then my ass I managed to make the doctor understand that I was worried about shitting, but he just shrugged his shoulders and told me not to worry about it.

When he was gone, the nurse who was feeding me said, "It'll be okay Mr. Black. We put stool softeners in the food, and your anus is healing nicely, so it won't be too bad."

I pointed to the straps that still held me in place, and then waved my bandaged hand around. My way of saying "How the hell do I get to the shitter when I'm strapped down, and even if I did, how can I wipe my butt with these boxing gloves on?"

She explained about bedpans, but I wasn't looking forward to the experience, and when my first shit came two days later, it was about as much fun as I expected it to be. I felt it coming on, rang my call button, and made the right signs when a nurse came in. She told me to hang on for a few minutes and went to get a male orderly who lifted me up and got the bedpan in position while she cranked the top of the bed up a little.

But then I just couldn't do it. The nurse was young and pretty, and there was just no way I could bring myself to try to take a shit while she watched. In fact, I didn't want either of them watching, and tried to sign for them to leave. In the end the nurse waited outside but I had to take my shit with the orderly standing right there.

When I bore down, my head started throbbing painfully. I moaned, and wanted to give up, but I knew that I'd just have to go through it again, so I kept trying and eventually felt something squeeze out. When it was obvious that I was finished, the orderly washed my ass and took the bedpan away. He was an older guy, and must have seen it all a thousand times, but that didn't make it any easier for me. The only good thing about the whole event was that at least my ass hadn't been too painful.

Later that day I had visitors. Two of them. I recognized Sergeant Wood, the head screw; the other one was an older man in a suit. Wood gave me a look that said he'd have been just as happy to see me go out of his prison in a body bag, and introduced the older guy as Mr. Allen, Warden of Folsom Prison. Where Wood was obviously a sadist, and full of hate, the Warden was harder to figure out. In fact, it was almost like he wasn't even human. No emotion at all. Just the palest blue eyes I'd ever seen, and a voice that might have come out of an alien.

He said a couple of things that didn't mean anything, then, "Do you know who did this to you?"

I shook my head. I hadn't a clue. I wanted to be alone. I couldn't tell what the Warden thought about my response, but Wood's reaction was obvious: relief.

It took me a minute to get it, but when I did, I went cold as ice. He'd been one of them. "No idea?" Wood added. "I suppose you didn't see them coming."

I shook my head again.

"Look kid, if you aren't going to help us help you, then you're on your own."

Now that he was sure that I hadn't seen my attackers, he could pretend to be pissed that I wasn't helping with his 'investigation.' I stared at the wall.

"You killed a cop, kid. That's enough to make it hard for any of us to worry too much about what happens to you in our prison, but we would have given you a chance. You understand that?"

I understood what kind of chance he'd been willing to give me.

"We'd have been willing for you to have a fresh start, but two days after you get here, you're already involving yourself in something that's got you a beating. That's a bad start, boy. A *bad* start."

The warden touched his arm, which shut him up. "They tell us you can't talk, and with your hands bandaged up you can't write either, so we're not going to ask you anything more at this time." He looked at his watch. "You'll be here for two or three more weeks, then transferred to the prison infirmary. Once you're back there, and recovered enough to talk, I'll convene a formal inquiry."

Whatever the fuck that meant.

"Enjoy your stay here while you can," Wood sneered at me and then walked out with the Warden.

Physically, I recovered fairly quickly after that. The doctors took the straps off one day and let me try sitting up. It hurt like hell, but I could do it. My reward for that was to be transferred to a room with barred windows and a locking door, which probably made sense, cuz there was no way I'd go back to Folsom if I could get out of this place, and I got no visits from doctors or nurses unless there was a big orderly there to make sure I didn't get violent with them the way they believed I'd been violent with everyone else in my life.

101

In the two weeks before my transfer back to prison, I had lots of time to reflect. I thought back through my life, thought about every event, every person that had played a part in my eventual sentence of life imprisonment. My childhood in the magic land of Australia. The death of my parents. Kids I'd fought. Teachers, social workers, and foster parents. My one friend, Robert Mandrake. Elizabeth and Bernie. The cop that had killed Elizabeth and tried to kill Robert.

I'd fall asleep wondering if there was anything I could have done differently. Some turn I could have taken that would not have left me raped and beaten in the basement of the Folsom Prison laundry. The conclusion I came to was that I really had done my best. Especially in the last couple of years.

Okay, okay, I wasn't an angel. I still stole, and I still got in fights, but I was trying. I was doing the best that I could to become a normal human being, but all my efforts were blown away by a guy with a badge who killed young girls for kicks.

For a while it seemed unfair that it was me suffering in here and not him, but in the end, I couldn't get too messed up over any of it anymore. All my rage and all my hate were now focused down on one person and one event. I couldn't change the event, it had happened and there was no way I could pretend it hadn't.

But Wood was another story. Right now, he was out of my reach. One day though ...

Maybe if I lived long enough the day would come when he wasn't out of my reach. I let that fire burn inside me and warm me. The idea of paying that fucker back almost made it possible for me to believe that life might be worth living.

And if I was wrong? If it looked like I'd never be able to give him his payback? Well, the cement was still forty feet below the Tier 4 railing, and nobody could stop me from diving.

CHAPTER NINE

My dreams of prison eventually woke me up. I found myself in a cold, sticky sweat. I wasn't in the hospital bed anymore. I was in a vastly more comfortable bed in the B&B in Montana. My clock read 6:00 a.m. and I knew I wasn't going to get back to sleep, even in this comfortable bed, so I got up and walked to the window. Montana's mountains were beautiful. Green with forest at the bottom and thrusting rocky and snowy summits up into the sky. No traffic jams, no people in my face, no old ladies taking forever to walk down a grocery aisle... Code Slow, Code Slow, Code Slow. This place was heaven.

The balcony door opened easily, and I walked out onto the sundeck. I was bare-balls and felt the cool morning breeze over my entire body. Birds sang, life was everywhere around me.

Below me I heard someone open a sliding glass door. "Mr. Black?" She must have heard me moving around.

"Yes?"

"Would you like to join us for breakfast outside, on the patio?"

A smile came over my face just from looking at this beautiful day. "Yes, I'd love to. What time would you like me down there?"

"How's thirty minutes from now?"

"Fine."

"Good, see you then."

I went inside, shit, showered, and shaved. I dressed myself in my clean clothes then ventured downstairs and out the back door, onto the patio.

"Good morning, Mr. Black. Did you sleep well?" Mrs. Deborcier asked. Either her husband had already left, or he wasn't up yet.

"Beautifully, thank you. Everything is wonderful. Well worth the money."

She had brought out a vast array of fried eggs, sausages, hashbrowns, toast, and fruit. "Ma'am," I said. "This is quite the spread."

"Wasn't nothing," she replied. "So, what brings you to our lovely town?" she asked as she served me.

103

"Relaxation," I answered.

"A vacation?"

"I'm not sure if 'vacation' is the right word for it or not. I'm here for a while. I don't know how long exactly."

That got her a bit suspicious. Well, I couldn't blame her, she was taking a stranger into her house, and someone who didn't have any kind of fixed plans was someone to be suspicious of.

"What do you do, Mr. Black?"

"I write. I've been a contract writer down in LA for seventeen years, and I finally just couldn't stand the rat race anymore." I'd told the story many times in the last couple of years, and it flowed out smoothly.

"I don't know for sure that I'm ready to retire, but I know that I need some time off. What I want to do is just find a quiet place away from cities, maybe with a lake nearby, and just take a year off." Her suspicion disappeared, but I continued with the story anyway. "I've always wanted to write a novel, but I could never do it where I was. This will give me a chance to finally do that."

"How exciting. Have you written anything I would know of?" she asked.

"I doubt it. I wrote advertising copy, annual reports, technical manuals, worked on some movie and TV scripts. I made a ton of money, but never got my name on anything."

"Oh well." She sounded disappointed. I wasn't a famous writer that she could gossip to her friends about, just another city slicker looking to get some fresh air, which was exactly what I wanted her to think. She spoke up again.

"My husband said you only wanted to stay for three days?"

"That's all I wanted to commit to. I'd like to look around the area, maybe find a cabin to rent somewhere if I decide to stay longer."

That brought a big smile to her face. "Well, don't that just beat all? We own a small cabin, my husband and I, up on Flatbed Lake. It's right on the lake, and real private. Now that Matt's moved out on his own..." She leaned forward, "Matt's our son. He's got an automotive shop up in Kalispell. I think he'd be about your age. How old are you?"

A nice old lady, and she knew how to throw a breakfast, but she sure did like to talk. "I'm thirty-five."

"Well, Matt's a couple of years younger than you then. Anyway, we used to go up to that cabin all the time, but we just don't seem to get around to it anymore, and we've been talking about renting it out. It would be just perfect for you. I know it would."

"Sounds like a possibility," I answered. "When can I see it?"

"Why, anytime you like. In fact, Matt's coming down to see us today, and I'm sure he'd be happy to take you up there and show it to you tomorrow, when he goes home."

My mouth was full of delicious food, so I nodded, and continued to shovel it in while she rambled on. When my plate was empty, she refilled it without my asking, and I started in again. She was about to give me thirds, but I stopped her.

"Delicious spread, Ma'am. Thank you very much indeed."

Relaxing with a full belly, my eyes went from focusing on her, to the vast countryside. So much land, so few people. So perfect for me.

When the coffee was done, I helped clear the table then went upstairs to my room and opened my suitcases. All the money, all two million of it, was still there. I took out a grand and filled my wallet, then lay down on my bed with all the windows open.

* * *

By the end of my fourth week in hospital the stitches were out of my ass and I could shit no problem. My ribs were still sore, it sometimes hurt to piss, and I was still sucking my food through a straw; but the doctors decided that I could finish healing just as well in prison as in their hospital, so I rode the chain back to Folsom and limped into the infirmary to finish my recovery.

The first couple of days were tough. No more Demerol, for one thing, so my pain levels went back up; and the fact of being back in the joint was hard for me to accept, made me think that maybe taking the high dive was the right choice after all. What kept me going was a dream I had the second night, in which my sister Susan was reaching out for help and I couldn't quite grab her hand. I woke up sweating and crying, but after I calmed down, I thought that although nothing I could ever do would help her, killing Wood might save some other poor soul.

That thought was reinforced by what I saw going on around me in the infirmary. Inmates were brought in almost daily, victims of beatings, stabbings, burns, poisoning, and rape. Attempted suicides landed there too. Inmates used whatever they could get their hands on. Some stuck nails into their own arms and tried to rip out the arteries—they weren't looking for attention, they meant to die. There were also victims of murder. The prison was a war zone, and the infirmary was like an emergency hospital on a battlefield. From what I had seen, that was the way Sergeant Wood liked it.

They kept me in the infirmary for two weeks, then sent me back to the hospital to get my jaw unwired. I spent a couple of days there, getting x-rayed, poked, prodded, and sampled, until they told me that as far as they could tell, I was healing fine. They weren't sure if I'd get back full use of my hands, but that I'd probably get pretty close; and as for the rest of me, as long as I stuck to soft food for a few weeks, and didn't try to do any heavy lifting, I'd soon be back to normal.

I said I hadn't seen any solid food in the three days I'd spent eating in the prison mess hall, so I didn't think that would be a problem, and asked them to tell the nurses that had taken care of me that I appreciated their work. Then, for the third time in about six weeks, I rode the chain to Folsom.

The guard on the bus signed me over to a guard at the prison. It was a moment I'd been dreading. I knew that I wasn't scheduled to go back to the infirmary, and I'd wondered if Wood was going to be waiting for me, to finish me off properly. The guard that signed for me didn't look like meeting me was the high point of his day, but at least he didn't seem outright hostile. I wondered if that meant that I'd be okay, or if it just meant that they'd come for me later.

The guard checked a clipboard, then escorted me to the infirmary to pick up my clothes, to the commissary where I was told I had enough credit to get some tobacco and papers, and then to a new cell in a different block than I'd been in before; this time on Tier 4, which was just fine with me. If my new cellmate was okay, then I'd try getting on with life; if it was some psycho who had won me by making the highest bid for my asshole, then I could walk out the door and go over the rail anytime.

My first cellmate crossed my mind. He'd reacted to my presence in his 'house' with anger and violence, but in the end had let me be. And he'd been right about the fact that sooner or later somebody was going to come for me. They had just come a lot sooner and a lot more violently than I'd expected.

The new cell was the same as the old one, except it didn't look like anybody's house. There was no chair, no bookcase, and no pictures on the walls. Toilet, sink, steel mirror, and two bunks. That was it. There were blankets on the bottom bunk, and some clothes folded at the foot, so I knew I wasn't going to be alone, but whoever it was hadn't done anything to make the place his own. I didn't know if that was a good sign or a bad one, but at least there was nothing obvious that said he was a psycho.

It was evening, and it wouldn't be long till I met whoever I was going to be sharing the place with, so I put my bundle of clothes on the top bunk and tried to climb up. Not much fun with ribs that were still healing, but I made it, sat down, and got out the tobacco and papers and tried rolling a cigarette.

I was still trying when I heard someone come in. Fear flooded through my whole body, and I dropped the paper and tobacco on the mattress, but when I looked up, I knew that whatever else happened, I wasn't going to get much trouble from this guy.

He was obviously a new fish too. Newer even than me, and scared shitless. Older than me, but still pretty young to be in a place like this.

He was staring at my face, and I could tell that it just about made him shit his pants. I'd seen it in a mirror, and while the stitches had all been removed, it was still a scarred-up mess. I'd probably be nervous about having to share a cell with Frankenstein's grandson too.

He got hold of himself and tried to act tough, but he was wasting his time. Eight years of violence had taught me how to tell who was tough and who wasn't, and this guy wasn't.

"Just get in?" I asked.

"Yeah."

"What's your deal?"

"Vehicular manslaughter. I got ten years."

I wondered how many of those ten years he'd live to see. "You got the bottom, so I'll take the top. That okay with you?" I asked.

"Yeah fine."

He was still trying to pretend that he was on top of himself, but that wasn't going to work in this joint. Things were going to be rough for him, maybe not as rough as they already had been for me, but he didn't look like he was going to be able to handle it. He looked like he'd shatter into pieces the first time he took a good punch.

Not my problem. I swept up the tobacco I'd spilled on the mattress and put it back in the package, then started making my bed.

The next morning was going to be another test for me, and as I lay on the bunk after the lights went out I wondered if I should have taken the big dive as soon as I'd had the chance, but eventually I fell asleep, and didn't wake up till the guards started hollering into the speakers in the morning.

The next morning in the showers brought me some attention. My bruises were starting to fade, but they were still visible from head to foot. My face and hands were scarred from the beating and burning, and my chest and side were scarred from the surgery. And then there were the old scars from jumping out of a window, and the huge one from when I got slashed with the bottle.

"*Jesus H. Christ* kid, you should be in a side show, not in here."

"What'd ya try to do boy, french-kiss a Mack Truck?"

"Nah. Looks like he had a fire in his mouth, and somebody put it out with a bicycle chain."

"A bit sore, are we? Try soap next time."

Laughter came from all around, but at least no one groped me. I shut off the shower and went into the change room, dried off, and headed back to my cell to wait for breakfast call.

Breakfast was the same slop as ever. They called it scrambled eggs, but it was just pale-yellow mush that I could have eaten through a straw if my jaw was still wired. The orange juice was mostly water, the coffee tasted like they'd washed last night's dishes in it, and the toast didn't taste like anything at all.

I sat at the table with the laundry guys, even though I didn't know if that's where I'd be working. Everybody sort of looked at me once and then acted as if I wasn't there, or as if nothing had happened. No teasing, no questions, no sympathy. My guess was that the word had come down to them that they hadn't seen anything, hadn't heard anything, and that if any of them ever said anything they'd wind up like me.

At mail call I got the word that I was headed back to the laundry. That frightened me a lot more than I thought it would and walking through the door and into the plant I was overwhelmed with a flashback to the day I was attacked. I felt the heat hit my body. I saw the steam. I saw the press machine. I smelled the sweat of men.

"Black!"

My thoughts were somewhere else.

"You listening to me, asshole?" It was the convict boss.

"Yes Sir," I replied.

"Back on the press."

That's not what I'd wanted to hear. I could feel the pain in my hands all over again. "Did you hear me, Black? You got shit in your ears?"

"No Sir. No problem."

I moved to the press and looked around before starting work. My new cellmate was loading wash into the giant washers, but otherwise everything looked the same as it had when I first got put there.

The day was hot, hard, and never-ending. I wasn't very strong after my hospital time, and the heat got to me a lot worse than it had before, but I kept my head down, and eventually got through it. We knocked off at five, and since I'd survived the day, I decided to see what yard-time had to offer before supper.

Not much, it turned out. Guys just stood around, smoking and talking. Or sat on benches or steps. There was a ball diamond, but nobody was using it. I sat on one of the bleachers behind home plate and let the sun work on me for a while, then headed up to my cell.

It was quiet in the block. Most of the prisoners were out in the yard, and the ones who weren't were just sitting in their cells reading or staring at the walls. As I walked along the walkway I stopped and looked down. Forty feet easy.

My cellmate was in, still scared, and still trying to pretend that he wasn't. We exchanged names, but I didn't really want to talk to him, so I got up on my bunk and told him I'd like to take a nap till supper time. I lay back, closed my eyes, and he left me alone.

Wake up. Shower. Breakfast. Work. Lunch. Work. Yard-time. Supper. Gate-time. Lights out. That's it. Over and over, and fucking over. Saturday and Sunday weren't much different except that there was no work. I didn't talk to anyone except Larry, the guy in my cell, and although I still got teased and catcalled sometimes, nobody bothered me much. I got slapped around by the guards a few times for being slow, or stupid, or ugly... Whatever excuse they needed when they felt like smacking someone, but nothing serious.

By keeping my head down and my mouth shut for a couple of weeks, I was able to learn by overhearing the conversations going on around me. I learned that the guards liked to be called 'Corrections Officers,' but that to the prisoners they were mostly 'badges' or 'bulls.' That I, and other kiss-asses and losers like me, were 'inmates,' but that guys who had their shit together were 'convicts.' And that the pay for working in the laundry was enough to keep me in tobacco and papers, but not much more.

I also learned how to roll my own cigarettes, which seemed like the most important thing to me.

Midway through that second week, at lunch call, I got the final answer to the question of my place in this new world. We all started trooping out to head for our chow but the trusty—the convict boss in charge of the laundry—grabbed my shoulder and said, "You stay here Black."

As soon as the others were all gone, two guys I didn't know, except for maybe seeing them a time or two in the mess hall, came in, and I knew what was going to happen.

I backed into a corner and got ready to fight for my life, but they didn't come at me, just stood, kind of looking me over, starting to smile.

"You enjoy what happened to you last time, Black?" It was the boss, staring at me with half a smile on his face too.

"Fuck you, asshole. You wanna kill me, then let's get started."

"Doesn't have to be that way, unless you really want it. I'm giving you a choice here, and if you got any brains at all, you're gonna get your pants off and give my boys a ride."

One of the boys was rubbing his crotch, almost drooling. "Yeah sweetcheeks, wriggle outta them pants and show us what you got for us."

I charged, swinging my fist for his face.

Might as well have swung for the moon. They were halfway expecting me to do just that, probably more than half hoping I would. The result was the same as if I'd just dropped 'em like they told me, except that I got kicked around as well as fucked.

It started with a couple of shots to the gut, and after that they got to do what they wanted. They ripped my pants off and forced me to my knees. One of them got behind me and slapped my head back and forth a few times, then grabbed my hair so I couldn't move. The other one stood in front of me and started rubbing his crotch again.

"Look at what I've got for you, bitch, look here." He slowly undid his belt and stepped out of his pants. His dick was pushing out his underwear like a tent pole. He rubbed it some more, then pulled down the underwear.

"Got something for you, fuckboy."

It was huge, and the end was dripping.

"Mmmm. A nice big sausage for the little boy's lunch." The one behind pushed my head forward. I tried to turn, but it was hopeless.

"You'll make us happy, won't you?" He yanked my head backwards and slammed a palm into my nose, breaking it again. "You *want* to make us happy, right?" He pressed the palm against my nose, and I almost passed out.

"Open your mouth and make my friend a happy man." He took his hand away from my nose, and leaned close and said, "And no biting, neither. Little boys that bite won't ever be able to bite again, cuz they won't have any teeth left."

He grabbed my head with both hands and made me move forwards and backwards over the other guy's hard-on until it hit the back of my throat, making me gag, then yanked me back while his buddy lay down on the floor with his legs spread and his dick sticking up.

"C'mon baby, get down here and suck."

The guy behind forced me over into the dog and fucked me while his buddy held my hair, yanking my mouth up and down over his cock. He moaned and groaned and started thrashing under me, and the other one pumped in and out, yelling at the top of his voice.

"You're mine. I own you. I'm gonna fuck your ass and you're gonna like it." In and out, slamming into my butt, hurting like crazy. "C'mon punk, get that ass movin'. Gimme some action back here."

So, tell me, what would you have done? Would you have fought them? Two men twice your age and each of them a hundred pounds heavier than you? In a place where they could kill you if they felt like it and no one would care?

I gave them what they wanted.

I kept my mind on the drop from Tier 4 to the main pit below and gave them what they told me to give them.

When it was over, I lay in the corner, cum leaking out of my ass, blood leaking out of my nose, while they got dressed.

"Not bad bitch, not bad." One of them walked over and toed me with his boot. Not a kick, just enough to roll me over where I had to look at him. "You got a lot to learn, but that wasn't too bad for a virgin." He smiled and tossed down a package of tobacco. "See ya soon, baby."

When they were gone, I staggered over to one of the sinks and threw up. After I'd washed the vomit away, I cleaned up my ass as well as I could, got dressed, with some paper towels packed into my underwear, and headed for the infirmary to get my nose taken care of. I pretended that I'd tripped and smashed my face against one of the machines in the laundry, and the infirmary guard pretended to believe me.

When my cellie saw me that night, and asked what had happened, I thought about telling him. But he was going to find out for himself soon enough, so all I said was, "You don't wanna know," and crawled into bed.

The broken nose got me a couple of days off, and during that time he did find out for himself. Showed up just before supper call the first night, eyes empty, walking like he didn't know what planet he was on. He was cut up and bruised some, not near as much as I'd been, but then, he wouldn't have resisted much.

That night, as I lay on my bunk listening to him crying in the darkness below, I thought about the choices available to me. There were only two: either I took what came my way, or I took one last jump over the railing outside my cell. I thought about it for a long time, but there really weren't any other options. Oh, I could try to fight, but all that would get me was beaten as well as raped, so there wasn't much point in that.

What it came down to was the fact that getting fucked, and being forced to suck dick, was the worst thing I could imagine—a lot worse than dying. I knew I could live with the pain; I'd lived with pain for as long as I could remember, but how could I live with the humiliation? What could possibly be worse than spending my life as a fuckboy for a bunch of criminal psychos?

It was as I was falling asleep, with the decision to go over the rail pretty much made, that I realized that there **was** something worse than getting raped like that. The thought that I knew who was responsible and that if I killed myself, I'd never be able to make him pay for what he'd done to me, was far, far worse.

Nothing that anybody could do to me now could be worse than what had already been done. There was nothing left of me for anyone to take away. All that was left was my need for revenge, and nobody could ever take that away.

So, I chose to live. I chose to learn everything I could about the way the joint worked in the hope that one day I'd learn how to get my revenge.

CHAPTER TEN

What was it like? If you haven't been there, there's no way you can ever understand, but believe me when I tell you that when I die and go to Hell, it's going to be a lot better than my first two years in Folsom Prison.

What I eventually came to understand was that Sergeant Rick Wood had a pretty good thing going. Prison takes men away from what they want, and if they want it badly enough, they'll give whatever it takes to get it. For some, it's nothing you'd really think much about. Books maybe, or their stamp collection. For others it's sex. Or power. Or drugs.

None of those things can be had in a prison unless guards are either bribed or intimidated into allowing them to be had, and guards can't be bribed or intimidated on any large scale unless The Man allows it. Wood was The Man, and not only did he allow it, he rolled in it like a pig rolls in shit. He loved it. He was a sadist who loved making people suffer and being head guard in a maximum security prison is the ultimate job for a sadist.

He could order people beaten or killed. He could beat them or kill them himself—and he often did. He was Judge, Jury, and Executioner. He decided who got rewarded and who got punished, and one of the favorite rewards he gave to the convicts and guards who worked for him was boy-toys in the rough. My cellmate and I were two of them.

The laundry was a major transit point for goods going in and out, and the convict boss who ran it got my services as part of his reward. He didn't use boys himself, but he paid a lot of his debts by providing entertainment services. I was the service.

Sometimes it was only humiliating. "Get down there and suck baby, and I wanna have you looking me in the eyes when you swallow."

Other times it was brutal. For some of these guys, violence was how they got off. They'd beat the shit out of me and jerk off on my face as I lay there bleeding. Make me suck them off after they'd put the boots to me so hard I could barely move. Fuck me while twisting my arm so far up my back that it dislocated.

But the worst time wasn't somebody's reward, it was my punishment for accidentally seeing something I shouldn't have. I'd gone to the back room of the laundry, where there was a toilet, to take a leak. That was all I wanted to do, take a simple piss. I never went back there when anyone else was there—no way I wanted to interrupt something that I wasn't supposed to know about—but this time I'd gotten back a bit late from lunch, and hadn't seen anybody go in for the half hour I'd been on the press, so I was sure it would be empty.

There were four of them. Three were sitting around the little card table that the boss kept back there, the fourth was leaning over a 'Block C' bin, and as I walked in, he stood up, lifting a brown paper parcel from the bottom.

He had his back to me, the others were all looking at him, and I was outta there faster than I've ever moved in my life, so I was pretty sure that they hadn't seen me. I hauled ass straight back to the press and was busy making shirts flat when the door opened. I didn't look up, but I could see out of the corner of my eye that the guy who came out went over to talk to the laundry boss.

Fuck. Had he seen me go in there? I didn't think so. He'd been doing paperwork, and he usually said something if he saw you heading for the toilet, and I hadn't noticed him looking up. And if he had noticed, he'd have told them that I was out of there instantly, that I couldn't have seen anything.

Wrong.

He must have seen me, and told them, because they came for me in the yard after work. I never even saw them. I was headed back to my cell, almost out of the yard when the blanket went over my head, and the first boot took me in the ribs.

They dragged me somewhere, I didn't know where—probably the janitorial room where I was found the next morning—and went to work on me.

They kicked me around for a while, then took turns raping me, then got back to knocking me around, which was what they seemed to enjoy most.

I passed out. More than once. But each time they'd manage to wake me up and carry on with the lesson they were teaching me, which was "You didn't see nothing." Wham. "You didn't hear nothing." Smash. "You ain't gonna tell nothing to nobody. Not ever." Boot. "Cuz if you do, we are going to come back and kill you one fucking inch at a time."

Then they raped me again; or at least some of them did, I was only semiconscious by this time, and don't know how many loads got blown in my ass.

When they'd all had as much of me as they wanted, they dumped me on the ground. "You there, bitch?" When I made no reply, one of them stood on my hand and grabbed a finger. Then broke it.

"*Aarrgh!*"

He pulled on another finger, broke it too, then yanked the blanket off my head and booted me into darkness.

I woke up in the prison infirmary. I wasn't as bad as I'd been after the very first beating—not bad enough to send me to the outside hospital—but bad enough that I was in pain for weeks. They'd broken ribs again, and an arm, and my nose, and the two fingers. But this time no lungs or kidneys had been punctured and I guess the prison doc didn't think a few broken bones was worth wasting a lot of real hospital space on.

My treatment? They yanked my nose into place and taped it. Put a cast on my arm, splinted my fingers, and taped my ribs. The blanket had done its job of keeping my skin from getting torn, so they didn't have to do any stitching, and my ass had been getting poked for two years, so last night's rape hadn't been anything special in that regard.

Officer Wood paid me a visit on my second day. "Black," he said.

"Sir." My lips were so swollen I could hardly talk.

"You pissed me off again." Everyone could hear the conversation. "You're causing me grief. I don't like grief. Do you?"

"No Sir."

"Then stop pissing me off."

"Yes sir."

"You know what? You are getting exactly what you had coming. You killed a cop, fucker!" He bent down to get closer. "Every CO in here knows what you did, and they don't like it one bit, so don't expect things to get any better." He stood up. "If you're thinking about making any kind of call over this, remember that Hell has many levels, joyboy, and I'm in charge of every one of them. This is my domain, and every time you piss me off, you are going to find out what the next level is like. You go looking for attention about this fuckface, and I will personally drag your sorry, cum-bleeding ass all the way to solitary and help you spend a month dying. You understand?"

"Yes sir."

With that he walked off.

CHAPTER ELEVEN

Looking back on it now, I'm amazed I survived those two years. Maybe, if that stay in the infirmary hadn't ended as it did, I'd have given up at that point. My cellmate, Larry Dalton, had taken that option after only a couple of months. He'd managed to get his hands on a razor blade, and I woke up one morning to find him lying on top of his blankets with his wrists slit the proper way, sliced all the way down from the top of the forearm to the wrist.

That hadn't been one of my better days, and the cellmate that replaced him was a real prick. He talked nonstop, was foulmouthed even by prison standards, and the only reason he didn't beat the shit out of me on a daily basis was that the first time he'd done it he'd had the shit beaten out of *him* by a couple of my boss's friends.

I might not have had any stature or power of my own, but I was property, and he found out what happens when you mess with someone else's property.

But I *had* survived.

I wasn't the same Todd Black that had gone in, though. Those two years saw all the humanity fucked out of me. I knew it was happening, and I wasn't too comfortable about it, but it was either become an animal, or die, and I didn't want to die until I'd given Wood full payback. Unfortunately, one of the things I'd learned was that there was probably no way I was going to be able to do that. He was bigger than me, and never came around the prisoners by himself.

I probably would have given up after that beating. If there was no chance for revenge, there was no point in living a life of pain and humiliation, and I'd have gone looking for my own razor blade or taken my long-promised high dive.

Why didn't I? Because after Wood walked out, a voice from the next bed said, "You're still alive, kid." It was more of a statement than a question. "Doesn't look like you learned anything since you moved outta my house though."

Who? I took a closer look and recognized my first cellmate. The one who'd been so happy to see me that he'd beaten me up and made me sleep on the shitter.

No anger or aggression in his voice or his face though, so I said, "Yeah, I did. I learned how to suck dick."

He laughed. Black humor makes a great icebreaker.

I think I may have passed out then, because it was semi-dark next time I was aware of anything.

I stumbled painfully to the head for a piss, and when I got back to my bed, he looked up from the book he was reading. One of his forearms was heavily bandaged, and I thought I could see more bandages under his pajama top.

He saw me looking at bandages, smiled, but didn't say anything about his arm. "You learned how to survive then, eh?" he asked.

"I do what I have to do to get by."

"You like doing it?"

"Like it? Sucking dick and getting the shit kicked out of me? Get real."

"Remember how I treated you when you first came in?" he asked.

"Yeah, you beat the shit out of me."

"Yes, I did, stupid! Why did I?"

"I don't know."

"Two years and you don't know?" He rolled his eyes like he'd never met anybody as ignorant as me. "Stay that dumb and you'll be a bitch for life. In here, you want something, you fight for it. I've been in here for five years now, and everything I got, I fought for. Anything more I want, I know I'm gonna have to fight for it. I have to. And you're gonna have to."

That pissed me off. "Yeah sure. Me and what army? I got about as much chance fighting these guys as you'd have fighting a fucking tank."

I thought he'd probably beat on me, bandaged arm or not, but all he did was roll a thin one and look at me through the cloud of smoke after he lit it. As if he was trying to decide something about me.

"What's your name, kid?"

I calmed down a bit and told him.

"Well Todd, I *have* fought a tank. In fact, I've fought a lot of tanks, and I'm still alive, and all the guys who were in the tanks are dead. But I'll tell you something," he took a big drag off the cigarette, "I sure as hell didn't beat 'em by pounding my way through the armor with my bare hands. You try to take on Wood and his perverts with your fists and all you'll get for it is hospital time."

"So how else am I supposed to do it, rent a machine gun?"

"That'd be one way." He said it like it was actually possible. "But then you'd wind up dead."

He stopped talking suddenly. He was still looking at me, but I could tell he wasn't really seeing anything, that his mind was turned inward, thinking hard about something. Then he snapped back to the here-and-now like he'd made a decision.

"You want a better life in here, boy?"

I started to say, 'Of course I do,' but then I stopped. All I'd wanted for two years was a chance to get back at the man who turned my life into such a living hell.

"What I really want is to see that cunt Wood, lying on the ground dying painfully."

"I thought so. But think about something else." He butted the cigarette in the ashtray on the table between our beds. "Life in here is never going to be easy—*nobody* in this joint does easy time—but it doesn't have to be as hard as what you're doing. Not by a long shot."

I didn't say anything. Either he'd tell me something or he wouldn't. I'd learned how to wait. "Right now, you're in no position to do anything about Wood. Maybe someday you will be, although you'll probably have to take a number and wait your turn behind about five-hundred other guys, but right now your choice is whether to do time, or to do hard time. Whether to suck dick or not."

"I don't remember anybody giving me a choice about it," I said sarcastically.

"In here, kid, not knowing how things are done isn't an excuse, it's a chance. A chance for someone to fuck you over." He picked up the book he'd been reading. "I'm outta the infirmary tomorrow, and I'll sort a few things out for you. Look me up when you get out and we'll talk about what you can do in return." He opened the book, and started to read, then looked up and added. "Just remember one thing."

"What's that?"

"Anything I do for you, I can undo, just as easily."

With that, he went back to his book and tuned me out of his world. I had about a million questions, but I also had the sense not to ask them. I'd been pretty good at reading people's intentions before I got thrown into the joint, and two years here had honed that instinct even more. I knew when to keep my mouth shut.

* * *

I woke up at two o'clock when someone knocked on my door. It turned out to be the Deborciers' son, Matthew.

"Pleasure to meet you Matt."

"Likewise," he replied.

He had a tough, but open and honest workingman's face. Not hardened like mine, but the face of someone who worked and played with the gas pedal all the way down. "I got down a little early, and if you're up for it, I'll show you the cabin this afternoon instead of tomorrow. Be good to get some more air, and it'll beat listening to my mother telling me how I shoulda been married years ago." He broke into a big grin. "She's a great mother, and I love her, but man, she could talk the leg off a pool table."

"Sure, whatever works for you. Is it far?"

"Eighty miles. Closer to Kalispell than to here, but it's great country all the way. Be a good ride."

"Let's go."

"Okay. Grab a jacket, we're going on my bike, and it's gonna be windy."

When we got outside and I saw the motorcycle my eyes must have lit up, because Matt said, "You like it."

"Beautiful."

"You ever ride on one of these before?" he asked.

"Never," I replied. We walked over to the bike. It was obviously his pride and joy.

"I got her from an old man who bought it in 1960, brand new," he said. "Traded it for doing some mechanical work to his car. He got bad arthritis and couldn't ride it anymore and I think he was looking for someone who'd love her the way he had." He patted the gleaming metal. "So, I fixed up his car, got this beauty, and restored her."

"It sure is a beautiful-looking machine," I said.

"Thanks," he replied. "It's a 1960 BMW twin. An R50/2 with 494cc displacement. She's always reliable and man, what a ride."

I didn't know anything about motorcycles, but it did look beautiful. "It's close to thirty years old. What do you do for parts?"

"There's a vintage BMW place down in Norcross, Georgia. It's called Blue Moon Cycle, run by a guy who's dedicated to keeping these things on the road. He's even on the Internet selling parts worldwide. These machines have quite a following."

He lectured me for a few minutes on things like horizontal pistons, the Earles fork, and the individual saddle seats. "The Germans built it for cruising pleasure. It's a touring bike and it's a swell ride, man. You ready to check it out for yourself?"

"You bet!" I answered enthusiastically.

The rear saddle was higher than the one in front. It made for a strange ride, being taller than the driver, but it gave me a great view and I embraced the wind as it hit my face. The wind danced through my hair and I held out my arms, flying on the ground. That is, I held out my arms until a bee hit my open palm. It felt like a fucking bullet. I stopped being stupid and did up my jacket, praying that one of those bugs didn't hit my face. A man on the highway on one of these things could feed himself by just opening his mouth and driving fast.

We turned off the highway after about three-quarters of an hour and went up a gravel road for about another fifteen or twenty minutes. There were thick trees on both sides but once in a while I'd catch a glimpse of blue water to the left. Then we turned onto an even narrower dirt road, and a minute later I was in Heaven. Beautiful little cabin, huge expanse of blue lake, mountains all around, no noise, no people.

We got down off the bike and stretched our legs, then Matt led me up to the porch and unlocked the door. It had that dusty smell of not being used lately, but it was clean and well furnished. The kitchen was in an L off the living room, there was a bathroom with new-looking plumbing, and a bedroom with a queen-size bed and a mountain view.

"Like it?" he asked. "I mean, it ain't much. Mom said you were some kind of writer?"

"Yeah, that's right, some kind of writer," I said. "I don't have a name you'd recognize, but I am a writer."

"No, no," he said. "I didn't mean that the way it came out. I just think that this would probably be a great place for you to relax is all. Mom said you were looking for a place to get away from the rat race and regain some focus."

"Yeah Matthew, you're probably right. This may be just what I need. What's your price?"

"How long you gonna stay?"

"Don't really know. But I'll lease it for however long you need. A month, three months, a year. Whatever."

"Okay, how's five hundred a month grab ya? That includes a full tank of propane, which you'll need to run the fridge and stove and heat, and the electricity, but you refill the propane tank yourself."

"Deal." I pulled out my wallet. "Here's a grand. I'll give you another five hundred tomorrow and we can call it mine for three months. That suit you?"

If he was surprised at being handed the cash on the spot, he managed not to show it, just counted out the ten hundreds and tucked them in his back pocket.

We locked up the cabin, walked around for a while with him pointing out names of mountains, which I promptly forgot, and then got back on his bike and headed for Missoula, and supper. It was an incredible ride. The bike didn't rattle or vibrate. Someone back in 1960 Germany deserved some real credit.

We drove up to the B&B. I got off his bike and shook his hand. "Thanks for taking me out there. There's just one small problem I overlooked," I said.

"What's that?" he asked, shutting down the machine.

"I have no wheels to get to and from the cabin. I need something."

"What do you have in mind?"

"How about a vintage 1960 BMW R50/2?" His eyes bugged out of his head.

"You want to buy my bike? No way, man! Sorry. We've worked together, you know? Blood, sweat, and skin. I restored this baby myself. You've got good taste Todd, but I can't sell you my bike."

"What about that place in Georgia you mentioned."

"Blue Moon Cycle?" he asked.

"Yeah. Do they restore bikes and sell them?"

"Sure, but they're gonna cost."

"How much you reckon? For one like yours."

"Fully done up?"

"Yeah, to the tits."

"Six or seven grand, give or take."

I made the decision then and there.

"Matthew, would you like to earn a few grand?" His eyes told me I had his attention. "There's no way I can go out to Georgia myself and bring the bike back because I've never driven one. Would three grand plus expenses tempt you to do it for me? Phone this guy, order a bike as close to yours as you can get, fly out, and drive her back?"

"Fuck man, for three grand I'd **walk** out there and **push** it back. But Blue Moon is gonna want the money up front."

"No problem. I'll give you cash, and you can pay them as soon as you're sure the bike is right."

"Cash? You're going to give me seven grand, in cash?"

"Why not? Plus three for your time and effort, plus some for expenses."

"Whatever you say, boss."

"And on the way back, stop at the biggest music store, in the biggest city you pass through, and buy me all the ska CDs you can get your hands on. That possible? You know ska?"

"Like the Bosstones, right?" he replied.

"Yeah. Get me a big variety. I can pick up a decent ghetto blaster here in Missoula, but I reckon the ska selection isn't going to be very deep. And pick up some oi and some punk too." I thought about some of the music I'd heard in the joint. Stuff that some of the old cons played. "And maybe some sixties soul and some Motown too."

"Sure man. I can do that."

Two days later, he was back in town, knocking at my door and asking, "You still for real on this, man?"

"Yup. You find something?"

"Oh yeah, did I ever. Blue Moon's got **exactly** what you want. An old R50/2 like mine. They're almost finished restoring it. It'll be ready in two days. They want seventy-five hundred, and they're not willing to bargain on the price. That still okay with you?"

I handed him an envelope. "There's fifteen grand in there. That'll pay for the bike, plus get you to Georgia and buy you gas and hotels on the way back. Should get me a big stack of CDs, and still leave you close to three. If there's accessories that aren't on the bike that you think I should have, just go ahead and get 'em. If the expenses wind up more than you expect, I'll make up your three grand when you get back."

He started to put the fat envelope inside his jacket. "Not till we count it, bro."

We counted. One hundred and fifty hundred-dollar bills.

"Fifteen K. Like you said." He put it back in the envelope and zipped it into the inside pocket of his jacket.

"Before you go, I need two more things from you, nothing big."

"Sure, no problem. What do you need?"

"A ride to the grocery store and then a lift out to the cabin, in a car. Can you get a car?"

"Sure, I'll borrow my mother's."

"Cool. Thanks."

We did the grocery thing, enough chow for two weeks; then loaded my suitcases, along with some books and the new ghetto blaster and the few CDs I'd bought the day before, into the trunk beside the groceries and hit the road.

CHAPTER TWELVE

When I woke up the next morning, my hospital companion was gone. I wasn't sure what to think about the things he'd said. I was certain that he was going to do something for me—no point in him telling me that he could help me if he couldn't. He wouldn't waste breath talking to a pillow-biter like me if there wasn't a good reason for it. On the other hand, he wasn't going to be giving me anything for free, so the big question was, 'What does he want from me?' And that's where I came up against a blank wall.

As far as I could tell, the only two things I had to offer anybody in this shithole were my ass and my mouth, and he could have those anytime he wanted. And I didn't get the impression that he was interested in my sexual services anyway.

So, what the fuck *did* he want?

When the orderly came around to check on me that morning, I asked for some help rolling a smoke.

"Kinda hard to do it one-handed," I said, lifting my casted arm off the sheets. "Roll one for yourself if you want." He would have taken one anyway, but I knew better than not to offer.

While he rolled, I asked, "What happened to the old guy on the bed beside me. Pretty big roll of bandage on his arm."

"Old guy?" The orderly laughed. "Sergeant-Major maybe look old to a baby like you, but he the *last* one you ever wanna tangle with."

Now that surprised me.

"Huh? You telling me he's tough?"

"Tough ain't the word." He handed me the smoke and started rolling another for himself. "Couple of big boys got into the pruno last week and made a call on him, figgered they'd make a rep, I guess. Last call they'll ever make."

I lit up. "Whadaya mean, last call?"

"They tough boys. Big fuckers, train in the gym all the time, and they

126

both had bangers."

"So, they cut him up?" I'd heard about bangers. Blades made from whatever was available. Bedsprings, chisels, whatever. Easy to hide, easy to get rid of, and instant death in a fight.

"Yeah, you saw his arm. He needed some stitches there, and there was a cut on his chest too, but that's all. And them two that tried for him, they went outta here in bags." He shook his head. "Two of the meanest fuckers in the joint, twice his size, and he kill both without getting more'n a couple of scratches."

"He have a gun, or what?"

"Gun? Sergeant-Major don't need no guns." He made a couple of show-off karate moves. "He a killer. He a *real* killer." He stuck the cigarette he'd rolled behind his ear, tossed the tobacco onto my bed and wandered off on his rounds.

Whoa, mama. What had I stumbled into?

It was a week before I got my first clue. I'd tried to pump the orderly a couple more times but got nowhere. The most he said to me was, "Only more thing you need to know 'bout Sergeant-Major is you **never** cross him. Not no way, not never."

I got discharged from the infirmary on a Sunday, and the guard that came for me said, "Looks like you got a new home, kid." He checked the clipboard he was carrying. "335-B. Says here that all your shit's been moved already, so there's nothing to pick up from your old hole."

What the fuck? Transferred to a new block? Getting away from the freak I'd shared my cell with for the past sixteen months was definitely a step in the right direction. Although, like Wood had told me, there were levels even in Hell, and maybe I was just changing levels. Maybe my new cellie would be worse, not better. That was not a comforting thought.

But Block B was where I'd spent my first few days. Where I'd met the 'Sergeant-Major'. Was this his doing?

My new roommate turned out to be a lean, but strong-looking black guy called Rope. I'd been right up close and personal with some black guys in the last two years, but they hadn't beat me or fucked me any worse than the white guys who beat me and fucked me, so I didn't have much in the way of prejudice to overcome, and Rope seemed okay.

His house was clean. He had a chair, and a bookcase with a lot of books on it, just like that first cell I'd seen.

"Sit."

He didn't sound aggressive, but it was clearly an order. I sat on the chair he'd pointed to. "Here's the rules. They're real simple. First, I have the top bunk. Second, you keep your self and your stuff clean. Third, there is no fucking or dick-sucking gonna happen in this room—you keep your hands on your own dick and I'll keep my hands on mine." He looked hard at me to make sure I understood.

"Fourth, you keep your hands off my stuff and I keep my hands off yours. You want to borrow a book or something, you ask politely and you can probably have it. Take anything without asking and you're outta here on a stretcher."

Reminded me of the rules Mrs. Fysh had laid out for me when I moved into her home. Although she hadn't had to say anything about dick-sucking.

"Sounds fair to me." But then I realized that if he was a hygiene freak he wasn't going to like the way I smelled after a day in the laundry. "Uh, you said keep myself clean … "

"Yeah?"

"I got nothing against that, but there's no place to shower after I get out of the laundry, so I probably won't smell too clean in the evenings."

"You're out of the laundry. Nobody tell you that?"

"Out of the laundry?"

"Didn't you talk to Ian yet?"

"Ian? Who's Ian?" What was going on here? "I just got out of the hospital about twenty minutes ago. I haven't talked to anybody but the badge that brought me here, and he was dumber than a fucking doorknob." I pulled tobacco and papers out of my pocket and started to roll a smoke, then decided I might as well try being friendly. "You want one?"

"Sure." Rope took the package and dug out a palmful. "Ian told me he talked to you in the infirmary."

"That guy? The one they call the Sergeant-Major?"

"That's the one. Sergeant-Major Ian James Douglas. Only we're not in the army, so we call him Ian."

"He got me transferred?"

"I think maybe you should talk to him yourself about that. No sense me guessing what he'd like me to tell you."

"I guess not."

We smoked in silence for a minute. I still hurt enough that I didn't really want to get up, but he had said to look him up when I got out of the infirmary.

"You know where he is?"

"Not for sure. Probably in his room. 241-B."

241-B was pretty much as I remembered it. Posters and drawings on the wall. Books. Chair.

And Sergeant-Major Ian Douglas reading on the top bunk. I rattled my knuckles on his bars. "Hello, Black."

"Uh, hello sir. I guess I came down to thank you for getting me transferred."

"Don't thank me till you've seen the price tag." He put the book down. "Come in and sit down, we've got some talking to do."

I sat and he talked.

"I told you I'd sort a few things out for you while you were in the hospital, and I've done that. You've got a new room, you'll be working in the woodshop instead of the laundry, and you won't be bending over for any of Wood's rough boys anymore."

I didn't say anything.

"Aren't you gonna thank me?"

"I did already. But you said something about the price tag."

"Ah. You *have* learned something." He got down off the top bunk and sat on the bottom one, where he could look me more in the eye. "There *is* going to be a price, and you'll find out what it is soon enough." He saw the look in my eyes. "Relax, it doesn't involve your asshole."

I still couldn't imagine what else he, or anyone, would want from me. My asshole was pretty much all I had to offer in this place.

"Here's the deal. I have a problem that I think you can help me solve. If I'm right, if you can help, then life is going to get a lot better for both of us. But…" He pointed a thick forefinger at me. "But I don't know for sure about you yet, and for the next little while, maybe a month or two, you are on probation. You do what you're told, work hard, learn what we teach you, and we'll go from there."

If he really was the kind of guy who could take on two giants with knives, the kind of guy who could arrange for me to get transferred, then I couldn't imagine him needing *my* help with anything. He was obviously miles ahead of me though, so I gave up worrying about it.

"Okay, I'll do my best."

"Good. First thing, you start getting in shape. Right now, all you're good for is sucking dick and pressing shirts. Rope'll show you what you need to do. Teach you. You got any problem with niggers?"

"I don't really know any."

"Well, Rope is a good guy. He's tough, and he's smart, and he knows more about fitness and strength than anyone I ever met. Do what he tells you."

"Yes sir."

"Next, you're going to be working in carpentry from now on. Douggie the Druggie is the boss up there, and he's going to be teaching you a whole lot of things you need to know. He's a big guy with red hair and a wild accent. He's from Australia."

"So am I."

"Yeah, I could hear it. You must have come over pretty young, your accent's nearly gone. Most people wouldn't be able to tell anymore." He leaned back against the end of the bed and pulled a deck of reals out of his pocket, took one for himself and held the package out to me, "Smoke?"

"Wow. Thanks. I haven't had anything but rollies since I got in."

We lit up and he said, "So when did you arrive in this shitcan of a country?"

Slowly, he pulled the story of my life out of me. I'd never told anyone before. Robert had heard some of it, but a lot of it had been locked away in the dark and never spoken aloud. It was weird to lay it out on the table like that. My childhood memories of Australia, moving to the US, my parents' murder, my sister's murder—yeah, I know, she killed herself, but it was murder as far as I was concerned—the many foster homes and schools, the journey into violence and petty crime, and the final irony, getting sent down for life because I'd tried to save a friend from a psychotic killer.

It didn't take long. I didn't give him the day-by-day version, but he seemed to understand pretty well. And I surprised myself by not crying. Maybe I just didn't have any tears left.

He didn't say much. Asked a question now and then, but otherwise just sat and listened. At the end he said, "Not much of a life, kid, but work hard for me and there'll be better days ahead." Then he stood up and motioned me toward the door. "Let's start by getting you healthy. Go see what Rope has to say about that."

What Rope had to say was a surprise. It didn't have anything to do with lifting weights or working out, it was about food.

"What they feed you in here gives you one thing, and one thing only, and that's calories. You want to get into any kind of shape, you are going to have to start by upgrading your fuel intake."

What?

"See this?" He opened a box that sat on his bookshelf and pointed to a bunch of little bottles of pills and capsules. "One of each, every morning after breakfast."

"You want me to take pills?"

"Bet your skinny white ass. Vitamins and minerals that a normal human could get in his food, but which you are most definitely not getting in what they serve here."

"Okay, if you say so."

"I say so."

He ran through a whole pile of rules about food and made me repeat them back to him till he was sure I'd remember. What things I should eat a lot of, what I should stay away from. Drinking lots of water and not much milk. Not smoking quite so much, taking care of my teeth ...

Once we'd gone over that stuff about twenty times, and he was sure I'd remember it all, he said. "How bad are you hurting?"

Normally I'd have lied, or said something noncommittal like, 'I'm okay,' but I figured that if this guy was actually trying to help me, I should be straight with him.

"Bad."

"Tell me."

"Okay, my arm's busted," I waved my cast at him "my fing..."

"Busted how?"

"I don't know. I was under a blanket, man. I think they probably did it with a pipe, but I don't know, could have been a boot, or a bat."

"I don't mean how did they break it, I mean how is it broken. Which bone? How badly? Complete fracture or greenstick?"

I didn't have a clue and told him so. "They didn't send me out to the hospital for x-rays, so I don't even know how the prison doc could tell." I thought about it. I had been awake when they put the cast on. I hadn't been tracking too straight, but I had been awake. "Uh, let me think." They'd been talking while they casted me. "The elmer bone. They said something about my elmer bone being broken."

"Ulna?"

"Yeah, that's right, ulner."

"Ulna. U-L-N-A." He spelled it for me. "It's the small one that runs along the outside of your forearm. Okay, what else? What happened to your fingers?"

I told him about the fingers, and about the nose, and the ribs.

"Let me see."

He unbuttoned my shirt and helped me get it off. Not much fun with broken ribs and fingers. He poked and prodded gently for a bit, then said "Hmmm."

What was that supposed to mean? He helped me get my shirt back on.

"Your ribs aren't too bad, but for a couple of weeks you're going to have to go pretty light, and no running for a couple of weeks either."

"Do *what* pretty light?"

"Weights. You ever work out with weights?"

"No. And how can I lift weights with a broken arm?"

"C'mon, let's go down to the iron pile and I'll show you."

Douggie the Druggie was another story entirely. He was taller than Rope, six-four or six-five, had flaming red hair, and must have weighed three hundred pounds. He had 'enforcer' written all over him. Tattoos ran up and down his arms and covered the part of his chest I could see at the neck of his shirt, and it was pretty easy to picture him riding a Harley in full outlaw colors.

I saw him as soon as I reported to the woodshop on Monday morning—shit, you could hardly miss him, and his Aussie accent came out on a big booming voice—but I didn't actually meet him till the end of the second day. One of the other convicts had spent those days teaching me how to use some of the machines and tools, and got me set up doing a simple job on the lathe, turning short lengths of wood into what he told me were going to be used as chair legs. About all I could do in the shape I was in.

I was getting ready to knock off when that Australian voice spoke softly behind me. "Right mate, you hang about when the others leave. Time for a talk with Douggie." I don't know which surprised me more, that someone that big could have got that close without me hearing him, or that the voice that was usually loud enough to break windows could be that soft.

He disappeared, but was back fifteen minutes later, after the others had gone.

"Welcome to Douggie the Druggie's School of Proper Mayhem. You comfortable with this thing yet?" He pointed to the lathe.

"I'm doing okay. My fingers and arm are a problem, but I can do the chair legs okay."

"Good. Now I'm going to show you how to do something a little more useful than a fuckin' chair leg." He picked up one of the finished chair legs and sort of waved it under my nose. "What I want you to notice is two things. First, this is nice hard wood. Take a good finish, no slivers. Second, it's not as big around as the average dick, which means that it can go up somebody's arse without causing any severe discomfort."

My eyes must have widened some, because he quickly added "Okay, I grant you it *is* longer than any dick I ever saw, but if we shorten it up some…" He turned on a saw and in about ten seconds had turned an eighteen-inch chair leg into half a dozen three-inch stubbies. He was so fast on the saw that I could hardly see his hands move.

"Righty-O." He turned the saw off and held up one of the short pieces. "Now mate, the question of the day is, why would you want this little woody up your butt?" He fastened the wood into the lathe, put on goggles and said, "Hang on a mo."

He was fast and efficient on the lathe, too. When he was done, he took the piece out, moved to a sander, worked on it for another minute, then handed it to me. "Recognize it?"

It was fat at one end, tapered a bit, but never got smaller than about half an inch thick. I looked at it, but it was just a piece of wood that fit smoothly into my hand. That's when it hit me. I pulled a screwdriver from the rack. It was a high-quality one, or so the guy who'd shown me around had told me, with a handle exactly like the piece of wood Douggie had made.

"Hey, good one. Now, the next question is, why would you want a screwdriver handle up your butt?"

"I've had enough up my butt lately; I don't need any screwdrivers, thank you."

He laughed. "Yeah, right. Well, in addition to being a decent poop-chute, your arsehole is one of the few places you can carry something that nobody can see."

"I know that. I saw a badge pull a condom full of blow out of a guy's ass the very first day I was here, but why would anybody want to smuggle a screwdriver han... Hey, wait, wait a minute." I remembered something that had puzzled me no end when it happened.

"That guy that got shanked in the showers last year. Somebody had to get the shank in there, and a naked guy can't walk past the bulls carrying a shank, can he?" I thought about it. It could work. As long as you made sure a tiny bit was still sticking out so it didn't cut your own ass. "So, what do you do? Sharpen up screwdrivers or something and stick them handle-first up your ass?"

Douggie looked at me like he was seeing something he hadn't expected to see. "Well, well, well. Maybe Ian was right about you." He pulled something out of one of the huge pockets on his coveralls. "Not a screwdriver. Screwdrivers work just fine, but they keep track of how many we got in here. So, we make our own." He handed a piece of metal to me.

It was like a pencil but made of steel. About six inches long, one end tapered to a wicked point, the other threaded, like a wood screw. I handed it back to him.

"Watch this." He mounted the handle in a vise, drilled a hole in the narrow end, then put the shank in a pair of vice-grips and screwed it into the hole he'd just made. "Voila! The Arsehole of invisible death strikes again."

He loosened the vise and handed me the shank. It fit nicely in my hand and five inches of pointed steel were at my service.

"Gotta sand and oil the handle some, otherwise you'll wind up with slivers in your arse, but otherwise it's a piece of piss."

I didn't know what 'piece of piss' meant. Probably Australian for 'easy as pie' or something.

"Now, you do it." He handed me one of the three-inch pieces.

I screwed it up, of course. It was a pretty small piece, and with one arm in a cast and two fingers in splints, I was pretty clumsy. He didn't seem to mind. Just handed me another piece and said, "Try again."

I messed up three of them but got the fourth just about right. It wasn't as smooth and clean as the one he had done, but as he said, a bit of sanding would make it serviceable, and anyway, I'd do better once my hand and arm were back to normal.

"You're all right, mate. I think you'll do just fine." Douggie was pleasant enough to me, but I didn't fool myself about how deep his feelings were. He was an enforcer. Everything about him made that clear, and I knew that if breaking one of my legs became his job, then he'd break one of my legs. Probably with the same good humor as he taught me how to make shank handles.

Six weeks later I was healthier than I'd ever been in my life. I don't know where Rope learned all that shit about nutrition, but he knew what he was doing. Proper diet, regular workouts in the weight pit, and, once my ribs were able to take it, regular runs on the track that ran around the perimeter of the yard were melting flab and building muscle.

It hurt. Fuck, did it ever, but Rope had promised that I'd get used to that kind of pain—come to like it even—and he was right.

And I'd learned how to make all kinds of weapons out of all kinds of raw material. I never really got to like Douggie the way I came to like Rope, but he was alright. He treated me fair, was patient with me up to a point, and in return, I worked hard for him. I learned to work with most of the tools in the wood shop and was looking forward to doing the same thing in the metal shop. In fact, I was all ready to start on metal one Monday after work when he said, "Shop's closed for the day. Ian wants to talk to you. Go get your running shoes and meet him on the track."

I'd hardly seen Ian since the day of the transfer, so I was both excited and a little afraid. Life had been sweet for six weeks, but I suspected that I was about to be told about the price tag. And I now had an idea about what that price might be.

He was in the yard, in his shorts and T-shirt, stretching, when I got down.

"Hey, Black, let me have a look at you." He made me turn around. "Not bad. Rope said you were coming along, but I wanted to see for myself."

As he was talking, he gradually lowered himself into a full split. I couldn't believe it. The guy must be almost fifty, and he didn't look like any kind of athlete, but Rope had been teaching me about stretching before working out and I'd tried that split thing, so I knew how impossible it was.

"C'mon kid, stretch a bit and then let's go for a jog."

So we stretched, him doing things a lot of gymnasts probably couldn't do, and me doing things that would have had a gymnast rolling on the floor laughing. He asked me a few questions about how things were going, and then said, "Okay, let's roll."

He set off slowly, which was good, because slowly was still about as fast as I could manage. We did a few laps that way, just jogging, not talking, but as we started the fourth lap he said, "When we go past the ball diamond this time, I want you to look at the guys that are standing by the bleachers on the first-base side. You got that?"

"By the bleachers on the first-base side. That's the side we come to first, right?"

"Right. There's four gooks there. Don't do any major staring but get as good a look as you can. I want you to notice the one that's sitting on the bleachers, not standing."

So I looked as we went by. Four Asians. Japanese or Chinese, I wouldn't know which. The one that was sitting didn't look any different than the three that were standing.

We were well past them when Ian spoke. "You get a good look?"

"Yeah, but they kinda look the same to me."

"Look more carefully this time. The one sitting has a scar on his face, about here." He ran a finger down the left side of his jaw. "It's still fresh, and pretty obvious."

I looked again on our next pass, and sure enough, the sitting guy had a big scar on his face. We did two more laps, then pulled over for some stretching and cool down. No one was close, and just before we headed to shower and change for supper, Ian asked, "So, you'll recognize him if you see him again?"

"Oh yeah. Pretty hard to miss that scar."

"Good. I want you to kill him."

So that was the price I was going to have to pay for not sucking dick.

Murder.

Well, I'd seen it coming. I'd thought about the price tag for most of the last six weeks, and murder is pretty much all I'd ever been able to come up with. I was too young and weak to do any kind of enforcement, I never got outside so I couldn't do any smuggling, and as for any kind of menial job, say turning shank handles, there was no need to have put out the effort with Rope and Douggie to get me to do that. I'd have offered to shape shank handles with my teeth if it had meant not bending over any more, and he knew that. Murder was pretty much all that was left.

And I'd thought about my answer, too. "Okay."

Ian was way more surprised with my answer than I had been with his demand. Hah. One for me.

"That's all? Just 'okay?'"

"Well, I'd like to know when and where and how, and maybe why, but I reckon you'll get to that on your own time.

"You aren't kidding, are you?"

"Come on Ian. I never got much of an education, but I'm not stupid."

"So, you've got it all figured out?" He was pretty sarcastic.

"No, I don't." I was sitting, leaning way forward, touching my toes. "I really don't have a clue what is going on between you and him, or why you think that I'm the guy to solve the problem, but if that's the way out of being Wood's favorite bumboy, then that's what I'll do."

I sat up straight, then stood. "And you know that I don't have a fucking clue how to kill anybody either, right?"

"Oh, I can teach you that. *How* is easy. Anybody can do the **how** part. What I can't teach you is to be mean and miserable enough to want do it in the first place." He smiled. "But Wood's already taught you that, so I don't have to." The smile turned into laughter.

CHAPTER THIRTEEN

I didn't do much of anything during that first week by the lake. Cleaned up the cabin, sat on the porch and read. Walked aimlessly along the shore. Nights were quiet and peaceful, and I slept the kind of sleep I hadn't had since I was eight years old.

My reading was interrupted on the afternoon of the eighth day when I heard a motorcycle coming up the gravel road. Matt honked the horn as he came into sight around the last corner, pulled up beside the porch and dismounted.

The bike was magnificent.

"*Whooooeeee*! What a beauty." The chrome shone, and the body gleamed a deep blue-black even under the dust of three thousand miles.

"It's an R50/2 like mine, but it's fully restored and all broken in. I had 'em add a few extras, and I picked up as much music as I could find."

"Fuckin-A, bro."

"Ready for a ride?"

"Soon, soon. Show me the tunes. Let's go inside."

He dug into the saddlebags and pulled out bag after bag of CDs, handing them up to me on the porch. I couldn't believe what I was seeing. "C'mon in. Let's see what we've got here." I picked up as much as I could and went inside. He followed with the last few bags and we dumped everything out on the table.

"God damn, I've never seen so much music in my life." The pile covered the whole table, there must have been over a hundred CDs.

"Hey man, Atlanta is a **big** city. Big and black, and music stores there really know about your kind of music. You asked for a variety. I hope I got what you wanted. Ska, soul, and oi. It's all there!" He poked at the mess on the table. "I've got receipts for everything. There's even a few hundred left over." He was reaching into his inner jacket pocket.

"I'll take the receipts, but you keep whatever's left over, man. Keep it. You have done wonders." I started picking up the CDs and could hardly believe what I was seeing. What a collection! I picked up one after another.

Some ska and punk bands I knew, like the Bosstones, Rancid, Selector, and the Pie Tasters, plus dozens I'd never heard of. Skankin Pickle, Area 7, The Porkers, Skapa, and Skaboom.

"Whoa! This *is* a fuckin' collection!" I looked at Matthew, who had been standing there patiently whilst I stared at my new CDs. "Man, I never heard of half of these bands. You did great. This is awesome!"

"I got lots of the stuff you asked for, ska, oi, punk, Motown, and soul, and I also picked up a couple of things that I like, that you maybe hadn't heard of." He dug around in the pile and came up with a couple of CDs. "Old stuff from the sixties that was sort of rock and sort of not." He handed them to me. "You ever hear The Ventures? Or Dick Dale?"

I shook my head.

"Wicked guitar, man. I think you'll like 'em."

I wanted to play them all, right now, then I remembered what was outside. "Take me for a ride!"

He did. We rode down to the highway, where he could put some speed on, then back toward the cabin. As soon as we were off the main road he stopped, told me to get off, and started teaching me the basics. How to get on and off, how to start the engine. Brakes, clutch, throttle, shift.

"You remember how to ride a bicycle?"

"Nope."

"Ah, come on, it might have been a long time, but nobody really forgets."

Matt seemed like a good guy. Someone I might even be able to get friendly with one day, but I wasn't ready to unlock any doors yet, so I just said, "Never learned to ride one in the first place," and left it at that. At least I'd learned to drive after getting out of prison, so the basic concept of shifting gears and using brakes and gas were there, but I'd never even thought about the problem of two wheels being different from four.

"No shit? Never?"

"Never."

He didn't push it, but he was obviously worried. "You don't want to be learning on this machine. You're gonna dump a whole bunch of times, and she's way too beautiful to do that to." He chewed on his lower lip for a while and then said, "Got it. I'll take your bike up to Kalispell with me and come back in my car. I'll bring you my mountain bike, and you can learn to ride on it. Soon as you're cool on a bicycle, I'll bring the Beemer down. Deal?"

I wanted to ride now. Not tomorrow, not next week or next month, but *right fucking now.* Get on the back of this beautiful lady and feel some wind in my hair. But Matt was right. And like I've said, I know how to wait.

"Deal."

* * *

I didn't see Ian for a long time after that. Oh, I *saw* him once in a while in the mess hall, or jogging laps in the yard, but the last thing he'd said was that from then until the hit went down, he wanted me to keep away from him.

"They see you hanging around me, they'll mark you. The reason that you get this one is that nobody knows you. Rope ain't in no one's corner, so seeing you with him doesn't mean much; and you work with Douggie after hours and behind closed doors." He stood up, dusted off his shorts, and motioned me to fall in beside him as he walked toward the block. "The gooks got no eyes in carpentry or metal anyway, but if I start hanging out with you, you'll never get near Tranh."

"But we just…"

"One day jogging don't mean anything. If they don't see you with me again, you'll be fine. Couple of weeks and they'll have forgotten you exist."

"But you said you'd teach me how to…"

"Douggie'll teach you everything you need to know, and explain what needs explaining, just remember one thing." He stopped walking and gave me a look that made me feel like the temperature had just dropped to forty below zero. "You want to ride in the car, you pay the fare. Blood in, blood out."

Blood in, blood out. The only way I was going to get in Ian's corner was by spilling someone's blood for him, and once I was in, the only way out was in a body bag.

He turned and walked away, leaving me shivering in the hot summer sun.

The next three weeks were a full-on crash course in Douggie the Druggie's School of Proper Mayhem.

"There's shanks and there's shanks, kid. But a virgin like you is almost guaranteed to screw up, and we want this bloke dead, not wounded, so you are gonna spend the next couple of weeks learning to dance with the Queen."

I must have looked more stupid than usual because he laughed. Then, right in the middle of his laugh, with no warning at all, I was suddenly spinning around, head flung back, and something weird rubbed all the way around my throat, from under one ear, to the other. It happened so fast that I didn't see Douggie move, didn't have any chance to react or fight. One minute I was standing there talking to the guy, the next I was on the floor with the sensation of whatever it had been going across my throat.

"On your feet, knave." Douggie helped me up, still laughing. "Now bow to the queen." He held up a toothbrush in front of me.

A toothbrush? I felt my throat. The weird sensation had been the toothbrush bristles. "Queen? You want me to kill some guy with a **toothbrush?"**

"Well, she's only a princess right now, but she'll be a queen right enough when she grows up." He reached into one of the pockets of his coveralls and came out with a piece of cardboard about six inches by two, which he unfolded, saying, "Like this."

Between the two pieces of card was something that had been a toothbrush once, but not anymore. Instead of bristles, there was some kind of blade growing out of the end of it.

"Go on mate, take it."

I picked it up and took a closer look. A razor blade had been melted into the end of the plastic handle where the bristles used to be. The way it was angled, it must have stuck out almost an inch and a half.

I didn't know whether to be impressed or not. Was this better than the shanks I'd been making?

"Puzzled, mate?"

"Yes sir."

"She's an elegant little solution to a serious problem. The problem is this: how does a skinny little inexperienced fucker like yourself take out a man that knows a thing or two about defending himself? If someone held him down, you could probably do it with an ax, but anything small enough for you to get close to him with just ain't likely to do the job."

He brought out one of the pointed shanks that I had learned to make when I first came to him. "I could do him with this, easy." The point was suddenly against my chest, and once again I hadn't even seen him move. "But he's never going to let me near him." He reversed the shank and slapped the handle into my hand.

"You could get close to him with this, but the chances of you getting a proper heart shot are pretty slim. Nine times out of ten you'd just poke a minor hole in him and make him mad."

I thought I'd be able to do it, but Douggie just laughed. "No way, kid. Hardly anybody knows how to kill with a knife. You catch bone, you hit the wrong spot, you catch clothing, you miss entirely... and even if you did manage to do it right, he'd be screaming and pointing at you while he died. But this baby, Her Highness here, she deals a different kind of death entirely."

He turned serious. "Sit down kid."

I pulled up a stool from beside one of the benches, sat down and started rolling a smoke. Douggie did the same.

"If you can pull this thing across someone's throat, then that someone is dead. End of story. It'll take him a minute or two to bleed to death, but nothing anyone can do is going to save him, and with his windpipe severed, he ain't going to be doing any yelling, either."

We lit up.

"And if we do our part, then this gook is going to be on the floor dead, with you well away from him, before anyone even knows he's been cut."

"Your part?"

"Yeah, our part. You think I was going to hand the lady over to you and tell you to go dancing with this gook by yourself?" He shook his head. "Not a chance. Here's what is going to happen."

So I spent the next three weeks learning one thing: how to spin a man around and expose his throat for a deep, ear-to-ear slash, and in the mess hall, one night at supper at the end of those three weeks, Nguyen Van Tranh, upstart importer of drugs into Folsom Prison and competitor of ex-Sergeant-Major Ian Douglas died just as Douggie had told me he would.

It went like this.

Two of Ian's boys started a fight about three tables away from where my target was eating with his buddies. At first it was just two bozos hollering and shoving, but then one of them landed in somebody else's dinner, and soon half the place was brawling. Food and fists were flying, men were cursing at the tops of their voices, and tables were going over.

I was behind Tranh when his table went over. He jumped up and back, and then slid to the floor with one more opening in his body than he'd had when the brawl started.

Five seconds later I was on the other side of the room throwing punches along with everyone else, and the Queen was already in the kitchen garbage.

The bulls waded in, as Douggie had said they would, swinging batons, and pulling fighting pairs apart. My sparring partner let them pull him away from me, and I started in on the badge that was holding me.

I'd never have landed a punch on him if he'd been prepared, but my reputation as a harmless fuckboy had him almost laughing at the idea of me in a fight. He stopped laughing when my boot took him in the nuts.

I had one moment of satisfaction, and then the roof caved in on me. Four bulls converged with batons and boots, and I woke up in the Shoe.

The SHU. Security Housing Unit. Solitary confinement. De-Seg. The Hole. Whatever you call it, you don't want to be there. *I* didn't want to be there either, but it was part of the price, and I was willing to pay it.

Douggie's script for the hit hadn't stopped with Tranh's death. The brawl hadn't just been a cover for me to sneak up on him. It was a multi-purpose brawl. First, it would grab Tranh's attention, allowing me to get close by pretending to be running from it. Second, it would grab the guards' attention too. The noise and general craziness would probably mask the fact of his death until everyone involved was well clear. Third, it allowed me to hand off the Queen without being noticed. And fourth, it gave me an excuse to swing on the guard.

I'd had some trouble with that one at first.

"Why the fuck do you want me going after a badge? Why set this whole thing up so that I can get clear, just so that I can grab the attention of every guard in the place?"

"Ian told me to be straight with you mate, so I will be. If any of Tranh's gooks see you doin' the dirty deed, you are going to find yourself invited to a little party to celebrate your own long and painful death. Last guy that pissed them off, they took three days killing him. But there's one place they can't get to you, and that's in the hole. You start whaling on the bulls, and they are gonna beat the shit out of you and throw you in the hole."

He offered me a tailor-made, as if that would somehow make up for getting the shit kicked out of me.

"And you ain't coming out for *at least* thirty. Guaranteed. Maybe even sixty if you really piss them off."

Wonderful. I lit the Camel and took a deep drag. "And you figure that's the safest thing to do?"

"Not me, mate. If it was me, I'd probably slip word to the gooks and let them do you. Safer all around if you're dead too, but Ian's giving the orders, not me, so you get to live." I choked on the smoke.

"Hey, it's nothing personal, kid. You're alright actually. But business is business, and I'd rather look out for my arse than yours."

Comforting thought. Not something that was going to help me get through sixty days in the box. He'd warned me that it wouldn't be fun. "Most blokes come out a bit berko after even a week in there. What you're going to be like after thirty or sixty, I don't want to think about. But whatever happens, it's gotta be better than sucking dick and getting booted around like you were."

The box was tiny. I'd been pretty much unconscious when they slammed me down, but now that I was awake, I could see a bare cell about eight feet by eight feet. Solid door with just a peephole window at the top and a little slot for my slop tray at the bottom. No window, no bed, no nothing except a toilet, a blanket, and me. And after about two days, no light either.

In the regs, it says that even prisoners on in the Security Housing Unit for Disciplinary Segregation—that is, stuck in the hole for punishment— are to be given half an hour of exercise per day. I didn't have a watch, or any way to mark the passing of days, but that door only opened once the whole time I was in there.

When I heard the lock opening, I didn't know what to think. I knew I'd been in for at least a few days, but I didn't think it had been more than a week. No way they were coming to let me out. Unless maybe Ian had sorted out some kind of deal for me.

I wish.

"Well, well, well, what do we have here."

After a week in the darkness, the light from the hall was blinding, but I knew that voice.

Officer fucking Wood.

"Black. How nice to see you again, you little cunt." I didn't see the boot coming, but I was expecting it. Didn't make it hurt any less. It took me inside of the knee, and I collapsed on the floor in pain. "I get back from holiday, and what do I find?" The next one was in the shoulder. "I find that not only are you a cock-sucking little cop-killer, but a danger to my staff too."

The third boot was on my upper arm, right in the bicep. I couldn't see them coming, couldn't do anything to defend myself, so I just curled into a ball and lay there, waiting for the next one.

He took his time. I could hear others, probably just inside the door, but it was Wood that was doing the talking and the hurting. He knew how to hurt, kicking me in the elbows, knees, shoulders, back of the neck, all the major muscles, a couple in the kidneys, and his voice told me he was enjoying it. Gradually though, even through the haze of pain, I could hear excitement replace enjoyment, and I knew what was coming next.

"Get his pants off."

Wood went first, and then the others took turns. At least it meant they weren't kicking me anymore.

"Get something straight shithead." They'd stopped fucking me and Wood was using his boots again. "I don't give a flying fuck what you slimeballs do to each other, but **nobody** touches my COs." In the gut this time. "None of you is fit to lick dogshit off my shoes." Next one in the armpit. "And **you** aren't even fit to lick dogshit out of a dog's asshole."

I was still conscious when they left. He'd been careful about that, wanting me to feel as much pain and as much humiliation as possible, wanting me to hear every word he said.

Sixty days in the hole. Doesn't sound like much, but after a while you start to lose control of your thoughts. Everything loses its meaning, and no matter how hard you try to stay in control, you wind up drifting away from sanity.

There are two fundamental rules of survival in the joint. Number one is, 'Do your own time.' Don't mess with other people, don't pry, don't get involved. I'd broken that rule in a big way. Not by choice, but I'd still broken it, and now I was in a position where I couldn't follow the second rule. 'Walk slow and drink plenty of water.'

That one's a little harder to explain to someone who's never done time, but it means something like this; you ain't going anywhere, so there's no point in rushing. Just keep moving along at as easy a pace as you can, and don't worry about the outside. If you think about what you're missing on the outside, your time just gets that much harder.

In that little eight-by-eight box there was **nothing** to occupy my mind, nothing to think about **except** how awful it was, and I think if I'd been anyone else, I would have wound up completely batshit crazy. True, life in prison had been two years of raging Hell for me, but not only had Ian promised that I'd have a better life once I got out of the hole, he'd actually given me a taste of it. For two months I'd been treated as a person worthy of respect, not a sex-toy to be beaten and fucked, then thrown in the garbage. He'd made it clear, through Douggie, that the price I'd have to pay for this better life included time in the hole, so I was prepared to pay it.

I didn't know if I'd get more visits from Wood and his friends, but even that wasn't really any worse than what had been happening regularly for the last two years, so I knew I could handle it. And thinking of Wood, and what I would someday do to him, gave me something to focus on, to hope for.

The pain from his shitkicking was so intense that all I wanted to do was lie absolutely still and find a way into unconsciousness, but I remembered that Rope had helped me heal faster after the last beating by making me do light exercise even with my injuries, and I forced myself to do that here. At first, just bending my arms and legs hurt, but I bent them a little anyway. Back and forth. Back and forth. And gradually I could do more. Stand. Walk. Stretch. Sit-ups. Push-ups. Jogging in place.

Maybe the weirdest thing about the hole was that the longer I stayed there in the dark, the more often the vision of the sunlit meadow came to me. The one my mother had told me about from her own childhood in New Zealand. I'd be lying there in the silent blackness, on the edge of madness, and I'd pull myself back to sanity with the promise that someday I'd find that meadow, and the mountains around it, and maybe even the beaches in Australia.

Another thing that helped was that I had learned to live inside myself a long time ago. It had been my way of surviving life in some miserable circumstances, and it worked for me here. Traveling through the inner universe would probably send a lot of guys over the edge, but I was used to it. Inside myself, I could fantasize, I could create, I could plan.

I looked at my past, my present, and my future. Time in the hole allowed me to chill right down to neutral and plan some serious *payback*. Not striking out in blind rage, but careful, well-thought-out revenge that would rid the world of some serious scum. Make peace with some of my inner demons and make the world a better place all at the same time.

I thought about the people who had abused me, the people who had tortured my sister. About the people who had knowingly allowed it to happen. About men in this very prison who had invaded homes and killed innocent people like my parents. Ridding the earth of people like that gave me a reason to live. At the age of nineteen, I was a man with a future.

So, I found my own way to walk slow, even in an eight-by-eight cell, and eventually the day came when the door opened and I stumbled into the light and started a new life. The light hurt my eyes, but I knew I'd get used to it again.

CHAPTER FOURTEEN

My new life *was* better. I got a cell to myself. I learned how to obtain some of the little luxuries that made life a little less harsh. A chair. A little table. Books. Walkman and tapes. Things everyone else takes for granted, but which don't come automatically in prison. Or cheaply. Everything I got, I paid for. I paid with loyalty, and with services rendered. I carried contraband. I made weapons. I killed men who stood in Ian's way.

In the course of six years, the Sergeant-Major had gone from being a new fish, to a convict, to being a minor honcho, to being the main man in Block B. With his devastating fighting skills, he'd never been in danger of being forced to smoke pole the way I had, but on the other hand, nobody had handed him anything on a platter.

He was quite a man. Over the following years I came to know him well, and in some ways, his story paralleled mine. He was a Brit whose family had moved to Canada when he was young, and he'd grown up hard on the streets of Vancouver, suffering neglect and abuse as a child, living by his fists and feet. He'd thought of himself as tough, but at the age of fifteen he'd had his ass whipped in a fight in a way that he couldn't understand. Every punch or kick he threw was turned aside, and he repeatedly found himself on the ground, unaware of just how he'd got there.

He realized afterward that the guy who'd whipped him had martial arts training, and Ian determined to get some of his own, mostly to even the score. He was lucky though. The place he stumbled into turned out to be a tiny *dojang* run by a middle-aged Korean who was one of the first teachers of hapkido in North America. Hapkido didn't mean shit to me. To me, everything that wasn't judo was karate. That there were different styles, or that one style might be better than another was all news to me, but Ian explained that there *were* differences, and that some of the differences were important.

Hapkido was close to a *total* defensive fighting style. Not just punches and flying kicks, but joint locks, takedowns, and weapons training.

Everything but ground fighting and attack techniques. A style in which there are no competitions, no board-breaking demonstrations, no flashy techniques that look good in a movie but don't work on the street.

He fell under the spell of the Korean master and devoted every spare minute to this new passion. Three years later he joined the Canadian Army, and did a tour of peacekeeping duty in the middle east with the Canadian Airborne Regiment, at the time when the Greeks and Turks were battling in Cypress, and the Israelis and Egyptians were fighting it out in the Suez. Here he made his first acquaintance with soldiers of the British S.A.S. At that time, the S.A.S. was probably the most hardcore commando regiment in the world, and Ian felt that he'd finally found a home.

When his term was up in the Canadian army he went to Britain and, with his British citizenship and military record, was able to enlist in the British Army. He did the required stretch in the 22 Para Regiment and applied for the S.A.S.

Only about two percent of the applicants pass the grueling six-month selection course, but Ian was number one in the whole class, and he spent the next ten years rising in rank and building his reputation as one of the deadliest men in one of the world's deadliest combat units.

The British Special Air Service taught a style of dirty fighting which focused on attack and silent killing as well as the usual defensive tactics. Ian developed it further on his own, by combining it with hapkido, and with the ground-fighting techniques that subsequently became famous as Brazilian jiu-jitsu. He called his system Defendo. It was death on two legs, and all based around the fundamental principle of K.I.S.S.—Keep It Savagely Simple.

He fought in Ireland, Cypress, and across Africa and the mid-east, but it all came to an end in a San Diego hotel room. He was on a training exchange with the US Rangers and came home early one day to find his wife in bed with a blond Californian beach bum. The guy made the mistake of taking a swing, and Ian killed him. His wife went berserk, pulled a knife on him, and he killed her too. A month later he was in Folsom, doing twenty-five years for Murder Two.

Why had he adopted me? Partly it was just business. I was a tool he could use in his struggle to take control of the drug business for the entire prison, but partly I think it was because he saw something of himself in me.

I reminded him of the kid he had been, the kid who had been dealt a losing hand in the game of life. He remembered how his old hapkido master had turned him from life in the streets, and I think helping me was his way of repaying the old man.

But business is business, and Tranh's murder had been far more than one guy dying. It had been the start of a corporate takeover, and by the time I got out of the hole, the Sergeant-Major was well on his way to being The Man. The one who controlled the flow of contraband goods and services into Folsom.

He ran his operation much as he'd run things in the army. There was a clear chain of command; orders were given and obeyed, and loyalty was paramount. I started off as a lowly soldier. My first mission had been a dangerous one, and I carried it out well, so I was well rewarded. But that was hardly the end. I stayed on easy street only as long as I paid my way, and paying my way meant doing what I was told to do.

Besides the smuggling and murder, I was told to take care of myself and prepare for the future. I continued to train my body, learning fitness and strength from Rope, and learning fighting skills from Ian. But he also insisted that I train my mind. At his orders, I enrolled in the prison's educational program, and finished my high school. After that I started a correspondence course in bookkeeping, something Ian told me would make me employable on the outside.

"Walkin' slow means not thinking about the outside, kid, but that only takes you so far. If you've got any brains at all then there's more to doing time than just doing time. You're gonna come out of this joint almost a middle-aged man, and if you don't do some preparing, you're gonna last about six months and then you'll be back in for sticking up a 7-11, or something equally stupid."

We were in the middle of a workout, him blocking anything I could throw at him, and putting me on the ground whenever he felt like it, then patiently showing me how he had done it, and making me practice it over and over and over. It was something the old Korean had taught him. 'If you practice a move ten times, your enemy will own it, but if you practice it a thousand times it will become yours.' He'd imitate the old man's Korean accent as I blocked the same punch or kick over and over.

"And this studying…" Punch, block. "This grade twelve and the bookkeeping courses..." Punch, block. "Not only are they gonna help you once you're out..." Punch, block, "but they're gonna get you out sooner." Punch, miss, **wham**.

Ian helped me back onto my feet and I rubbed my jaw where his punch had connected. I knew he'd pulled it, or I'd have a broken jaw, but it still hurt.

"Parole board, they like to see that you've done something to better yourself." Punch, block. "You were just a kid when you offed that cop, and they're gonna take that into account." Punch, block. "But **only** if they see something that makes them think that you're on the path to being a responsible citizen."

Punch, block. Punch, block. Over and over.

The perks he got for me, the cell to myself, the vitamin supplements, the training from himself and Rope and Douggie, were all great, but one thing that I really wanted, I couldn't have. Revenge on the animals that had abused me.

"Kid, there's a time for revenge, and that time ain't here yet."

"Why not? I know how to take them out one at a time. No one will know."

"You don't get it, kid. You are gonna leave them alone because I tell you to leave them alone."

Why was he doing this to me? It was the one thing I wanted more than anything else and he knew it.

"I need them where they are, doing what they're doing. You think I want to start from scratch? The laundry is the perfect distribution center for the whole fuckin' joint, and those guys are already in place." He stared me down, but then his expression changed. "Besides, you already got some of that revenge when you took out Tranh."

"Huh?"

"Who do you think they were working for?"

"I know fuckin' well who they were working for. Wood."

"And Wood was working for Tranh." Ian broke into wicked laughter. "God Damn, but that was great. Wood hates gooks even worse than he hates niggers. **Hates** them. Taking orders from Tranh must have been like having a fishhook up his asshole." Suddenly he was deadly serious again. "Doing Wood is going to be a real pleasure for somebody, and a service to the human race at the same time. Might even be you that gets that pleasure kid, but it ain't gonna happen soon. Right now, he's bought and paid for, and I don't want him, or any of the dickheads he's got working for him, touched."

There was the beginning of a promise in there, and I jumped on it. "Okay. You're the boss. But when the time comes, he's mine."

Ian thought that over. He didn't make promises lightly. "Wait and see. You're not the only one who wants him, but he's probably done you worse than anybody else, so maybe you deserve the chance." He dug out his tobacco and papers and started rolling. "Things work out between you and me, then I don't see why you shouldn't be the lucky one, but that's a long way down the road. For right now, I need him."

"Okay. I can live with that."

We took a smoke break and then got back to the business of tossing each other around.

Being The Man, Ian got all kinds of perks. Including a real woman. So did the convicts who were his senior lieutenants. They may have been paid hookers from the outside, but they were pure fantasy to every inmate in the joint.

You had to marry in order to get the conjugal visits, but there were ways around that, just as there were ways around everything else, and I still remember the day I was sitting in my cell, working on my bookkeeping course when Ian walked in and said, "You're getting on in years, kid. Man your age oughta be married."

I was older and wiser by then. "And what's the price tag on this little gift?"

"Warren the Walker made parole, so it's time for you to put your asshole back in service."

Which was just fine with me, because I knew that the service he was talking about involved condoms full of coke and smack, not cocks. If it meant me getting laid, I was more than happy to walk back from the boneyard with a load of drugs up my ass, or in my stomach. I got a boner on the spot just thinking about it.

Ian arranged my sham of a marriage to a hooker named Kylie Spence. When I finally saw her, I understood why she was commonly known as 'Ten Cent Spence'. She may have been only twenty-four, but she looked like she was a hundred and twenty-four. She'd fuck for anybody with money and spent all the time she wasn't on her knees with a cock in her mouth shooting up whatever drugs she could get her hands on. She was the most fucked-out piece imaginable, and just looking at her I knew that it wasn't going to be long before death parted us. If she'd ever had a soul, it had died a long time ago, and her body wasn't going to be long in joining it.

Conjugal visits took place in the boneyard, a group of trailers adjacent to the cell blocks. It was a place where wives and families could see their incarcerated husband or father in an atmosphere that wasn't as cold as the main visiting area and that offered some privacy. Sure, there were fences and armed guards all over the place, but once inside the trailer you could forget that for a while.

Standard procedure called for full cavity search and shit watch after you returned from the boneyard, but money spoke louder than the rulebook, and conjugal visits were just one more way for Ian to bring drugs—and occasionally other things—into the prison, and for a few select guards to put their sons and daughters through college. Or buy themselves a new boat or whatever.

When I finally got into the trailer and met my new wife, I wanted a divorce. She was the ugliest, scrawniest, fucked-out scarecrow of a human being that I'd ever seen. Face pitted out with coke sores, broken nose, scraggly, matted hair. Track marks and sores over every vein in her body, and no life at all in her eyes.

She was sitting on the bed, naked, smoking a cigarette. I stared at her saggy, pruned-out tits.

"Hey baby," she said. "So, you like my tits, huh?" Her voice was as empty as her eyes.

"Been a while since I've seen any." I didn't add that hers weren't exactly the ones I'd been dreaming of.

"Oh yeah?" She put out her cigarette in an ashtray. "Come on over here in front of me."

The ugly thing unzipped my pants and pulled out my cock. She started sucking and stroking, but the sight of the sores around her mouth was too much for me and I pulled back, still only half hard. She must have known how repulsed I felt because she gave me a resigned look and said, "Okay then, let's fuck."

She sprawled back on the bed and spread for me. She had rough, coarse pubic hair an inch thick that went halfway up to her belly button. God only knows what was hiding in that bush. Somewhere in there was the lost lagoon.

"You wanna eat me," she barked.

I gagged at the thought. I'd rather lick dogshit out of a dog, as Wood had suggested, than lick that pussy, but six years without a woman was enough to stiffen my dick, so I dropped my pants, rolled on a safe, and climbed on. She grabbed my cock, rubbed it around in her bush for a while, then pulled me in.

It was like entering the Black Hole. I was no expert on pussy, but this was the fuckin' Batcave. As I thrust in and out of her it felt like I wasn't even touching the sides. Pussy was supposed to be warm, wet, and tight. This thing belonged on a cow. She moaned and groaned, but it was strictly for show—no way she was feeling anything in that cavern of hers.

But six years is a long time, and I soon shot my load.

After a few moments, I collected myself and quickly dismounted the creature that I had married.

"Happy, baby?" she asked. "Was it good?"

"Yeah, right." I lit a smoke and started playing with a tit but stopped when she began probing her anus with her finger.

I knew what was coming and watched despite being disgusted with myself as she dug around and then slowly pulled out a condom filled to the circumference of a D-size battery, about eight inches in length.

She let out a giant fart as it came out, and smiled a big gap-toothed smile at me, as if it was the funniest thing she'd heard in a year. What a pig. Then she held the thing out for me, but there was no way I was going to touch it until she'd cleaned it up and repackaged it. I think she knew that and trying to hand it to me was her way of telling me to go fuck myself.

She tried to get it untied, but soon gave up and bit the end off. Jesus Christ! Didn't she care that it had been up her ass? It contained four more condoms, each about two inches long, and stuffed with what I assumed was either smack or coke. Or it could be speed or Angel Dust. Didn't matter to me one way or the other.

I told her to drop them in the sink, and after washing them carefully, and wrapping each one in a clean condom, I squished one into the false heel of each shoe, then got out the tube of K-Y that I'd been allowed to bring in with me and lubed the other two and stuffed them up my own butt.

I thought about fucking Kylie again before leaving, but one look at her killed that thought, and I headed for the door.

Ian had shit coming in and money going out every month, but he alternated his boys, and I got a turn about once every five or six months. If my 'wife' had been even halfway human I'd have been begging for more turns, but with Ten Cent Spence, once every five or six months was almost too often. Still, anyone with eyes could tell she was going to die soon, and I knew that my next wife couldn't possibly be even half as revolting.

She wasn't. Ten Cent didn't even last two years, but my conjugal visits with her were so awful that I was almost scared as I was being led to the trailer for my first meeting with the new 'wife' Ian had arranged for me. Her name was Brandi. Or so I was told. I doubt that was her real name, but I never saw the wedding certificate, so I really didn't know.

When I entered the trailer, she was sitting cross-legged on the bed. She had her clothes on, and actually looked pretty good. Waist-length black hair, pale skin, and big brown eyes. Horsey teeth though, which were obvious because she was enthusiastically chewing gum, but what the hell, I wasn't in a position to be really critical.

"Hi Todd!" she giggled.

"Hey Brandi, how about losing the clothes?"

"Are you *horny*?" she shrieked.

"Hell, yeah. You bet I'm horny. Gimme some of that pussy."

Brandi stood up on the bed and quickly threw off her clothes then twirled around slowly, letting me see what I'd married. Yum yum. Flat stomach, cute ass, sizeable round tits with big pink nipples, and *no* big scary bush on her mound. And feisty to boot. She was actually decent looking, and my cock was already dripping pre cum even before I got it out of my pants.

"*Ta daaa!*" she yelled as she flopped back onto the bed and spread her legs. I was almost—almost—tempted to eat her pussy, but then I thought about all the dicks that had been in there before me and decided that until someone invented a tongue condom I'd stick to fucking. Especially now that word was out about AIDS—thank god *that* monster hadn't got loose in the joint until I stopped taking it up the ass every few weeks. I shucked all my clothes, rolled on a condom, and jumped onto the bed with her.

"Ooh Todd, do you want me? C'mon, stick it in!"

"It'll be my pleasure, lady."

I positioned myself above her and she spat out her gum. I rubbed the head of my cock over her clit and pussy lips. Slowly, slowly I eased Dicky D in, hoping for tight. But no, it was another cavern. Not as big as the Batcave between Ten Cent's legs, but not exactly a tight fit. The condom didn't help matters either, but Brandi grabbed my ass and wrapped her legs around me, pushing me in hard.

"Todd, oh Todd! Pound it into me baby!" she moaned.

Her dirty talk turned me on and I gave her the pounding of a lifetime. I could feel her tits pressed against my chest, and to my surprise she grabbed my face and kissed me, pushing her tongue right into my mouth. I forgot she was a hooker and gave back as good as I got.

Her little squeals and moans, and the way she writhed around beneath me, drove me crazy. Every muscle in my body tensed up and I grabbed her shoulders and shot my load with a series of grunts. I doubt that she got any more out of it than Ten Cent had, but then her satisfaction wasn't really part of the deal. She was there to provide me with gratification and Ian with whatever he had ordered.

"Was that fun, baby?" Brandi asked sweetly.

"Fun? Yeah. Hand me my cigarettes."

That time around, Ian had ordered information, as well as the usual condom-load of smack. Wood was nearing retirement, and Ian wanted to know the exact date, and who was going to replace him.

I wanted to know the date too, because if he was leaving, then he wouldn't be of any use to Ian, which meant that I could look forward to my reward. And it worked the other way, too. As soon as he didn't need us anymore, there was a chance he'd turn on us. Especially on me, whom he'd hated since day one.

But in the end, Brandi's information about his retirement date didn't help. The prick decided that saving his hide was worth more than trying to settle any old scores and used about six months of accumulated sick leave to bug out early. Chickenshit bastard.

But the info on the new head bull *was* worthwhile. Some guy named Anderson, who was known throughout the entire state as a total square. A guy who walked around with a broomstick up his ass, and whose mission in life was to rid the California Department of Prisons of corruption.

So, we had a plan in place before he even arrived.

Ian had been saving Crazy Carl for exactly this kind of problem. No sane convict was going to take out the senior CO, but Carl was so far from 'sane' that he didn't have a clue what the word meant. He was a duster who was so paranoid that he'd believe anything. Including Ian's story that Anderson had been brought to Folsom for the specific purpose of getting Carl transferred to a secret cell where he would be tortured until he died. Crazy motherfucker believed it, no question. But that's what PCP does to you. Turns you into the kind of batshit weirdo who **likes** being in solitary, because in solitary they don't bug you about decorating the walls of your cell with your own shit.

As it turned out, Carl decided not to kill the guy right off, but rather to make him suffer the way he believed Anderson was going to make him suffer, so instead of going for his throat, he dived down and severed an Achilles tendon. But it worked out well enough. Anderson had to retire on a medical pension—and his replacement was more than willing to supplement his retirement income by working with us.

After that, life wasn't bad. It never got easy, but I'd been in since I was sixteen, and it was the only life I knew as an adult. The hard part was that Ian's empire was constantly under attack. There was an endless stream of new convicts who had been tough on the outside, or who had big connections, and figured that they could take over inside. No surprise there. Taking over by force is how Ian had got where he was, and he had to be vigilant always. We all did. But Ian was a world tougher than anyone else, and we survived.

Most of us did, at least. We lost people now and then, but never anyone important enough to the organization to make a difference. I came close a couple of times, but the years in the weight room, on the track, and under Ian's instruction had made me a hard target.

Ian could take me anytime he felt like it, but other than that, I don't think anyone else in the joint would have had a chance. Maybe Douggie, but definitely no one else. The scars I did collect came from the two or three times I was ambushed by several at once, but even there, I was able to handle it. There were some tough guys in that shithole, but I had learned from one of the deadliest men in the world.

So, I walked slow and drank plenty of water.

I studied, I worked out, I rose through the ranks to join Douggie as a sort of joint number-two in Ian's organization. I helped run a business, and I helped recruit new people.

People like Johnny the Needle.

Over the years, I got pretty close to Ian, but he was not just my boss, but also my teacher, and, yes, a kind of father figure, so I can't say that we were friends. Or maybe I can say that. We **were** friends, but there was always that distance between us, whereas Johnny the Needle was my age, and we could be regular friends without anything standing between us.

He was a tattoo artist. He and his brother ran their own chain of shops, but he got busted for dealing mescaline. The so-called 'War on Drugs' was just getting into full swing at that time, and it made for some huge changes in the prison system. Up till then, there'd only been three serious joints in the whole state, but when the courts started handing out big numbers to everybody caught with more than a reefer in his pocket, the prisons, which were already full, couldn't cope, and the state went on a building spree that's still going on. High security prisons have sprung up everywhere. There must be fifteen or twenty of them now, and they're all full.

Anyway, Johnny's bad luck was our good luck. He was a stand-up guy, hard as nails but with a great sense of humor. I'd run into him when he'd come down to check out the iron pile and took a liking to him right away. I also saw a business opportunity and talked to Ian about adding tattooing to the list of goods and services we provided. He liked the idea, but wasn't about to trust some new fish, so it took a while, but eventually Johnny the Needle got to set up shop inside.

There was no comparison to a real-world tattoo shop, but he was a true artist, and a true artist will find a way to do his art no matter what tools are available. He designed and built a tattoo gun out of weird bits and pieces. The motor out of a tape deck wired up to run off a wall socket. Needles smuggled out of the infirmary. Ink faked up from ash and water. He was an inventive genius.

His system was primitive, but it worked, and like I said, the guy was an artist. Did a back job on me that still blows people away when they see it, a dragon that seems to flex its wings when I flex my lats. Pretty soon he was working almost full time, and as far as I know the lucky bastard **never** had to bend over.

I wish I could say that Rope and I got to be friends too, but I can't. He was a cool guy, and he taught me a lot. I liked him and respected him, but while he always treated me well, he couldn't let himself get close to a white boy, which was too bad. He'd been a pro football player, so he got special treatment from everybody, both guards and cons, and managed to do his time without having to get into anybody's corner. Training me had been strictly a business deal for him. We got along, and I wanted to get to know him better, but the racial barrier was just too strong.

Douggie I respected, and he respected me, but friendship was never in the cards for us. Sometimes the chemistry is there and sometimes it isn't. This was one of the times when it wasn't. Not that I disliked him, or ever had anything bad to say about him, just that he wasn't someone I ever felt comfortable around. We could work well enough together, and there was never any friction between us, but really the only friends I had were Ian himself, and Johnny the Needle.

There were many things that I admired about Ian. He was the first adult to talk and make sense all at the same time. He put his words into action and didn't do anybody wrong unless they were threatening him or his possessions. I grew attached to him, and the day he announced that he'd made parole was a pretty tough day for me.

Obviously, I was happy for him. But I knew I'd miss him, and I worried about what would happen when he left.

"Don't worry about it, Todd. I've talked to Douggie, and he understands that there can't be two bosses. He also knows that you'll do a far better job of running things than he will, so he'll support you all the way."

That was a load off my mind. A power struggle with Douggie the Druggie was not going to end until one of us was dead, and if we were at each other's throats someone else was bound to step in and take over, probably leaving **both** of us dead.

"So, what are you going to do with yourself? Go back to the S.A.S.?

"No way. It'd probably be okay with me, but they gave me a dishonorable discharge about two minutes after the guilty verdict, and there's not a chance in hell they'd take me back. Especially not at my age. But the French Foreign Legion'll be happy to have me. I know a bunch of Legionnaires from the old days. They'll get me in."

He gave me a playful shot on the shoulder. "You should think about it yourself. Not much place in the world for what you've become, and with your record there's not many doors that'll be open for you. Track me down when you get out and I'll see that the Legion takes you in."

When his release date came, we got the goodbyes over with quickly.

"Well kid, it's been a slice," he said.

"Thanks Ian. Thanks for everything."

"Sure kid. You remember what I told you about the Legion, eh? I'm not much of a writer so I doubt you'll hear from me again unless you track me down and show up yourself. Think about it, kid."

"Well, first they gotta let me out. But if they ever do, I imagine you'll see me again."

We shook on it, and I felt a piece of paper slide into my hand. I slipped it into a pocket, and Douggie and I escorted Ian as far as we could, shook hands one last time, and watched him walk out the door.

When I got back to my cell, I pulled out the paper. Ian's parting gift to me was Officer Rick Wood's new name and address.

In 1996, I got my own parole hearing. I had a lot of good shit to show for the time that I had served. I had my GED, a correspondence degree in accounting and bookkeeping, and a certificate in counseling. I also had the good behavior recommendation I'd bought from the head bull, which I think counted for a lot.

The hearing wasn't easy. I did my best to appear repentant and humble, but it was hard for me to sit there and let three fat-ass rich guys who'd never had a stroke of bad luck in their lives pass judgement on me.

I must have been convincing, because a month later I got my papers, and a month after that, fifteen years after I got sent up, I walked out the door. The light was somehow brighter outside, but I knew I'd get used to it.

* * *

I put more scratches than I care to think about into the paint on Matt's mountain bike, and plenty into my skin, too, but before long I had it down. After that, I spent what was left of spring, and half the summer trying to keep the fun meter redlined. I rode that R50 just about every day. Sometimes with Matt, mostly by myself. I explored every highway and back road in western Montana. I got myself outdoor gear and camping equipment. I learned how to fish. I hiked up and down mountains.

How do you make up for twenty-five lost years? You can't, not really. But I did my best.

What I'd seen and done in those twenty-five years was the stuff of nightmares. Somewhere along the way I had lost my soul—what I'd done in the last two years was proof of that—and I wasn't sure I'd ever get it back. If there was any chance, it was here in the Montana wilderness. Blue sky, fresh air, lakes and mountains, and people who were friendly but not nosy.

I'd been shafted by life. I knew that. But did that mean that what I had become was not my fault? Would a better, or stronger, person have dealt with it in some better way? Would the world be a better place if I *had* done the dive off the Tier 4 railing at Folsom? Or was the world a better place because I'd stuck it out and then spent the second and third years of my freedom on a killing spree, ridding the planet of some of the sickest, cruelest, people imaginable?

This was all going around in my mind one night at the cabin. It was storming like it was the end of the world. Rain pounded on the roof and rattled against the windows, thunder and lightning regularly lit up the inside of the cabin, then shook it like a dollhouse. I started up a fire in the wood stove and put on a pot of tea, then dug into the bottom drawer of my bedroom bureau and pulled out the notebook I had started keeping six months after my release.

Two years of single-minded payback were recorded there.

I grabbed a blanket, poured a mug of tea and sat down in front of the fire with the little journal and started to read. Maybe in these notes, these stories of the people I'd killed, I would learn whether I was just as much a psychopath as they were.

Or whether I was a saint with a sword.

PART III

CHAPTER FIFTEEN

Long-term prisoners often have difficulty readjusting to the world. Life in the joint is not much fun—a man may be beaten occasionally, or even raped—but his life is stable and predictable. His daily routine is decided for him by authority beyond his reach and he never has to worry about paying the rent or whether there is enough money to buy food.

Little wonder then that after spending ten or fifteen, or even twenty or twenty-five years in prison, many ex-cons can't cope with the uncertainty of life outside. A world that changes daily, unpredictable people, lack of supervision, all conspire to make life in the world seem impossible for the man who has not had to think, who has been required *not* to think, for so long.

With no job, no social support, and considerable prejudice against him, is it any wonder that he turns back to the life that led him to prison in the first place? Not me though. I had never set foot outside as an adult, but I left the prison with considerable support already in place.

I had business skills: I'd done the bookkeeping course, and I'd run what amounted to a fairly successful small business for the last five years.

I had money: Every gram of dope coming into the prison meant money for me. Much of it had gone to expenses, particularly to guards, but over the years I had amassed a decent stash. No bank for me in the joint, but Johnny the Needle had a brother who took care of that for me.

I had connections: Doing what I did inside meant building up a network of business connections outside. They weren't family, and they weren't friends, but I'd been good for them, and, up to a point, they were more than willing to help me.

I had a job: Johnny the Needle's brother had done well with the tattoo business, and the four shops, all called The Primal Urge, were doing okay in cities from LA to Seattle. Like Johnny, he was a genius with a needle, but he wasn't much of a businessman, and he was more than happy to hire me as a sort of general manager on Johnny's recommendation.

All those things made it possible for me to cope with the world, but they sure didn't make it easy. Johnny's brother, Paul, was a big help. He was really fond of his little brother and was grateful to me for helping him out inside. He had fixed up the garage behind his house as a self-contained apartment and he rented it to me cheap. He also helped me with some of the simple stuff that everybody else takes for granted. I'd never shopped for food or cooked a meal in my life. Shit, I didn't even own a coffee cup. I didn't know how to drive a car. I didn't know where to buy a TV or how to get cable installed.

He showed me where the supermarket was, how to use the bank account that he'd set up for me, how to get telephone service, how to deal with the million-and-one little things that had not been a part of my life in prison.

It wasn't all one-way though. Three months after I took over the business end of things at The Primal Urge, I'd almost doubled his profit. No magic there, just basic common sense, starting with keeping track of income and expenses and then introducing the idea of discipline so that income got maximized and expenses minimized.

For a few months I was fully occupied. Between sorting out the business and learning how to live on my own, I didn't have time to scratch my ass, let alone think about my promise to myself that I'd one day pay back the people who had destroyed my sister and me. I took driving lessons and then bought a used car. Nothing fancy, just a seven-year-old Toyota that Paul told me was a good deal.

Once I had my wheels, I found an iron gym and got back to pushing weights. I also bought a computer and learned how to use it. At first, I just wanted it to help with the accounting for the business, but I soon discovered the internet, and that was a revelation, let me tell you.

Eventually though, everything was under control, and I started thinking about taking the first step toward delivering some retribution.

The coroner had ruled my sister's death suicide, but in my mind, it had never been anything but murder. At the time, I hadn't understood exactly what was going on, but the one thing I did know was that someone was doing something bad to Susan, and taking her own life was the only way she could deal with it. By the time I was hanging out with Robert and the street kids at the lot, I had heard enough stories to know what had happened.

Her foster father was fucking her. That was obvious, and he was going to die for it. Her social worker had known. Mia Pridy wasn't a rookie when Susan and I had been added to her caseload. She was an experienced social worker, and there was simply no way that she hadn't recognized the signs. Whether her sentence would also be death depended on what I found out in the next couple of months, and the same would go for the foster mother.

Bookkeeping wasn't all I'd learned in prison. Ian Douglas and Douggie the Druggie had taught me to dispense death as easily as most people could breathe, but Ian also taught me that without planning and patience, violence was pointless, likely to end up doing as much harm to me as to my victim.

I'd learned from others as well. The thirteen years I spent working in— and eventually running—Ian's organization had put me in close contact with men who were walking encyclopedias of criminal knowledge. Robbery, arson, bribery, extortion, police procedure, explosives, blackmail, torture, weapons procurement, drug trafficking, prostitution… you name it, I'd studied it.

I'd put it to use in the settling of my sister's account with Daniel Rebernick and recorded it in my journal.

My little blue binder. Probably should have burned all the pages before I left Seattle. It had been the passport to Hell for nineteen people already, and it would certainly be my ticket to the stainless-steel ride if anyone ever saw it.

I didn't open it right away. Just sat by the fire and drank my tea and listened to the storm rage outside. Did what was in the book mean that I should be in Hell, as well? Burning right alongside the nineteen monsters I had sent there already?

I had spent the last few months trying to leave all that behind, trying to find out what it was like to live without being consumed by rage and fear and pain. Riding my bike on empty highways and letting the wind cleanse me. Camping by mountain lakes and looking up at the billions of stars overhead as I fell asleep, wondering if maybe the beings who lived on the planets that circled those stars were just as fucked up as we were, or if maybe there was a decent world out there somewhere. A world in which young orphan girls were cared for with love and respect, not used as sex toys by perverted monsters like Daniel Rebernick.

I flipped open the cover and the first of the tab dividers...

* * *

The flight from Oakland to LA is a short hop, just over an hour, and for most people it's probably about as exciting as taking the bus to work. For me, flying for the first time, it was a big fucking adventure. Paul got me to the airport and showed me how to check in, but after that I was on my own. I half expected to accidentally wind up on a flight to Germany or Australia, but somehow managed not to get totally lost, and by mid-afternoon I was checked-in to a small hotel not too far from the Los Angeles branch of The Primal Urge.

I spent a couple of days earning my salary, but by then I was getting responses to the phone calls I'd made the first evening, and decided to stay for a week conducting my own investigation of my sister's death over twenty years ago.

When I got back to Oakland, I took all my notes and typed them up in the format that eventually became my blue book.

Subject: Daniel Rebernick
Crime: Sexual and physical abuse of my sister Susan, leading to her death.
Sentence: Death

DETAILS
Address: 4312 Dixon St., Santa Barbara, California
Current age: 58
Occupation: Cash register repair tech, Foster care provider
Marital status: Married to Maria Rebernick

CASE HISTORY
[SOURCE: Warren the Walker bribed someone in the Social Services office and got photocopies of the Rebernicks' records. He also had someone talk to a few of the surviving foster children.]

Susan is not the only child to die in The Rebernicks' care. One other girl killed herself and two went 'missing.' Two of the survivors (both now hookers) confirm that they were sexually and physically abused by, get this,

BOTH of the Rebernicks. They both claim they informed their social worker, who promised to help, but never came through for them. That social worker was Mia Pridy.

How these people managed to avoid official investigations following the deaths, and what part Mia Pridy played in all this is not certain, but I imagine I'll be able to convince them to tell me before they die.

ACTION PLAN

Background: Several days of clandestine observation showed a pattern, at least on weekdays. Daniel Rebernick leaves for work at about eight in the morning, returning at about five-thirty. Friday evening, he came home at eight, quite drunk. Maria Rebernick does nothing at all, other than watch TV and cook. They do not seem to have a foster child at the moment.

Unobserved access to their house should be easy as there is an alley behind their property, and they have nice high fences.

Action: Since there is no foster child in their home now, it is the perfect time for their punishment. Best bet would probably be to take the bitch out in the afternoon, and her husband when he gets in from work. Friday would be the best day, because no one would miss them until he didn't show up for work on Monday.

The executions themselves should present no problems. Both are old and unhealthy, so the only thing to be careful of is that they do not make enough noise to attract attention from the neighbors no matter how much pain I inflict on them.

So now I was going to become a true murderer. I had killed several times in prison, but that had been a matter of survival, and I never really thought of myself as a murderer. This time however, there was no threat to me, and I was going to kill anyway. I was planning it carefully in advance, expected to cause a lot of pain, and expected that more murders would follow.

I thought about that for a week or so after I finished typing out the notes. Since my parole, I'd learned that most people were decent, quiet folks. A different world to what I had known in childhood and in prison. But the fact that most people were decent did not excuse the behavior of those who were not. If anything, it made it less acceptable.

In a desperate world, maybe there was a case for cruelty; but the Rebernicks, and people like them, did not live in a desperate world. They had a comfortable middle-class existence and gained no benefit from the suffering they imposed on the children in their care beyond their own sick gratification.

The stories the two hookers had told Warren were proof enough of that. Stories of thirteen- and fourteen-year-old girls being forced to eat Maria's pussy while Daniel gave it to them up the ass, of Maria shoving beer bottles up their twats while Daniel jerked off on them, of beatings if they resisted, of death threats if they made any attempt to seek help.

The thought of my sister enduring that hell was enough to end the discussion in my mind. The Rebernicks were going to die, and if that meant that I would be labeled a murderer, then so be it.

Two weeks later I made the following addition to the Rebernicks' chapter of my Blue Book.

Conclusion: Sentence carried out. Daniel and Maria Rebernick will abuse no more children.

Twelve little words on a five-inch by eight-inch page, but what a story lay behind them ...

CHAPTER SIXTEEN

"Hello Maria." She moaned and rolled her eyes, trying to come to terms with her disorientation and nausea. I'd walked up their dumpy suburban alley one Friday afternoon in March, opened the gate into their back yard, walked through the garbage that they filled it with, and tested the door. It was unlocked, so I opened it as quietly as I could and followed my ears toward the sound of the TV.

She hadn't heard me coming and the first she knew of my presence was when I tapped her on the shoulder. She'd jumped in fright, tried to turn, and taken a shot to the side of the head from the sap I'd bought two weeks before. Woven leather filled with lead shot. I know that they've gone out of fashion, but some of the old lags I met in Folsom told me there was a time when half the cops in the country carried them. No good in a real fight, but just the thing for working over a helpless suspect.

"Feeling a little woozy, sweetheart? Maybe this'll help."

I heaved a bucket of cold water over her and she snapped to attention. Must have been strange for her. One minute she's sitting in her living room, watching some mindlessly comforting TV program, then she's naked, strung up in her basement, with a splitting headache, coughing and spitting out water, and no recollection of how she got there.

I'd hung her up so that her feet reached the floor—no sense having her pass out from the strain of her two hundred pounds hanging from her wrists—but high enough that she couldn't really move. And with each arm tied to a separate beam, she couldn't turn either. Just stand there like the winner of the "World's Ugliest Hippo" contest, with breasts drooping almost to her waist, and fat hanging in huge rolls.

I was behind her, and she tried to turn her head to look at me, screaming in pain when I pressed the tip of the soldering pencil into the flesh of her bare shoulder.

First rule of torture: Establish the victim's total helplessness.

Second rule: Establish with absolute certainty that even the slightest deviation from your command will be met with instant and excruciating pain.

Compared to some of the people I'd had to extract information from in the joint, Maria Rebernick was nothing. She caved in at the first touch of the iron and answered every question I had. Crying, moaning, pleading, even offering herself to me.

"I'd sooner slit my own throat than let your revolting body touch mine, you ugly, perverted, sadistic old cow."

Once I heard from her own lips about the arrangement she and her husband had with Mia Pridy, I suddenly couldn't stand the thought of another word from her. I gagged her securely, told her that this was payback on behalf of all the little girls she'd destroyed, then broke both her elbows and went upstairs to wait for her husband. Hanging from broken arms like that, she'd torture herself, and I wanted nothing more to do with her. If she hadn't died of heart failure by the time I brought Daniel down to see her, I'd put her out of her misery.

"You're late, Dan."

I'd waited till he had closed the front door behind him before stepping into his sight and speaking.

"Huh? Who are you?"

I snap-kicked a knee and heard it break.

"I'm the last person you ever want to see, Dan." He was writhing in pain on the floor, but I knew he could hear me. "But don't worry about it, fucker, cuz I'm the last person you ever *will* see."

He tried to speak, but I cut him off by grabbing the ankle of the broken leg and dragging him across the floor and then down the stairs.

When he came to, he was hanging about six feet from his wife.

"Watch this, Danny Boy." I pulled her head back and slit her throat with my Spyderco. Blood spurted and gushed, some of it even splashing onto him, then subsided. She was off my list.

"Does the name Susan Black mean anything to you, Dan?"

He was in a lot of pain, and at first, he didn't react. Then I saw the expression of recognition flash onto his face. It had been twenty-two years, but he still remembered. Good.

"She was my sister."

It was the last thing I said to him. I gagged him and bound his wrists behind his back with a roll of duct tape that I'd found on his work bench. I then let him watch me smear the soldering pencil with oil. He tried to squirm away when I slid it up his ass, but nobody squirms much with a broken knee, and soon it was all the way in.

I picked up the extension cord and made sure he could see me as I plugged the soldering pencil into it.

A minute later he started to dance. Even with the broken knee, he danced. When the dancing finally stopped, I unplugged the pencil, slit his throat, and left.

What I'd learned from the Rebernicks got me started on the second chapter...

Subject: Mia Pridy
Crimes: Procuring children for abuse. Knowing accessory in the sexual and physical abuse of my sister Susan, leading to her death.
Sentence: Death with extreme pain.

DETAILS
Address: 534 West Esplanade Blvd., Santa Barbara, California Current age: 63
Occupation: Retired social worker
Marital status: Single

CASE HISTORY
[SOURCE: Maria Rebernick —under *extreme* duress.]
Mia Pridy had a kickback deal with the Rebernicks (and others?), through which they got sex slaves, and she got 15% of their foster-care payments.

It was a sweet deal for everybody but the kids. Pridy got free money, the Rebernicks got their rocks off, and if the girls complained, Pridy buried the complaint. Or maybe assisted in their 'suicide' or disappearance.

How did she get away with it? By picking girls like Susan who had no relatives or friends to turn to.

COMMENT For all I know, the Rebernicks were victims of just this sort of abuse in their own childhoods. Maybe they were unable to control their own actions and deserve some sympathy. But Mia Pridy deserves only pain and suffering. She was no pervert who couldn't control her actions, she was a greedy bitch who sold children into slavery and death simply to pad her bank account.

What I wanted more than anything else as I left the Rebernicks' house that Friday evening, was to find Mia Pridy and kill her as slowly and painfully as I could. If she'd been the last name on my list, I might even have done that, not caring what happened to me as long as she paid for what she'd done to my sister. But to do it without planning almost guaranteed that I'd get caught. Until ex-Corrections Officer Rick Wood was dead, I wanted to stay alive and free, and that meant not being stupid about Mia Pridy.

So, I extended my visit to LA, staying through much of the next week, mixing work at The Primal Urge with work on my own project—gathering intelligence about Mia Pridy.

ACTION PLAN

Background: Pridy is retired, lives by herself in a small house in the Rosemont area. She is fairly active, walking her dog in the neighborhood, and working in her garden. She has a moderately active social life—she went out three nights during the week I observed her.

Getting into her house may be more difficult, because it is not fenced off, so middle of the night is probably the only option.

Action: Given her activities, she will probably be missed fairly quickly, so I will have to get away quickly and carefully.

Middle of the night it was. With what I'd learned in prison, breaking into her house was easy enough, so the only problem was getting to and from it in the middle of the night without getting nine-elevened by some nosy insomniac neighbor.

She may have heard something as I came in, or maybe she was just insomniac herself, because she was half-awake when I got to her bedroom. Not enough to cause any problem, but I was glad it hadn't taken me any longer to find her.

I sapped her gently, then stripped her, gagged her, and tied her to the bed. When she started bringing things into focus again, we began our chat. There was only one thing I wanted to know:

"I know about the deal you had with the Rebernicks. Who else was there?"

She was surprisingly tough for someone who'd never lived the hard life, but I'd learned so much about pain that there was never any question that she wouldn't talk. Once she had given me the names of the two other foster families that she'd supplied sex toys to, there really wasn't much left for us to talk about. I explained that what I was really there for was to make her suffer as much as possible until I killed her.

"You said you'd let me go if I told you."

"I lied." I tied the gag back on, then thumbed open my knife and let her see the wickedly serrated blade.

Her eyes nearly bugged out of her head, and she started struggling, not just in fear, but as if trying to tell me something.

I let the knifepoint rest against her stomach, but didn't press. Then loosened the gag. Almost before it was out, she was whispering, "I can pay you. Let me go. I'll pay you." I didn't say anything, just let her feel the knife move slightly.

"I've got money hidden. Let me go and I'll give it to you." Stupid woman.

Half an hour later I was well away from her house. She was dead and I had the fourteen grand that she kept stashed in the kitchen, in a teapot of all the stupid places. I also had the names she had given me, although I wasn't entirely sure what I'd do about them.

Pridy made the news the next day. All the newscasts were full of "the brutal sex slaying of an elderly woman."

She may have been over sixty, but she hadn't seemed 'elderly'. Maybe it made for a better headline. The sex part was one hundred percent wrong too, but I was pleased that they'd bought it. I'd worked hard to make her death look like the work of some kind of psycho-rapist. The cum they'd find in her wasn't mine, but it was real cum—it's easy enough to find a used condom in the back alleys of Los Angeles—and the pain she'd felt was real enough, even if there was no sexual motive in the mutilation.

Quite a different story from the Rebernicks, who hadn't been found for almost a week. Which maybe says something about how many friends they had, and how much of an impact old Dan made at work.

The cop that was interviewed on the news said, "We have several good leads and expect to apprehend the sick bastard that did this before he can strike again."

'Good leads' my ass. There were *no* leads, and he knew it. No thread of my clothing, no fingerprints nor footmarks, and no trace of my hair, flesh, or bodily fluids was going to be found in either Mia Pridy's house or the Rebernicks'. Likewise, no trace of them or their blood would ever be found on me. The clothes I'd worn, including the gloves, hairnet, the plastic bags that went over my shoes, and the Spyderco were all in a dumpster a dozen miles away, and would soon be lost forever in a landfill.

Motive? My connection with these people was buried over twenty years in the past and was indirect at best. No, I was safe. Knowing the LAPD, they'd find someone to arrest and convict, but it wasn't going to be me.

Which left one more score to settle ...

Subject: Rick Wood, now living under the name Donald Livingstone

Crimes: Rape, torture and murder of inmates while he was chief CO at Folsom.

Sentence: Death with extreme pain.

DETAILS

Address: 41573 Lincoln Road, Monroe, WA

Current age: Fifty-something

Occupation: Retired, although he's probably involved in something ugly

Marital status: Unknown

CASE HISTORY

[SOURCE: Firsthand personal knowledge.]

A violent and sadistic sexual predator who took advantage of his position in the judicial system to make Folsoma living Hell for anyone who crossed his path or aroused his passion.

"Hey Paul!"

"What's up?" He was bent over some woman's bare back, inking a Celtic design just above her right shoulder blade.

"Gotta talk to ya. Got some ideas."

"Sure. I'll be done here in about fifteen."

We went for coffee and I explained my plan for adding piercing to the business. "It's popular. Tats are popular. The people who go for one usually go for the other. Why not hire a good piercer for each of the shops? Or at least for LA, Oakland, and probably Seattle. Don't know if Portland's got enough demand for that kind of thing."

I slurped my cappuccino. Just one more thing that hadn't been part of my life in prison. "I visited a couple of shops in LA that do that, and man, they are turning business away. Ditto in San Francisco."

"So, what'll it take?"

We talked money and plans for a bit, and he agreed that the first thing was for me to get my ass up north and check out the piercing scenes in Portland and Seattle.

Portland's an okay sort of place. Not a lot happening there, but kind of pleasant. Relaxing. The kind of place that ordinary people like to raise kids in. Seattle is a different story entirely. It's got that same kind of reputation, the 'great place to raise a family' rep, but the reality is a little different. It may be a great place for families, or parts of it may be, but it's also got a dark side. Rough trade walks the streets, and whatever you want in the way of sexual or chemical stimulation is easily available if you know where to go. Probably one of the reasons ex-Corrections Officer Rick Wood had moved to the area.

After what I'd gone through in the first two years in Folsom, my appetite for kinky sex was nonexistent. My idea of great sex was me and one woman. It also usually involved a hotel room and a couple hundred dollars, but it satisfied me, and what more can you ask than that? As to chemicals, I'd learned a long time ago that alcohol was stronger than me, so other than the odd beer or glass of wine, I didn't touch the stuff. Ditto for drugs. Fifteen years in the joint had given me plenty of opportunity to observe the ugly side of drug use. Smoking a reefer a couple of times a year was all the chemical stimulation I needed.

This was my third trip to Seattle though, and I'd learned a lot from the guys at the shop, so even though I didn't fish in that side of the pond myself, I could tell you all about it. And about the music scene, which I did take part in. Clubs everywhere. Any kind of music you could think of, including plenty of my kind of sound.

Once business was out of the way, and I'd satisfied my music jones, I got down to the real purpose of my trip north. I bought a Washington State Gazetteer and sat down in my hotel room to plot a route to 41573 Lincoln Road, Monroe, WA.

Soon it would be time for Rick Wood to pay the devil his due.

Back in Oakland a few days later I finished filling out Chapter 3 of my Blue Book.

ACTION PLAN

Background: Wood lives near Monroe, about half an hour east of Seattle. He must have made a ton of money in the joint, because he's bought himself an acreage and a fancy house in some expensive-looking country. And I was right about him wanting to be near Seattle. I followed him in one night and watched him pick up a couple of boys to take back to Monroe. I bet he's got a dungeon in the basement!

The house is isolated enough that I'll be able to deal with him without worrying about nosy neighbors, and if he's bringing his joy-boys home, then he probably doesn't have a wife or kids.

Action: The first problem will be the dogs. Don't know what kind they are, but there's two of them and they both look big enough to rip me to shreds and mean enough to enjoy doing it. A pistol with a silencer is probably the answer.

Knowing Wood, the place is going to be fully alarmed, so breaking in is not an option, even after the dogs are dealt with. Best bet is probably to wait till he's home alone, walk up and ring the doorbell at ten in the morning, or catch him in the yard.

"Mornin' Todd."

I was on my second cappuccino at The Roastery, just down the block from the Oakland Primal Urge.

"Hey Paul, how's it going?"

"Real good. Hang on, I'll get myself a jolt and join you."

When he came back to the table he said, "So how did it go in Portland

and Seattle?"

"Portland's probably not gonna work, but Seattle's definitely ripe for it—every second person you see on the street has about eight piercings. In fact, the guys in the shop were going to suggest it to you. They've even got somebody in mind."

"What about money?"

We went over the budgets I'd prepared, and in the end, he said, "What the fuck do I know? You're the brains in this organization; if you think it's a good plan, then go for it. Go back up to Seattle and set it up."

Music to my ears.

Conclusion: Sentence carried out. Rick Wood will kill and rape no more. The world is a safer and better place, but I have more work to do.

Is it possible for one man to make retribution for the misery of many? Retired Corrections Officer Rick Wood died a painful, slow death; but did that really make up for all the deaths and misery he had caused? If only it could have.

No amount of suffering that I could impose on him would make up for the lives he had ruined or ended, **nothing** could make up for that, but what I learned while killing him may help me save a lot of others.

It went like this...

I left Seattle a little after five on Saturday morning, and got to the side road that led to his house just before six. I parked my car out of sight and eased up to the fence that surrounded his house. The dogs came running, barking loud enough to wake the dead, and I dealt with them as quickly as I could, then hopped the fence and ran for the porch, flattening myself beside the door.

I heard him coming downstairs, heard him muttering, "What the fuck are you guys barking at?" The footsteps stopped and I could hear the beeping sound of the alarm being deactivated, and then the lock turning.

When the door was halfway open, I launched into it with my whole weight, smashing him between it and the frame, then yanked it back open and kicked the gun he'd dropped out of reach.

"Why, it's Officer Wood." He staggered, clawing the doorframe. "Fancy meeting you here. What a surprise!"

"Black!" The scars on my face make me easy to recognize, and he'd put quite a few of them there himself.

"What the fuck did you do to my dogs, you shitlicking cunt?" If I was him, I'd have tried to dive back into the house, maybe get a door between us, go for the telephone, or grabbed something to use as a weapon, but all he could think of was what I'd done to his dogs.

He took a swing, but it was a long time since I was a helpless sixteen-year-old for him to do with as he pleased, and I caught his hand, twisted it a bit, and broke one of his fingers.

"*Aaowww*!" He jumped back, sort of cuddling the finger. "You shit-eating little cocksucker, you are *dead*. Ya hear me, Black? You're fucking dead."

He didn't seem to understand that the script had been changed since we last met, so I gave him a shot in the solar plexus, sapped him into semiconsciousness, cuffed him to the stair railing, and took a quick look around for the best room for him and me to party.

When he finally came to, he was strung up pretty much the same way I'd strung up the Rebernicks. Feet just touching the ground, and arms tied to separate weight machines, naked. We were in his basement, in the fully equipped iron gym he'd installed there.

I lit a smoke. "Sorry to drop in on you like this, but I kinda thought that if I asked for an invitation, you'd just say no."

"Go fuck yourself."

"Hey, that's no way to talk to your old prison pal."

"Eat shit, pillow biter."

A whirling heel kick to the left quadriceps shut him up. Another to the right quad left him unable to do much with his legs.

"We got all day, and all night Wood, and I've got a lot of questions. You can answer them straight up, or we can do it the slow, painful way." I let him think about it while I opened the pack I'd brought with me and pulled out the little butane torch. "Me? I'd rather do it the hard way, but it's up to you."

I turned the knob until we could hear the hiss of gas, then pulled out my lighter and lit the torch.

"What do you want?" He was finally starting to understand.

"What do you think I want? I want to see how long I can stretch out the pain before you die, but I do have a couple of questions to ask along the way." Wood wasn't some overweight cash register repairman who'd shit himself at the first touch of pain, and he'd know that nothing he could do would stop me from killing him in the end. He'd hold out as long as he could.

That turned out to be almost an hour. Pretty impressive, in a way. But he was only human, and in the end, he started talking.

It was quite a party. Not much drinking and dancing, but plenty of conversation. We talked about money, and about the ways he had found to make it and hide it since he left the California Corrections Department. We talked about his preference for fucking young boys, and how he found out where to get them. We talked about the other people he knew who used children for sexual gratification.

I took notes and prodded him with helpful questions when he seemed to have run out of things to say. Eventually though, all my questions had been answered and it was time to leave. I blinded him, poked out his eardrums, cut off his tongue and his dick, severed enough tendons to make sure he couldn't get out of the room, and went up to where I'd left the dogs.

He thought I'd killed the dogs, but he was wrong about that. The tranquilizer gun had worked just like it was supposed to, and they were both unconscious, but still alive. I'd looked them up in a dog book after my first visit. Rottweilers. Big fuckers that must have weighed close to a hundred and thirty pounds each.

I carried them down to the basement, left them in the weight room with the thing that was flopping around on the floor, and closed the door behind me. He'd thought I was going to kill him, but he was wrong about that too. I didn't have to. The dogs would do it for me when they got hungry enough.

* * *

I tore out the pages on the Rebernicks, Mia Pridy, and Wood and tossed them into the fire. There were fifteen more names in the book. All people who had taken part in the ruination of the lives of children. Some were like the Rebernicks; people who got their rocks off abusing children. A few were like Mia Pridy; soulless ghouls who provided children to these perverts. And some were dealers who sold drugs to children and lured them into the dark world of pornography.

Mia Pridy had given me the names of two couples with whom she had the same kind of arrangement that she'd had with the Rebernicks. Wood had given up the names of two pimps in Seattle, who ran stables of kids.

He'd also told me all about the drug dealing and kiddie porn that he was involved in, how he laundered the money he made, and where he kept the stash of cash waiting to go to the laundry. Over fifty grand that had been, in a small wall safe in his bedroom.

* * *

I was restless. So much death. I put the book down, took my cup to the sink and rinsed it. The storm outside was easing off and I went out on the porch. The wind was still wild, but there wasn't much rain coming down, and I could see stars to the north. Looked like tomorrow would be a good day for a ride. And maybe some company.

"Matt."

"Yeah, man."

"You got any big plans for tomorrow?"

"Got a job to finish in the morning, but nothing else. Why?"

"If the storm clears, are you up for a ride? Maybe up into the mountains? Catch us some trout?"

"Storm's already cleared up here. So sure, a ride would be good. Not before lunch though. Promised a guy I'd have his car running by lunch."

"Great. I'll come by the garage around noon."

"See ya then."

I hung up the phone and tossed more wood into the stove. A ride might blow the memories of those evil days out of my mind. At least for a while. Tonight though, I was into those memories big time. I picked the blue binder up again and began reading.

CHAPTER SEVENTEEN

My work for The Primal Urge let me travel up and down the coast from LA to Seattle, and I spent the next eighteen months following the leads that Pridy and Wood had given me, then the leads that those leads gave me, until I was sick of blood, sick of pain, sick of death.

I'd like to say that I hated it. That killing nineteen people had been an almost impossible thing for me to do, that I couldn't sleep, that I must have been insane... But I can't say any of those things. Oh, I had some unhappy moments, but I never once doubted that what I was doing was not only right, but necessary.

America, and I guess most other 'civilized' countries, has done a pretty good job for eighty or so percent of its people. They've got good lives and are better off than any other time or place in history, but somehow the other twenty percent have fallen through the cracks. They live in poverty, filth, and ruin. No government—not federal, not state, not city—really cares about them. They're there, they suffer through unhappy lives, and everybody else pretends they don't exist.

The young ones are easy targets for predators. No one cares if they live or die, no one even notices if they disappear. A woman like Mia Pridy can ruin dozens of lives. A man like Wood can ruin hundreds.

I killed nineteen people, but I saved thousands. That didn't make it fun, but I never questioned the rightness or wrongness of it.

In the end, it even made me wealthy. Three of the people I took out were drug dealers. Two of them had stashes like Wood had, but the third was about to leave for a major buy when I got him. He had two-and-a-half million in a suitcase in the trunk of his car.

I hadn't really had to use much of it. I made a good living working for Paul and Johnny, I didn't have any appetite for drugs or fast cars, and I don't gamble, so it was now in a suitcase under my bed.

All of it except for the amount I'd spent on false IDs. Two separate sets of full IDs; credit cards, driver's licenses, passports—the works. It had cost me over a hundred grand, but Warren the Walker said they were all good enough to get me through US Customs or through any police Driver's License check.

He'd told me something else, too, in his roundabout way; something that made me believe that he was giving me the straight goods on the quality of the ID.

"What the fuck you need two sets of ID for, man?" Warren had asked. "I mean, what the fuck you need *any* bent ID for? I thought you said you was walkin the straight line now."

"Yeah, well, you never know."

He smiled and offered me a beer, which I turned down, and a smoke, which I took.

"You been tellin' stories to old Warren, aintcha?" He was about twice my age, of indeterminate race, and had the rep of being able to get anything you asked for. Anything.

"You asked for info about those chickenhawks, those Rubberneck scumbags, or whatever their name was, and a couple months later they are not just dead, but real *messy* dead." He nodded his head slowly a couple of times and took a pull on his beer. "Good riddance, and nobody's gonna hear nothing about it from me." He held out his hands, in loose fists, and shook them gently. "I had a stepdad like that after my real dad died, so you get no grief from me."

It's an endless fucking circle of violence, that passes from generation to generation. I wondered if Warren would have wound up selling insurance or autoparts instead of guns, intelligence, and forgeries if he hadn't had that stepfather.

"What I'm sayin' here is that I understand why you might need to change your name one of these days, and I want you to know that the paper you get from me is going to be fuckin' first class paper. If the ID I give you says you are Charlie Smith, then there ain't no police nowhere going to be able to prove you ain't."

I didn't really expect to need the ID, but having it was a comfort. Somebody, in a police department somewhere, had to have noticed that there was a common thread connecting a lot of deaths up and down the west coast in the last two years.

I'd been careful. I'd covered my tracks, I'd planted false evidence, I'd tried to leave no trace of myself, but cops are nothing if not tenacious, and there are a *lot* of them. All it would take would be one slip and I'd have myself a ticket to the stainless-steel ride. The big jab. Lethal injection.

If I ever did find myself on the run, I wouldn't get far as Todd Black, cop-killer and ex-con. But for now at least, I had come to rest. Here in Montana I could live as Todd Black the ex-writer. The quiet guy who rented the Deborcier's cabin up at Flatbed Lake. You know, the one with the old motorbike, and the scars that make him look pretty tough, but who's always willing to lend a hand if you need help.

No more killing for Todd Black.

PART IV

CHAPTER EIGHTEEN

Matt had his head under the hood of an ancient-looking car. Something that would probably have looked old even before I went into the joint. He didn't hear me coming, and when I gave him snap in the ass with a rag that was lying on his tool tray, he jumped in surprise, only to bang his head on the hood above him.

"*Ahh fuck*!"

"Hey Matt! How's it going?"

"Pretty good till you got here, ya dumb fuck! Is that how you always greet your friends?"

"Yup," I replied.

"Wouldn't want to be your enemy then, would I?"

"No, I don't think anyone would. You hungry Matt? I'm buying!"

"You're gonna have to if you want to get back on my good side."

"Alright. Deal." I looked at the car he'd been working on. I don't know much about cars, but it looked about as old as I was, only not as badly scarred up. "So, what are you working on here?"

"You know Pete? Pete Transky? I think I introduced you to him once."

I had a vague memory of a guy about Matt's age who dressed like a country singer. "The cowboy?"

"Yeah, that's the guy." Matt was wiping himself clean and putting tools away. "He got this old Ford from his dad. I think it belonged to his granddad. Anyway, it got driven for twenty-some years, and then parked in the old guy's garage for the last ten or so. He asked me if I could restore it, get it running smooth and looking good."

I closed the hood, which felt like it weighed about fifty pounds. "Jesus. They used to put real metal in these things!"

"Yeah, not like that plastic crap they make today!" He spat. "Cars they're making now are designed for eight-point-five years of use and then you're supposed to buy another one."

He walked over to the clean-up stand and lathered up with cleansing gel, continuing his sermon as he scrubbed.

"You take one of these vintage cars, an old Mustang say, or a Plymouth Valiant. Those babies weren't designed for eight-point-five years. They were made to last indefinitely. They were made with solid steel and engines that would go five-hundred thousand miles. It was a different way of thinking, man—seriously!"

Matt paused to look over at the old Ford, shook his head and said "C'mon, let's get outta here and get some vittles. You ever eat at Greasy Joe's?"

Greasy Joe's turned out to be anything but greasy. The two women that ran the place were obvious lesbians, the full dyke variety, but when I asked Matt what he made of them, he said, "The way they cook, they could fuck green reptiles from Mars for all I care."

Half an hour later, I'd decided that, for food like that, I'd go to Mars and *get* the green reptiles if they wanted me to. "That was probably the best meal I've ever had."

Matt burped. "Yeah, and it's like that every day. I don't know where they learned to cook, but I plan to move there when I find out."

"Maybe I'll come with you." I signaled for the bill. "But not today. Today we're going riding. Pack your fishing gear and your sleeping bag and let's hit the road." I patted my full belly. "Let's catch a whole mess of trout and bring 'em down and give 'em to the lezzies here, let them cook 'em up for us."

* * *

"Look at that sky, man, just look at it. You ever see that many stars?"

We were lying on our backs, wrapped up in our sleeping bags, on the shore of a lake just below tree line. Yesterday's storm had left the air crystal clear, and at our altitude in northern Montana, the night sky was like nothing I'd ever seen.

Matt seemed to like it. "Makes ya realize this old earth isn't such a bad place." If only he knew. "You ever think about what might be out there?"

"Whaddaya mean? Like aliens or something?"

"No. Well, not exactly. I mean, how many stars are there? A million or something?"

"Shit, way more than that. Billions."

"Right. So, do you ever wonder if there aren't planets like this one around some of those stars? If there are really that many stars, then for sure there's gotta be some of them that have planets we could live on. Planets that weren't as messed up as this one."

"Huh?" Matt was surprised. "Messed up? You some kind of greenpeacer?"

"No man, I mean the people. Living out here in Montana the way you do, you have got just *no* idea what kind of people are walking the streets of LA. Or any other big city for that matter."

Matt leaned up on one elbow and looked at me. "You sound kind of bitter, man. You run into someone unpleasant?"

I liked Matt. In fact, I thought of him as a friend, but there are some things that you don't go into even with your friends, so I just said, "Yeah, a few. Enough to make me appreciate it out here, that's for sure."

The women at Greasy Joe's were surprised when we showed up the next afternoon with a pile of fresh trout.

"No, they're a gift." Matt tried to explain. "You two cook the best food either of us has ever eaten, so we just figured you'd do a better job than we could with these babies."

They looked at each other, then at us. Finally, one of them said, "Okay, Matt. Thanks. We'll put them on the menu tonight, and you guys eat free."

I laughed. "That's what we were hoping to hear."

We left the restaurant and headed back toward Matt's garage.

"You're a lucky man, Matt."

"Hmm? What do you mean?"

"Living here. This is heaven." I waved my hand indicating the town, the surrounding country, the mountains above. "You have no idea how lucky you were to grow up in a place like this."

"Yeah, I suppose." He was thoughtful. "I guess I don't think about it much. I mean, I was born here, grew up here, went to school here…" He pointed to a school yard we were approaching. "That's where I went to school."

The playground was full of kids, running, laughing, playing games.

"Pretty good school, I think. Or at least I liked it. I guess I had a couple of dorky teachers, but then, who doesn't?" He laughed. "You probably had some loser teachers too."

"Yeah, I guess I did."

"I sometimes wish I was a kid, back in school again." He pointed to the children goofing off in the playground. "Remember what it was like? No worries, no problems, nothing to do but have fun?"

Fuck. I wish.

We turned and cut through the forest behind the school, taking a shortcut to the garage. Neither of us was speaking, which is probably why the two kids that were hiding behind the Atco trailer at the end of the playground didn't notice us approach. That, and the fact that they were pretty much occupied with each other. Or with what was in each other's pants to be more precise.

Matt gave me a nudge and whispered, "Hey man, look at that. Coupla kids behind the barn sneaking feels. Reminds me of..." He stopped dead as he realized what I'd known from the moment I saw them. "Jesus H. Christ on a Harley! It's two **boys.**"

Welcome to the world, kid.

"This ain't right man, not here, not in this town!" Matt yelled.

The two of them looked up at us, and the blood just about froze in my veins. I knew that look. Oh, God, how I knew that look—not the guilty look of a couple of kids experimenting with their sexuality in a homophobic world, but the dead-eyed 'I don't care' look of the abused.

I slapped Matt on the arm to shut him up and tugged him further into the trees, away from the boys' view. Matt looked hurt and confused that I had hit him.

"They're kids, man, just kids. They couldn't be more than eleven years old." He rubbed his arm where I'd whacked him. "That hurt, Todd. What's the matter with you?"

"Sorry Matt, I really didn't mean to hurt you, but there's a big problem here." I could feel the joy and relief of the last six months slipping away.

"I'll say there's a problem." He tried to see through the trees to where we'd left the boys. "I mean, Karen and Leslie at the Spoon, that's one thing. But they're adults. These guys were children."

"Someone has had a go with them, Matt, the signs are all there."

Silence between us, with Matt staring at me in bewilderment. What to tell him?

"Matt, you only know me as a writer, but I've also done a lot of work with disturbed and abused children, and I can recognize the signs a mile away."

"In this town?"

"Any town, Matt."

"But who?"

"Not you, and not me. Other than that, you'll never know."

"But I grew up here, man. I *know* everybody in this town."

"Not as well as you think. Someone here is getting his rocks off poking it to young boys."

"Jesus." He grabbed my shoulder. "Shouldn't we do something? Report it to the police or something?" He was clearly shaken.

"How do you know it isn't one of the cops who's doing it?"

"*What*? A cop? Are you nuts?"

"It happens. Believe me, it happens." I pulled out my smokes, lit two, and gave him one. "Can I ask you a favor, Matt?"

"Huh?"

"Put what you saw in the back shelf of your mind, and let it go."

"But we've gotta do *something.*"

"Something will get done, but you aren't going to be involved in it." I squared off to face him and put a hand on each of his shoulders. "Matt, there are a lot of things that you don't know about me. Things that you don't even *want* to know. One of those things is that I know how to deal with the kind of sick fuck that abuses kids."

He looked at me like I was from Mars.

"You gotta believe me, Matt. You are way out of your depth in this, and you don't want to know *anything* more about it. Just believe me when I say that I know what I'm doing, and that I've got those kids' interest at heart."

He didn't have a clue what I was talking about, but he could tell I was serious, and he believed me. "Okay. And you know something?"

"What?"

"I don't think I'd want to be that guy when you caught up to him."

"You wouldn't." Maybe he did have a clue.

When we got back to his garage, I rolled out my bike. "I'm heading down to the cabin. I'll be back here either tonight or tomorrow morning, but I'm not going to be very good company, for you or for anyone; so, if I see you and ignore you, don't worry about it." I mounted up and kicked the starter. "And if you see me, just ignore me, okay?"

He took my hand and shook it, slapping me on the shoulder with his other hand. "Be careful, Todd."

"I always am."

For the first time since Matt had brought it back from Georgia for me, the bike gave me no pleasure. I rode from Kalispell to my cabin without really feeling the wind in my hair or noticing anything around me. My mind was crawling with snakes, and life had gone from joyous to bleak. Back at the cabin, I did what I had to do. Packed the things that I'd need for an indefinite stay in Kalispell plus the things I'd need for dealing with whoever had gotten to the two boys, closed the place up, and was back on my bike within half an hour.

But I had only ridden for ten minutes when I had to stop. I didn't want to do this. I'd sworn six months ago that I'd never do this again. Nineteen deaths in two years was too much. I pulled the bike off the road and scrambled down through the trees to the edge of the lake. No beach to speak of, but no people and no houses, either. I found a boulder that jutted out into the water and sat down on it.

'Go back to the cabin.' I said to myself. 'Go back to the cabin, go for a swim, cook some supper, drink some of that wine you've been saving, and go to bed.'

I don't know how long I sat there. A minute? An hour? No idea. As long as it took to convince myself that I should forget what I'd seen and go home.

With that thought firmly in mind, I stood up and was about to head back up to my bike when I glanced down and saw my reflection in the still water. All those scars. I'd been a kid once, with no scars, and no snakes in my mind. I knew that unless someone rescued the two kids I'd seen this afternoon, they'd wind up with scars just as bad as mine.

It was dark when I got to Kalispell. I left the bike behind Matt's garage and started walking toward the forested area behind the school. It was probably another beautiful starry night, but I wasn't noticing that. I was in full predator mode, and the night sky was only relevant insofar as there was no moon, and therefore not much chance of anyone seeing me once I was off the street.

That trailer the kids had been hiding behind. It had had an abandoned look about it. Would it do as an observation post? I shone my Maglite into a window. Desk, chairs, table, hotplate, and coffee pot. Papers strewn over the desk and table, tools and hardhats lying around. Definitely in use for something—maybe a construction office for an addition to the school. So, I kept prowling, and eventually lucked out across the road from the other side of the school where I found a gas station with a big "Closed Permanently. Moved to 15th Street" sign in the window.

The back door was easy, and soon I was looking through the front window at the deserted schoolyard across the street.

There was a bathroom with running water, an enclosed office where I could hunker down out of sight, and plenty of room to bring in the bike. If I opened the office door a bit, I could see the school, but no one could see me. The place stank, and it didn't look like my comfort level was going to be too high, but other than that it was a perfect observation post. I checked my watch. Eight thirty-five. Time to get my bike and get to the Safeway and do some food shopping before it shut. If I hurried.

The first morning was about what I expected. Teachers arriving early, kids arriving singly and in groups, the older ones walking, the little ones being dropped off by parents. From nine till ten-thirty I didn't see any activity except for one kid running in late, then the playground exploded with kids out for their morning recess.

It wasn't hard to pick out the two we'd seen the day before. They were picking on younger boys, and I wondered if I was going to be in time to break the cycle of abuse that had obviously started, or whether I was already too late. How much had they been put through? No way to know.

I spotted one other likely victim as well. A boy, about a year younger than the first two, who sat by himself on a swing set meant for kindergarten kids. Not swinging, not smiling or interacting, just staring at his feet. Withdrawn from everyone—trying to get away—just as I had been, just as my sister had been. Maybe he'd simply had a bad morning. If I didn't know about the other two, I probably wouldn't have thought twice about him, but knowing that there was an abuser active, I assumed the worst.

Most of the kids went home for lunch and returned by one o'clock. The ones who returned early played on the schoolground, under the supervision of a couple of teachers. In the afternoon two of the classes came out for P.E.

At three o'clock they all burst out again, some heading home, some staying to play, including the two I'd been watching. None of the teachers approached them, nor did any of the adults who had come to pick up other children. I wondered if it was their parents, or a sitter, or a neighborhood "uncle." If it was, then I'd have to find out where they lived and do some reconnaissance in their neighborhood.

Eventually all the kids were gone, and the last teacher had driven away. A man who I assumed to be the school janitor carried several wastebaskets out and emptied them into the dumpster and returned to the school. A few minutes later he came out, locked up, and walked over to a small building that I'd assumed was an extra classroom, or maybe a woodworking shop. He unlocked it, went in, and didn't come out again.

Shit. If the janitor lived on the grounds, I would have to be a lot more careful skulking around at night. And I needed something to keep me occupied during the day. Another day of watching a schoolyard that was empty half the time and I'd go nuts.

I eased out the back door and walked down the alley that ran behind the garage, coming out at the other end of the block, on the street that Greasy Joe's was on. I was tempted to head straight there for supper, but I wanted to get to the local mall before the bookstore closed, so that I'd have something to read in the days to come.

I made it just in time, arriving just as the woman who worked there was about to close up. "Can you stay open long enough for me to buy up a couple of books?"

She looked me up and down. My scarred face usually made people wince, but she didn't seem bothered. "Sure, no problem. I'm not exactly late for anything."

"Thanks, I'll try not to take much time." Clever, Todd. Well, *you* spend fifteen years in prison and see how aware of pickup lines *you* are.

I walked around, but I was worried about keeping her too long, so of course I couldn't keep my mind on what was on the shelves in front of me.

"Are you looking for anything in particular?"

I hadn't heard her walk up behind me. I turned around and actually noticed her for the first time. Short, compact body, long reddish-brown hair, great smile, and amazing tits.

She followed my gaze to her chest, then looked back up at me. I gave her the 'OK, you got me' look, and she surprised me by laughing.

"Interests other than female anatomy, that is?"

"Umm, out-of-the-ordinary fiction, revenge, survival, sex, you know..."

She led me across the room and pulled a book off a shelf. "This novel just came out from Australia. It is called **Davo's Little Something,** by a writer named Robert Barrett. You'll find revenge in it in spades!"

"Okay, I'll take it, but I want at least one more. Maybe something nonfiction." I thought for a minute. "I know. A friend of mine was in the S.A.S., a British Army Regiment. He used to tell me stories about it. Would you have any books on that?"

She handed me the first book and said, "I don't know, but if we do, it would be in the military section." She led me to another aisle. "Here, have a look."

I spent a couple of minutes looking and found not one, but two books on the Special Air Service. "I'll take them both plus this one."

As we walked toward the cash register, she looked over her shoulder at me. "I haven't seen you in here before. Are you new, or just passing through?"

I couldn't believe it. A good-looking woman actually talking to me. "Uh, neither really. I live down on..." I was about to say that I lived on the lake, in the Deborcier cabin, but old habits die hard. "... Down in Missoula. I'm just up this way camping and wanted to take a couple of books along in case the fish aren't biting."

She rang up the books, and I worked up some courage. "I'll probably be passing through on my way back. I could look you up if you wanted."

She stopped what she was doing, and I was sure I'd blown it. "Uh, I'm sorry, I didn't mean to upset you or anything..."

"Hey, it's okay, I was thinking about asking you." She smiled. "When will you be back?" Shit. What to say. What day was it? Thursday?

"Well, I'll probably camp for a couple of days, then come back in on Saturday, maybe grab a meal at Greasy Joe's and then, depending on the weather, either head back south or go do some more fishing. Would you like to have supper with me?"

"Sure, sounds like fun." She finished ringing up the sale. "Tell you what. You give me a call when you get into town. I'm off at noon on Saturday, and if I've got the time and the energy, I'll cook something up for us. If not, well, Greasy Joe's is pretty good." She wrote something on the receipt and handed it to me.

"Julie. 673-8188." I read it aloud.

"That's me. What about you. You have a name?"

"Todd." I stuck out my hand. "Todd Black."

"Well, Todd Black, you have fun camping, and don't forget to come back Saturday night." **Whooeee!** I think I floated most of the way back to the garage. A date. Thirty-five years old, and I was going to go out on my first date. An actual date with a real woman. God damn.

CHAPTER NINETEEN

I slept soundly that night in my observation post. I had to jerk off first, but I did sleep soundly.

I awoke at sunrise and cleaned myself up as best I could in the bathroom sink, then set about cooking some breakfast—ham omelet from a boil-and-serve package. Once I'd eaten and cleaned up the pot, I pulled out one of the books I'd bought the night before, the novel by the Australian guy, and started reading.

Interesting book, with some parallels to my own situation. It's a story about a guy, an ordinary guy, who was beaten into a coma because he and a gay friend had stumbled onto a group of white power skinheads who were breaking into the gay friend's car. When he wakes up from the coma, he finds he's developed extraordinary senses, so he hones his fighting skills, then starts hunting down and killing the skinheads who attacked him. I didn't have anything against skins, but I could sympathize with his situation.

Movement outside caught my eye. The janitor arrived first, checking into his workshop, or whatever it was, then opening the school. After that it was pretty much a repeat of the day before.

Cars arrived and mothers and fathers got out and escorted the kids into the schoolyard. There were a couple of grandparents too, but none of them was flying any of the flags I was looking for. Same for the teachers. All I was getting was quick looks, so it was possible that any one of them could be involved, but they weren't advertising it.

The rest of the day passed reasonably quickly, mostly thanks to the book, and soon enough it was three and the kids were flying out the door and heading home for the weekend. A few stayed and played in the schoolyard, but not many. Among those that did was the kid I'd seen on the swing set the first day. He didn't join in the games, just hung around by himself, and through my binoculars I could see that he wasn't really aware of what was going on around him.

Maybe it was his father, or stepfather, that was doing him, and he just didn't want to go home.

Ten minutes later I had my answer. The janitor came out, looked around, and walked over to the little guy. He didn't touch him, and I couldn't hear what they were saying, but I didn't have to—their body language told me everything I needed to know.

Now what? Follow him home? In a small town like this where there wasn't much traffic, following him would be easy, but with my scarred-up face and my motorcycle, he'd almost surely notice. Even if he didn't, someone else might, and then when he turned up dead… I decided that it made more sense to break into the school tonight. Surely his name and address would be in the principal's office, and once I had those, I could make an intelligent plan.

So, I read, cooked and ate supper, washed up, read some more, and then went to sleep with my alarm set for two-thirty.

The school was easy. Finding his name and address in the mess that the principal called an office was harder, but eventually I struck oil.

Herbert Jansen. 14121 Aspen Road. The address didn't mean anything to me, other than it sounded kind of rural, but that was a problem that would be easy enough to solve in the morning once I picked up a city map.

The next step was the outbuilding that he used. I wanted a look into his custodial office, or workshop, or whatever it was, but here I struck out. Oh, I could have got in. With what I'd learned in prison, I could get into pretty much any building, anywhere. No, the problem was that I couldn't get in without leaving some obvious evidence. The place had only two windows, and they were both covered with metal mesh—probably to keep them from being broken by stray baseballs—and the door was heavy, solid wood, secured with a big deadbolt and hinged from the inside.

Cold rage was building inside of me, and I wanted to rip off one of the screens and smash in a window, or get on my bike and roar out to Aspen Road, wherever the fuck *that* was, and break every bone in his body. I fought hard to control myself, and eventually calmed down. Herbert Jansen would pay for what he had done to the children. He would pay with his life. But not tonight. With that thought firmly in my mind, I returned to my squat in the abandoned garage and crawled back into my sleeping bag.

I slept till ten and woke up feeling dirty and used. I had come here to escape this sort of thing. This was not supposed to happen here. A mixture of anger and sadness overwhelmed me, and the only thing I could think of to cleanse myself was to get on my bike and ride as fast and as far as I could.

Three hours later I was at a lake high in the mountains. I'd walked the last half mile in on a trail that was too rough for the bike, and when I got to the shore, I stripped off all my clothes and dove in. The freezing water overwhelmed me and drove everything out of my mind. I stood it as long as I could, then laid on a rock and let the sun dry me while I watched big, fluffy clouds sail past and thought of nothing at all.

I stayed on the rock for a couple of hours, at first with my mind empty, then trying to think of a way out—report the guy to the local law, write a letter to a newspaper—but in the end, I knew that no one else was going to deal with it if I didn't. The kids probably wouldn't testify, and if they did, it could ruin their lives. The guy would wind up with a wrist slap and move on and do the same thing in some other town. No, like it or not, this was my task.

I dressed, hiked back to my bike, and headed toward Kalispell, stopping at every gas station I passed until I found one that had a street map of the Kalispell area, one that would show me where Aspen Road was. When I opened my wallet to get the money to pay for it though, the first thing I saw was a bookstore receipt with "Julie 673-8188" written on it.

Shit. I was supposed to be coming back from my "camping trip" today and having supper with her tonight. I paid for the map and went outside and sat on the curb. Was there any point in even calling her? Wasn't it my duty to keep my mind focused on my job?

I looked at the map. No sign of Aspen Road. Not listed in the street index either. Nothing to do but follow him home on Monday as carefully as I could. Which meant either sitting around eating my liver for the rest of the weekend, or going through with my supper plan, hoping that I could at least pretend to be human for a few hours.

"Hello, is Julie there please?"

"Speaking."

"Hi, it's Todd, the guy you kept the bookstore open late for."

"Hey, Todd, good to hear from you. How was the fishing?"

Fishing? What the fuck was she talking about? Then I remembered the story I'd told her. "Oh, well, actually I wound up not doing any fishing. Just hanging out and hiking and reading. How about you?"

"Things are pretty good with me. Are we still on for tonight?" Her voice was doing things to me. Or to part of me anyway.

"Well, that's why I'm calling. I'm still a few miles out of town, and I'll need a bit of time to clean up, but I'm up for it if you still are."

"You bet. I'll start cooking, you just come over whenever you're ready."

"Cooking? Fantastic. See you in about an hour."

I hung up, feeling like maybe a night with this woman was exactly what I needed. I'd drop in on Matt, beg a shower and then head over to her place and…

"Uh, hi Julie, it's me, Todd, again. Um, where do you live?" Bonehead.

She lived in an old, Victorian-style house, right in the middle of town, and at 7:30 p.m. I was knocking on her door.

"Hi Todd." She was wearing a sexy sundress, and I wanted her instantly.

"You look great, Julie," I said, trying not to be too obvious about staring into her wonderful cleavage.

"Thanks, come on in."

"Wow, what a great place." I looked around. The house was spacious and airy. Hardwood floor, high ceilings, leaded glass windows, decorative moldings, big winding staircase to the upper floors. Much too big for a clerk in a bookstore to afford.

"It *is* great, isn't it? We really love it." Whoops.

"We?"

"Oh, I share it with a couple of other girls." She paused and then smiled at me. "Don't worry, I've sent them away for the night."

Well, well, well.

"Are you hungry?" She asked.

"Famished."

"Good to hear. Come on the kitchen and have a drink while I finish the salad."

She carried the conversation through supper, keeping it light and a bit suggestive. She'd made a chicken potpie, which was simple and delicious, and she offered apple pie for dessert.

"It's store bought. I do chicken pie, but I don't do apple pie."

"Hey, no worries. You've already done wonders for me." I picked up our plates and carried them to the sink, and on my way back stopped behind her, looking past her, out the window toward a view of the sun going down over the mountains. "That was a great supper, Julie."

She tilted her head back and looked at me without speaking for a couple of seconds, then reached up and pulled me down toward her, and kissed me deeply.

With our mouths locked together, I slid my hands under the shoulders of her dress and eased it down, then let my hands slide back up over those perfect breasts, rolling the nipples gently between thumb and finger.

Her nipples stiffened into little rocks and she moaned, deep in her throat, then broke free and stood up, letting the dress slide to the floor.

There was nothing under it and she pulled my head down, down, until I was kneeling in front of her, pulling her lips apart, and tonguing her. Then pulling me to my feet and mashing her mouth into mine, licking her own sweet juices from my lips.

And that was just the beginning. She was on fire with something halfway between lust and love. What I mean is that she'd been so horny for so long that she was ready to screw anything that moved, but at the same time, she was picky, and didn't want to give herself to someone that she didn't like. For whatever reason, she'd taken a shine to me, much as I had to her, and we spent the next eight hours in an all-out sexual marathon.

It was all new to me. Except for Bernie, so many years ago, my sexual experience was limited to hookers, and even Bernie had been a hooker. Or at least an apprentice hooker. Julie took me to places that I didn't know existed, taught me things I could never have imagined.

We both knew it was a one-nighter. Oh, sure, we probably thought that we'd do it again sometime, if I ever passed through town again, but we weren't fooling ourselves about it. We'd clicked, we'd helped each other make the world a less lonely place for one night, and the future would take care of itself.

We never did get around to the apple pie...

At four-thirty she finally fell asleep. I lay beside her for a while longer, wanting nothing more than to fall asleep beside her, and wake up to make love again in the morning, but the meter was running out on at least three young lives, and I was the only one who could do what needed to be done. As quietly as I could, I got out of bed and covered her up, took a shower downstairs, got dressed and let myself out the door.

I'd left my bike behind Matt's autobody shop but walking back to my squat that morning as the sun rose was a wonderful, sad, pleasure. Julie had opened a door in me that had been closed since I was eight. Shown me that there was joy in this world, that people can be good and kind to each other. I knew that I would taste that pleasure again, but I also knew that I would never be free to enjoy it fully.

I had seen too much. I knew too much. I had lived for so long on the dark side that the darkness would haunt me as long as I breathed. Still, the morning was cool and clear, autumn smells were in the air, and up in the mountain lakes, trout would be rising to feed. I promised myself that I would pack my fishing gear and go visit those trout as soon as I was done here.

The first order of business, though, was to get some sleep. Once I'd done that, I could look for a better map, and then see about arranging a personal visit with Herbert Jansen. I watched the schoolyard as I passed it, wondering if I should check out the custodian's office on the off chance that he'd left it unlocked. Who knew what he might keep in there? Maybe something that the police would be interested in knowing about after they discovered his body.

I firmly believed that police, especially local police, were a lot less likely to put real effort into a murder investigation if they knew that the deader was a child molester, or a child pornographer, or a dealer of drugs to children, and I made sure that there was as much evidence of that kind of thing as possible around the corpses I'd left behind me.

I started across the grounds, then realized that there was a light on in the building. And a car parked in front of it. Jesus. Was he in there?

I about-faced, ran to my squat, and grabbed the little pack with the tools of my trade in it. Could I do it now? I looked at my watch. Six o'clock on Sunday morning. No traffic, no people, dawn just breaking… What were the chances of anyone coming to the door of a school custodian's office at this time?

I hadn't had time to plan anything, and planning is what had kept me safe through nineteen killings, but this was a golden, God-given opportunity. I thought of the faces of the three boys I knew he was using, and my decision made itself.

Go. Don't ask questions, just go. Do it.

Thirty seconds later I was silently testing his door. Locked. Well, I'd expected that. I knocked.

Something crashed. I'd probably startled the shit out of him, and he'd knocked over a cup or something. Then there was a shuffling and, "What is it?"

"Hi. Mr. Jansen is it? I'm Bill Thompson, the substitute who's taking the Seventh-Grade class this week. I left my briefcase here on Friday and when I noticed your light on, I thought I'd take a chance and knock on your door, to see if you could let me in to the school to get it."

He grumbled about 'did I know what time it was?' but the fact was that he was up, and he could hardly refuse to walk thirty feet across to the school door for me, and he finally said, "Oh, alright, hang on while I get my keys."

Yeah, and get your pants back up, and hide whatever porn you were jerking off to. I waited, heard rustling inside, then steps approaching the door. As soon as it was open enough for me to be sure that this was the guy I'd seen with the kid, I pushed in, drilled him in the solar plexus, and had the door closed and locked before he finished collapsing onto the floor.

I cuffed one of his hands to the doorknob, leaned down and whispered in his ear, "If you make one sound, just one, I will cut your nuts off. Do you understand? I'll slice off your cock and balls and shove them down your throat." I flicked my Spyderco open under his eyes and repeated, "Do you understand?"

He could hardly breathe, but he nodded his head violently up and down.

I took a quick look around. The place was divided into two rooms. The small front one that we were in now, and a larger one that was obviously his workshop. Nothing fancy, just the basic equipment and tools to allow him to build and repair whatever was needed around the school.

And on the little desk that he'd been sitting in front of when I knocked were half a dozen Polaroids. Pictures of boys mostly, fondling their own dicks, but also two in which he co-starred, one showing him riding a kid from behind, the other with the kid sucking his dick. I picked that one up and walked over to him.

"You know what this is?" He didn't know what to say, what kind of answer I wanted. "What it is, you animal, is your death warrant."

His eyes went wide and he tensed, ready to scream for help, but I was way ahead of him, with a boot to the chest cutting off all sound.

I had a syringe in my pack. I had enough smack to kill a horse. I knew that I had to shoot him up and make his death look like an accidental overdose. If I left him in the chair with the spike still in his arm and those pictures spread on the desk in front of him, no cop was going to look any further. In fact, if a cop did spot something not quite right, he'd probably take one look at the pictures and decide that "Death by Suicide" was the only sane way to close the case.

I knew all that.

But I lost control. I made the mistake of looking again at the picture in my hand and that was it. I drove a boot straight into the middle of his face, breaking his nose. There was no way this soul-destroyer was going to float out gently on a needle full of smack.

Rage flooded through me and my next boot burst an eyeball.

I don't really remember much after that. When I came to my senses and looked at my watch, I realized that I'd been there over an hour. There was blood everywhere, and Jansen was still alive, barely, and pretty much beyond pain. I hunted around till I found a broom. I didn't bother greasing it, because by that time his asshole was slippery with blood anyway; just eased it in, then pushed. And kept on pushing, feeling things rip and tear, until he convulsed uncontrollably and died. I think the broom handle had ruptured his heart.

Once I was certain he was dead, I threw the tools I'd used back into my pack, took a quick look around to make sure I hadn't left anything that could be traced to me, then ran across the street to my squat in the garage, hoping that no one saw me in the few seconds I was on the road.

Jesus Christ! The bathroom mirror showed me a picture from the ninth circle of Hell. I was bathed in blood, and the cold rage in my eyes would have petrified the devil himself. With that vision of myself, the bloodlust of the last hour released me from its hold and my gut spasmed uncontrollably, dropping me to my knees, vomiting what was left of last night's supper onto the floor.

For a while I lay there in my own rancid spew, not caring, not knowing where, or even who, I was.

Eventually I came to my senses.

"Oh Todd, oh Todd, oh Todd. You fucked up big time with this one."

I peeled off my clothes, using my shirt to wipe up as much of the barf as

I could, rinsing it down the sink. With a T-shirt and tap water I wiped myself as clean as possible, then put on fresh clothes and stuffed all the bloody things into my large backpack.

Now what? There was probably evidence of my presence smeared all over the janitor's shop. How could I have been so fucking stupid? I took a deep breath. "Okay, Todd, think." I said out loud. "You wore gloves. At least you did that." What else? "C'mon Todd, what else?"

But really, there wasn't anything else. They might get a footprint in the blood, but the shoe that had made it was in my pack and would soon be disappearing from human sight. No doubt there was a hair or two, some dandruff, some flakes of skin, but they would be lost among the tons of other bits of human debris that was bound to be floating around the place.

And what cop was going to push it anyway? They'd almost surely believe it had to be one of the parents, and the parents would all have alibis, and shit, the cops probably had kids themselves, so how far were they going to push it?

I'd been incredibly stupid, but it looked like I might luck out anyway. As long as I got the hell out of town fast. I looked at my watch. Seven-fifteen. Ten minutes to pack everything up, five minutes to look around as carefully as possible, wiping whatever I could think of that might hold a fingerprint; then I was easing the bike out the back door and rolling it quietly to the end of the alley. When I was sure there was no traffic coming in either direction, I kicked the engine to life and got my ass out of Kalispell.

Back at the cabin I stripped off all my clothes, grabbed soap and shampoo and dove into the lake. It was bone-chillingly cold, but I didn't care. I scrubbed and lathered and scrubbed and lathered, over and over. When I was sure that I was as clean as I was going to get, I went inside and rinsed off in a warm shower, dressed in clean clothes from my bureau and put the stuff I'd stripped off in the pack with the bloody stuff.

What to do with it? Burn it? Bury it? Take it down to Missoula and drop it in a dumpster? The pack had to go too, and it was big enough that it could attract attention when the dumpster was emptied, so that meant a hike into the mountains to find a safe place to burn it all.

It was at that point that I realized that even though no one had seen me going to or from the janitor's shop, I had left a witness behind. I ran for the phone.

205

CHAPTER TWENTY

"Hello."

"Matt, it's Todd."

"Hey man, how are you? Get lucky last night?" Lucky? Oh, right, my date with Julie.

"Matt, is anybody there with you?"

"Huh? No, just me and this plate of beans and toast. What's up?"

"That kind of depends on you, bro. Sometime in the next day or so you're going to find out that I didn't spend the whole night with Julie, and when you do, you're going to have to make a choice."

"Whoa, you lost me on the last turn. Say it again."

"You heard me. You're going to have to make a choice tomorrow, and what you choose is going to affect me."

"You been smokin' weed again?"

"Matt, this isn't funny. This is deadly serious, and I don't want to talk about it on the phone. You'll know exactly what I mean soon enough."

I think my urgency finally got through to him. "Okay. What do you want me to do?"

"Just one thing. It's all I can ask without putting you in a bind. If you decide to make the choice that affects me, then give me a day's warning, okay? Will you promise me that?"

"Of course. You in trouble, dude?"

"Depends on you, Matt. Depends on you."

I tossed a can of the white gas that I used in my little stove into the pack with the soiled clothes, strapped my camp shovel on the outside, and headed uphill.

Two hours later I found what I was looking for. A hollow in the forest with plenty of dry wood, and well out of sight of civilization. I scraped away all the topsoil and built a fire. Once it was roaring hot, I soaked the clothes in the white gas and tossed them in, one article at a time, finishing with the pack itself. I stayed there, feeding the fire, for two more hours, till there was nothing left but ash. Using dirt, and water from a nearby stream, I made sure the fire was completely out, covered it back over with the topsoil, then set off downhill, barely making it back to the cabin before dark.

I slept well that night. I'd covered my tracks well, and the rest was up to Matt. Sometime in the morning they'd discover the janitor's body, and then all hell would break loose. With a little luck, the cops would see the pictures right away, and keep the whole thing as quiet as they could, but it wouldn't take long for the word to spread, and sometime during the day Matt was going to find out. He'd been pretty upset at the idea that someone had molested the kids, and we were friends, so I didn't think he'd turn me in, but I had no way to know for sure.

Maybe I ought to run. Take no chances. Use one of the sets of ID that I'd spent so much on. Sure, and while I was at it, why not kill Matt to make sure he couldn't tell any tales.

No. I was done with running. I'd only been here six months, but this was my home—the only place that had felt like home since I was eight years old. And Matt was my friend. If my friend was going to send me on the stainless-steel ride, then what was the point in living anyway?

On that thought, I fell asleep and didn't wake up till almost noon, when the phone rang. "*Urnnhh?*"

"Todd? Is that you?"

"Umm. Yeah. Just waking up."

"Oh, sorry, man, but I heard the news while I was having breakfast at Joe's and thought I'd better call you."

So. Now I'd find out.

"I don't know all the details, but from what I do hear, the guy was fucking kids, so whatever happened to him is exactly what he deserved. Go back to sleep and don't worry about me."

"Thanks, brother. I owe you."

"You don't owe me. Everybody around here owes *you*."

I was about to hang up when he said, "Listen, when this settles for you, I mean, when you feel up for it, give me a call and we'll go get some more trout for the girls down at Greasy Joe's. You missed a good feed that night, and they said they'd be happy to do it again."

"Deal."

But I doubted that it would be that simple. There'd been no time to be thorough in my clean-up of the abandoned garage. There would be bloodstains, bits of barf, no doubt some fingerprints if they looked hard enough. The question was how hard the cops would push it. Eventually they'd realize that it wasn't a parent, or a teacher, or anyone else with a personal involvement. When that happened, they'd have to decide whether or not they really wanted to find out who killed someone that was better off dead.

If they did, then I wanted to be prepared. I wanted to be able to hit the road with zero notice the instant I felt that I was in any danger. So, I got on the bike and headed south for Missoula to make some preparations.

I visited the Deborciers and laid a year's rent on them. Told them I liked the place and that I'd be happy to stay there indefinitely, but that I wanted to be sure that I could go away for a couple of months whenever I felt like it without having to worry about them renting the place out while I was gone.

Then I hit a department store to replace the stuff I'd burned and pick up some extra clothes that would see me through the winter at the cabin. Last stop was the biggest outdoor store in town where I replaced my pack and my knife, picked up a supply of dehydrated food, more fuel for my stove, and some better camping and hiking clothes. Matt told me I didn't owe him anything, but I got him a new fly rod that I knew he'd been dreaming of for a long time, along with a reel. I hoped that if I ever got real serious about fishing, that I had plenty of money left—that rod and reel set me back over two grand.

It was dark by then, and the Deborciers had told me I was welcome to stay at their place, but I really didn't want to be around people, so I made the night drive back to the cabin, and settled in for another good sleep.

I had no remorse about killing Jansen. I'd settled that issue in my mind long ago, and what the police did was out of my hands. I dreamed of Julie.

Two days later Matt and I were pulling fish out of a lake high in the mountains. He was ecstatic about the rod and reel, and he'd accepted the fact that, beyond a bare outline, he'd never know much more about my past than he already did.

"Todd, it's okay. It really is. The man I know came to this town six months ago, and every day that I've known him, he's shown himself to be the kind of friend that I really want."

"Thanks."

"No, really. I've seen you helping people out of a ditch when it was raining and you could have ridden on home to your woodstove. I've seen you go out of your way to be helpful and polite a dozen times, and I know that if I was ever in trouble, you'd be there for me." He threw an arm around my shoulder and gave me a good thump on the back.

"You're no more a writer from LA than I am, but I've known that for months, and accepted it, so don't worry about trying to keep your stories straight with me. When the time comes to tell me, you'll know, and you'll tell me. Till then, I'm cool with it if you are."

And that was that. He honestly accepted me for what I was and didn't care what I'd been.

We camped and fished for three days, then headed down into town with a cooler-full for the girls at Joe's, and the next morning they fed us a breakfast of trout almandine. I don't have any idea what trout almandine actually is, but whatever it is, it sure does make a great breakfast. At nine-thirty we were walking back to Matt's place with nothing more on our minds than when we should go fishing next, when the Red Alert bulb started flashing in my head.

Suits. The town was crawling with suits. Okay, okay, in Kalispell, where nobody wears anything but jeans, it only took a few of them to make it seem like the place was infested; but even two or three meant that the local police had called in the pros.

Fuck. Fuck, fuck, fuck.

Matt started to draw my attention to them, but I cooled him. "Just keep walking."

"Huh?"

"Matt, it's big-city cops. I can tell a cop at a thousand yards, and these guys are just across the street. They're cops, they're here to take over the murder investigation, and that means I gotta hit the road."

"Right now?"

"Soon as we get to your place, I'm outta here."

"Hey, you don't have to run. I'm not gonna tell them anything."

"No, I don't expect you will. But that won't stop them. Those guys aren't from Montana, and if the federal government has stepped into this, then we are dealing with a kind of cop that you don't know anything about."

We'd passed out of their sight, around a corner, and I stopped and turned to him.

"Listen, there are only two people who know I was in town that night, one is you, the other is Julie, and Julie has no idea that I stopped at your place, or that I even know you. She can spill everything she knows to the feds, and all that'll give them is that I arrived at her place for supper and left again sometime after four-thirty when she fell asleep."

"But how would they even know to ask her?"

"In a small place like this? Get real, that's the first thing they're going to do, ask around to see if anybody noticed any strangers hanging around. Now listen. If they ever do find out about me being here, they'll eventually come to you, because they'll find out we're friends. All you've got to do is tell them that I left here on Thursday, to go fishing somewhere. That's what Julie will have told them, and there's no reason that they'll think you're lying. You're clear and safe."

"Okay, man. I'm with you all the way. And if it looks like they're getting anywhere, I'll call you as soon as I hear about it."

"Do that. But not in those words. If you want to tell me that you think they're on to me, just tell me… lemme think… Yeah. Tell me that you've heard the fishing is really good at some lake to the east and suggest that we go wet some flies. Can you do it that way?"

"Sure, no problem."

"Good. I'll tell you that I can't go, cuz I'm headed down to Missoula or something, and you'll be clear."

"And you can get away? Are you sure you'll be okay?"

"It's what I do, Matt. Don't worry about me."

Four days later I was sitting on the porch, reading one of the S.A.S. books I'd bought from Julie when the phone rang.

"Hey, Todd, how are ya?"

"Doin' fine Matt, what's up?"

"Well, I just talked to a guy who came down from Sawtooth Lake, you know, out to the east, and he said the fish were just about jumping into his net. You wanna go get some?"

"Oh, shit. I'd love to, but I told Doug I'd meet him in Missoula day after tomorrow, so I can't go till the weekend at the earliest. Would that suit you?"

"Sure. Have a safe trip to Missoula and see you soon."
"You bet bro."

PART V

MATT'S STORY

It's funny, I guess I figured out that Todd wasn't a writer almost as soon as I met him. Kalispell, Montana isn't exactly the center of the universe, but I've met a couple of writers, and I've read a fair bit about writing, even attended some writing seminars myself, and Todd just wasn't even close. I didn't know what he was hiding, but it was obvious that the whole writing thing was just a cover for something else. I didn't know what, but he was definitely playing his cards close to his vest. I mean, I've worked on engine blocks that showed more emotion than he did.

And then there were the scars. We never talked about them, but it was pretty clear that his face had been used by people who didn't like him a whole lot. He radiated this air of controlled violence that would have scared the shit out of me if there hadn't been something else coming from him at the same time.

I'm not sure how to describe it. Vulnerability maybe. A sense that he was lost and looking for a way back home. Not that the feeling of violence wasn't real, just that there was more to him than that.

My mom didn't pick all of it up, but then she operates on some strange wavelength of her own and picked up enough to satisfy her. Maybe the maternal thing enabled her to tell that he was really a child who needed help, and not a man to be feared. Or not by her anyway.

She bought the writer story, but I think she believed that he'd been in some kind of tragic accident, and that she could help him. She gets off on that. Helping people who are in tragic circumstances. Kind of like being in her own romance novel or something, I guess.

So anyway, when I got that long letter from him, I thought that his story needed to be told, and I rewrote it as well as I could.

People think that child abuse has finally been dealt with. That because somebody can go on Oprah and talk about how their daddy diddled them, that the problem is almost over. I guess I thought that way too, but after reading what Todd wrote me, I realized that the Talk Show thing is as far as most people want to think.

That even while we prosecute the odd child molester, there's no slowdown in the amount that goes unknown and unpunished. Getting Todd's story published could really rip the lid off and make people understand that we've got a long way to go.

One problem with what he sent me though, was that he took off before he knew how the FBI had got onto him so fast after he killed that sicko who was porking the little boys—Jansen, the janitor at the school.

So, I'll add what I learned afterwards to the story, writing it like a crime novel.

* * *

Metros Makrides was staring at the picture on his desk. It was the usual thing: the picture of spouse and kid, that sits on ten million office desks around the world. This one showed a blond woman of about forty, with her arm around the shoulder of a ten-year-old boy. Both squinting into the sun and standing on a small dock, with a boat behind them and what looked like a cottage in the background.

The usual thing, but after what he had just finished reading, it was special and precious in a way that it had never been before.

As head of the FBI task force on serial killers, Makrides had seen the aftermath of hundreds of killings, so it wasn't the gruesome nature of the deaths he'd just read about that disturbed him, but the thought of what the victims had done to bring about those deaths.

How could people do that to children? What kind of person could use a child for his own sexual gratification? Could sell a child into prostitution or sexual slavery? Could sell hard drugs to a child?

Whoever was putting these people away, no matter what kind of psycho he was, was doing the world a service, and for the first time, Makrides questioned his desire to bring a serial killer to justice. But to let even one get away with murder was to open a door that he believed must never be opened. He picked up the phone on his desk and dialed.

"Trevor. It's Metros… Yeah, not bad. Listen, I've got something here that I want you to look at… No, it's one you probably don't know about. Hawkins over at LAPD homicide put it together, and it's new to me too. He was looking at similarities in several killings in the LA area when he heard about one in Seattle that was almost the same, and since then he's found another three or four more up and down the west coast."

He listened for a few moments then said, "Yeah, me too, but he's giving it to us. I guess he's got enough on his plate without this and probably figures that the chances of catching the guy are so slim that he'd rather have us take the heat from the press than him ... Sure. Ten minutes. I'll be here."

Two days later Trevor Avey was back in Makrides' office. He dropped the stack of reports on Makrides' desk and sat down.

"So?" Makrides asked.

"Hawkins had seven. Two days, and I've got three more." Avey stood up again. "You want a coffee? I'm going to go down to the Cafeteria and get one."

"Sure. Black."

Five minutes later they were both drinking their coffees and going over the stack of paper that Avey had dumped on the desk.

"See, look at this one. Portland. And another here in LA, and one in the Bay Area. All of them within the last eighteen months." He prodded the papers with a finger. "I've put Powell and Santiago to work on it, and I'll bet they turn up a few more. Our boy gets around."

"Yeah, and he seems to know more about who's poking it to kids than the child protection agencies do."

"Maybe he's in the welfare or child protection game himself. Sees these abuses going unreported and unpunished and decides to play judge, jury, and executioner all by himself."

"That's pretty much what I thought at first, but I'm not so sure now. If that were the case, you wouldn't expect this kind of spread. They'd all be within one jurisdiction. Or at least in one metro area, LA, or in the Bay area, or whatever. What kind of social worker knows who's selling kids into sex slavery in foster homes in LA, *and* who's pushing drugs on schoolgrounds in Seattle?"

They both stared at the folders on the desk, then Avey said, "A fed of some kind? But I don't really know of any federal agency that would have all that data."

Silence. They both knew the probable answer, but neither wanted to be the first to say it. Finally, Makrides spoke. "We're probably looking at a cop here, Trevor. Who else has access to this kind of information?"

"Yeah, I know. Or a group of two or three cops. Shit." Avey pulled a notepad and pen out of his briefcase. "Okay, I'll summarize what we know and email it to Powell and Santiago, with a copy to you. Give them a day to digest it, and then the four of us can meet on Thursday morning."

* * *

"Let's deal with the facts first, and then we can start in on the theories." Avey put the first of the overheads he'd prepared onto the projector and the four of them got down to work.

One by one they went through the details of twelve grisly murders. Dates, times, places, forensics, investigating officers' reports. When the tenth overhead came off the projector, Makrides spoke.

"You saw most of this in the emails Trevor sent you. He and I have prepared more material—the conclusions that we've drawn—but before he puts it up, I'd like to hear your thoughts." He turned to Powell. "Helen?"

"Pretty obvious that they're all connected, but what I can't figure out is how anybody could know so much about who's abusing kids over such a wide geographical area." Helen Powell was a tall woman, lean and strong, with an odd combination of young-looking facial features and very gray hair.

"I mean, if some sicko is looking for runaways, or prostitutes, or middle-aged gay businessmen to kill, it's pretty easy to find them in any city. But who would know that..." she riffled through the stack of paper in front of her "...that Maria and Dan Rebernick were abusing foster kids in LA, and also that..." more paper shuffling "... Annette Allison was procuring sub-teen boys for porn films in Seattle?"

She leaned back in her chair and scratched her head. "That is just not the kind of thing that you can drop into a bar and find out for the price of a couple of beers. Somebody has put a lot of intelligence work into this." She turned to her partner, "Rafe?"

Raphael Santiago didn't say anything for quite a long time. No surprise there, because he hardly ever said anything at all. When he finally spoke, it was short and to the point. "Helen's right. One or two bits of this information could fall into anybody's lap, but very few people could gather it all. I'm not even sure we need a profiler on this one. Just figure out who could possibly gather this information and we'll be knocking on his door twenty minutes later." He stopped abruptly, then added, "I don't mean to imply that it'll be easy to figure out how someone could get this kind of data, just that I think that's the way to approach it."

Makrides spoke up for the first time in the meeting. "Why no profiler, Rafe?"

"Oh, I think we can profile this one pretty well ourselves, sir." Santiago shrugged his broad shoulders. "I certainly don't **object** to having one in, but I suspect we can profile this guy pretty accurately. Look at the kills. Every one of them was perfect. There hasn't been a single shred of evidence left behind, and that's with a dozen kills investigated by the three biggest homicide departments on the west coast, and…" He waggled a finger to emphasize his point, "… and, he knows how to kill, how to do recon, how to inflict pain, how to break and enter. This guy is a stone professional."

"A hitman? You're saying someone's hired a hitman for this?"

"No, not at all. Most hit guys can't kill a mosquito without leaving a ton of evidence. No, what I mean is that this guy has had some **real** training somewhere along the line. CIA, Secret Service, Army Rangers. Something like that."

Makrides and Avey exchanged glances, and Avey spoke for both of them. "What about a police officer? That'd help explain how he knew about some of these people."

"I don't know about that, Trevor." It was Powell who answered. "A vice cop would probably know as much about this as anyone but cops just don't get the kind of training that this guy has. Not even SWAT guys get that kind…"

Avey interrupted. "True but think about this. FBI agents don't get that kind of training either; but Rafe here could do everything this guy's done, and he's an FBI agent." He turned to Santiago. "Right?"

"Yeah, sure, but I didn't **learn** that shit in the FBI."

"Exactly."

Makrides and Powell both looked puzzled.

"My friend here," Avey pointed at Santiago, "spent quite a few years in the US Army Rangers before joining the Bureau." He paused, trying to decide how to explain his point.

"Think about it this way. Suppose we had a guy who was killing serial killers the way our guy is killing child abusers. We figure he's gotta be in our task force, because we're the ones who have the knowledge; and we figure he's got to have Ranger or CIA training in order to do the kills the way he does." He looked at the other three. "Who does that leave us?"

"Yeah, right, me," said Santiago.

"So, you're saying let's look for vice cops with Ranger training?" Powell asked.

"Not necessarily vice cops, and not necessarily Ranger training, but that's definitely the idea. Let's figure out what kind of person could have this extensive knowledge of the child-abuse scene, and what kind of person could have the training to do the kills this way, and then crossmatch 'em."

"And with the kills spread all over the west coast, we'll be able to eliminate just about everybody, because no one but our guy is going to have been in those cities at those times."

They worked on details for the next hour, and finally Makrides said "Alright, that's enough for today. Rafe, I want you to put together as complete a summary as you can of the training you think this guy had to have in order to do what he's done, and then give me a list of all the places where someone could get that kind of training.

"Helen," he turned to Powell, "you do the same kind of thing for the information end of it. Summarize all the kinds of information he'd have needed access to in order to know that these people were involved in the abuse of children—drugs, porn, sex-trade, whatever—then give me a list of the workplaces and occupations where that kind of info is available."

He stood and stretched, then turned to Avey. "Trevor, I want you to get onto every jurisdiction you can think of on the west coast, plus maybe the mountain states, and ask them to send in full details on any death of any person in any way connected with the abuse of children. I'll bet that we find a few more, and maybe somewhere along the line our guy will have slipped up and left us his calling card."

He picked up his notepad and pen, started to leave the meeting room. "Helen, Rafe, if you could get those reports to me by tomorrow afternoon, I'd appreciate it. Let's meet here again on Tuesday at three in the afternoon, that should be long enough to have some results in from Trevor's request for information."

They met again on Tuesday, and at least once a week for several months after that. They cross-checked the records of dozens of men, and a few women, who had both the training and the information required to make the kills. They investigated murders reported to them by police departments who had received Avey's request for information. They called in a profiler.

All to no avail.

"This is nuts." Avey was drinking coffee in Makrides' office early one Tuesday morning. "Either the guy has stopped killing, or he's dead. He'd already killed a dozen when Hawkins first noticed him, and he's done at least six since. In a two-year span we had almost twenty murders that fit, and in the last six months, nothing. Nada. Zip."

"You want to call it off?" Makrides pulled a folder from the tray on his desk. "I'll be happy to give this one to you if you think you're not going to get anywhere."

"Which one's that?"

"The corpses that have been turning up in pairs, wired together at the wrists and ankles."

"Yeah, I actually had a look at some of the files on that one, and I've got a couple of ideas that might be worth following up."

Makrides put the folder on his desk, unopened. "What about the child-abuser killer?"

"We've looked at every single one of those cases a hundred times. He didn't leave a single clue anywhere, in fact he deliberately planted false clues at some of the sites, and we are not one step closer to him now than we were when we started. And on top of that, he's stopped killing. Not one in almost six months. It's almost like the guy was doing a job, and now the job's done and he's disappeared back into the woodwork."

Avey leaned over the desk and picked up the folder. "I think maybe it's time that we got on with the rest of our business too." He opened the folder and scanned a few pages. "Yeah, this one we've at least got a chance on."

"Okay, why don't you ... "

The door opened and both men swiveled to see who was interrupting.

"Trevor, Boss, sorry to barge in, but we've got a fresh one." It was Santiago, out of breath from taking three flights of stairs instead of waiting for an elevator. "I mean *real* fresh."

"Go on."

"I just got a call from a trooper in Kalispell, Montana. They found a guy dead in a room with drawers full of kiddie porn. Really savage death, fits perfectly. They found the body this morning, and it looks like the guy's been dead less than a day."

"Where the fuck is Kalispell?" Avey asked.

"I asked that myself. The trooper says it's a small city, maybe ten, twelve thousand, up near the Canadian border."

Avey tossed the folder back on Makrides' desk. "Looks like I won't have time for this today after all." He turned to Santiago. "Where's Helen?"

"She went for lunch just before this came in, but she should be back in about fifteen minutes."

"Right. Get on the phone. Get back to the trooper that called you and give him the standard drill, then organize a flight for the three of us to wherever is closest to Kalispell, and make sure there'll be a State cop with a fast car waiting for us at the airport. Get back to me as soon as you're done."

He turned to Makrides. "This is the first one outside of a major metropolitan area. If our guy's not a local, then someone will have noticed him. I'll question all twelve thousand of them myself if I have to."

Ten days later Trevor Avey was once again sitting across a desk from Metros Makrides. "Welcome back, Trevor. Did you bring me a killer?"

Avey pulled a slim binder out of his briefcase and dropped it on the desk. "He's in there. Name, description, photos, fingerprints, last known address, everything except the man himself."

Makrides made no move to open the folder. "You want to tell me about it?"

"Yeah, sure. We got lucky with flights and were in Kalispell by the evening of the day that Rafe got the call. Quite a pretty little town actually, mountains all around, forests, lakes, just like in a movie or something."

"Trevor."

"Yeah?"

"You ever been more than ten miles outside LA?"

"Sure. I've been to New York a couple of times, and I was up in both Seattle and San Francisco this spring looking for our guy. Why do you ask?"

"Never mind. Go on with the story."

"Right. First thing we did was go out to the crime scene. The corpse was the janitor at the local elementary school and from the photos he had in his filing cabinet, it's obvious he was fucking kids from the school. Mostly eight- to ten-year-olds, and all boys."

Makrides looked at the picture of his wife and ten-year-old son that sat on his desk, and shivered, despite the warmth of the office.

"He paid for it, boss." Avey had seen the glance. "The gory details are in my report, so I won't bother you with them right now; but believe me, he paid for it."

Makrides thanked God that his own son had never had to face something like that. "He may have paid, Trevor, but no matter how painfully he died, it doesn't wipe out what he did to the kids."

"No, it doesn't, but he won't be doing it again." They sat silent for a minute, then Avey pointed to the picture and said, "My daughter's four now, and my son is two. If I found out someone had done to one of them what this creep did to the kids in his school, I'd probably have killed him too."

"We all feel that way Trevor, but if we act on those feelings, are we any different than the people we're trying to put away? Some things are better left in the hands of the law."

"I've thought about that a lot in the last few days, and with respect sir, I just don't know. Look how many of the psychos that we pull in were already convicted of murder or rape and are out on parole. Or were charged and got off."

Makrides didn't say anything.

"Anyway, it turns out that the cops in that town are no dummies. They might not have the training that you'd get in LAPD Homicide, but at least they know how to preserve a crime scene. And they're a fair bit more polite than most of the LAPD Homicide guys I've had to deal with. Anyway, we put in a shitload of hard work, we had a little luck, and we now know that a man named Todd Black is our guy. Here's how it happened.

"The crime scene was exactly like all the others. A child abuser met a really painful and messy death, and there wasn't a single goddam clue in the place. We flew in an M.E. and a forensic team from Seattle and they didn't find anything that could help us. But my first hunch, about it being a small town and maybe somebody noticing something, paid off.

"First thing I figured is that our guy had to have been there for a while or he'd never have found out about Jansen ... "

"Who's Jansen?"

"Oh, sorry, that's the name of the janitor that was putting it to the kids. So, we asked around about people who were new to the area in the last few weeks or months and came up with a list of about a dozen names. We talked to some of them and were able to eliminate them right away, but there were a couple who we either couldn't find, or who we couldn't clear at first."

"Including this Todd Black?"

"Yeah, he was just a name at first, one more guy who'd moved to the area recently, but when I started checking it out, one thing after another just clicked into place. I'm actually kind of proud of us all on this one boss; I don't think there's very many teams you could have sent in there who would have got it."

Makrides stood up and said, "Well, I can't give you a medal, but I'm going to get myself a coffee and I could probably afford one for you, do you want one?"

"Sure."

When Makrides returned, Avey continued the story. "Like I said, there were three or four possibilities, but when we got a description of this Todd Black guy, Helen jumped on it. Clean cut, badly scarred from a lot of fights, pale skin, tattoos, kind of a loner ... "

"A con, right?"

"God damn, you're as fast as she is."

"Not as pretty though." Makrides felt good about guessing right. He hadn't been in the field for a long time. He missed it, and sometimes wondered if he still had the edge.

"Yeah, anyway, I made the next step, which was that I remembered a report we got from the Washington State Police in response to my request for information about dead child-abusers. It was something that we had a laugh about when we saw it, but thank God that someone up there in Washington had too much time on his hands one day, and sent it in."

Makrides tried to remember all the reports they'd received, but no lights flashed on in his mind.

"It wasn't a murder, which was why we never really considered it at the time, but as soon as Helen said 'I bet he's a con', it flashed back to me. It was some guy whose partial remains were found in his basement. He'd apparently been attacked and mostly eaten by his own dogs—two big Rottweilers I think it was.

"Anyway, the Washington people sent it down because it was a violent death, and they'd found a lot of kiddie porn in the guy's house. What triggered it for me was that they'd said the guy was a retired Corrections Officer from somewhere down here. I phoned in and got a couple of people here working on it, and guess what?"

"I bet that Todd Black was a con who took a dislike to a CO who wound up as dogfood."

"**Ding ding ding.** His name was Rick Wood, and he was the kind of guy who gives the Corrections Department the reputation it's got."

"And Black?"

"Black?" Avey stood and walked over to the window, not saying anything, just looking out into the sunshine. "Black, sir, is something else. I left Powell and Santiago up there to finish up the investigation, and flew back to Sacramento to see what I could find out about Black and Wood at Folsom, which was where Black did his time and Wood was the head screw." He fell silent again.

"And … ?"

"And all I've got to say is that you should pray that your name never comes up on Todd Black's list."

"That bad?"

"No sir, I don't think bad is the right word. I've spent the last three days going over everything I could find out about him, talking to people who did time with him, and if there's one thing he's not, it's bad. What he is though, is deadly. Remember what Santiago was talking about, all that stuff about Army Rangers?"

"Was Black in the Rangers before he got sent up?"

"Rangers? Hell, he was only sixteen when he went in, but he got taken under the protection of a guy called Ian Douglas who, according to anyone who'll say anything, is the deadliest thing that's ever walked on two legs. Douglas turns out to have been in the British S.A.S, which Santiago tells me is an outfit that makes the Rangers look like boy scouts."

225

"So, he got his Ranger training in the joint. Kind of ironic."

"I guess so. Anyway, I went back further and dug out his records as a kid. Guess what?"

"Abused?"

"You got it. His parents died when he was eight, and he spent the next eight years in foster homes, getting the shit kicked out of him. But the clincher, the absolute clincher, is that he had a sister who was also in foster care, and who died while living with a couple named Daniel and Maria Rebernick—the first known victims of our 'child-abuser killer.'"

"Jesus. You don't miss much do you."

"Neither does Santiago. He called this morning with hard evidence. Black's first slip-up in the eighteen kills we know of."

"What was it?"

"He got thinking about how our guy always seemed to have done homework on his victims. Knew their routines well enough to get to them at times when he wouldn't be disturbed, or when their bodies wouldn't be found for a while. So, he started thinking, how could the guy have spied on this janitor without being seen? I mean, he's a stranger, with a scarred-up face, so he can hardly hang around the school yard.

"So, Santiago cases the area and figures that the only place the guy could have used as an observation post is an abandoned gas station nearby, and sure enough, he got prints. The guy had cleaned up, but he must have been in a hurry, because he missed a couple of spots, and I just got confirmation from Sacramento that the prints Rafe lifted out of the gas station came from Todd Black's fingers."

Avey had forgotten about his coffee. He was still over by the window, and still mostly looking out into the sunshine. "I think I was right about him having stopped his killing spree six months ago. I think he took his revenge on the people who had abused him and his sister, plus a few other child abusers that he found out about along the way, and then retired. A couple of the people he hit were drug dealers, so he may have scored some cash along the way.

"Anyway, he'd been in Montana, living in a cabin by a lake about thirty miles from Kalispell for over six months. He had a reputation as a loner, but I also ran into a lot of people that he'd helped in small ways. You know, fixed a flat tire, did some shopping for them when they were sick, that kind of thing."

Avey walked back to the desk and picked up the picture of Makrides' wife and son. "I think he was a lot like you and me sir, or like we would have been if we'd been kicked in the teeth when we were young instead of raised in loving families. He got savaged by the system, took a savage payback, and then let it go."

He replaced the picture on the desk and returned to the window. "As far as I can find out, all he was interested in out there was camping and fishing and trying to leave his past behind him. My guess is that he stumbled onto this Jansen totally by accident, and just reverted to savagery. I also guess that he's probably in some small town in Nebraska now, or Maine, or Tennessee, and that he's not very likely to start up again."

He returned to the desk, picked up his briefcase and headed for the door. "It's all in my report, sir. Not really a job for us anymore. Just put out his description across the country and eventually some Sheriff's deputy will spot him." He opened the door but stopped before leaving.

"With your permission sir, I'm going to take the rest of the week off. I'm going to go home and spend some time with my kids. Maybe take them to a lake in the mountains somewhere and let them look at trees instead of cars and cement."

It took Metros Makrides over two hours to read everything in the binder, and when he finished, the building was empty, and the sun was going down. For a long time, he sat, almost still, moving only his hands as he held the picture of his family.

What would his son have become if he'd been born Todd Black? Finally, he picked up the phone and dialed a number he knew by heart.

"Hi princess. Sorry I'm a bit late, but I've been sitting here thinking that maybe I'll take the rest of the week off. Maybe next week too. Would you like to spend a couple of weeks up at the lake? Just the three of us?"

He smiled at whatever she said, hung up the phone, and, after staring at it for a long minute, put Avey's report in the bottom drawer of his filing cabinet, the drawer where he kept material that he felt he'd likely never look at again.

"Up to you now, Todd Black. Up to you."

HELP US

If you'd like to help us out please go back to where you ordered the book from online and put up your review with your comments. Let us know if you'd like to see this expanded into a series or not. We'd appreciate this very much and we look forward to reading your review. Thank you and have a great day!

OTHER BOOKS
BY SIMON WELLINGTON

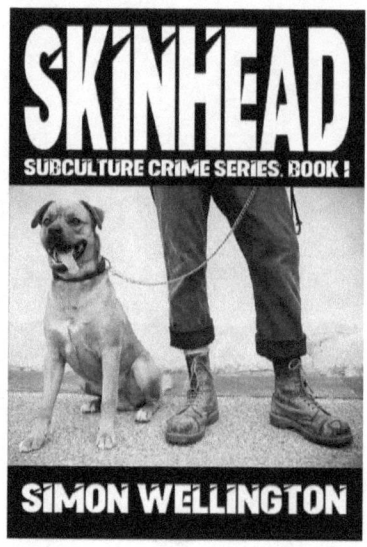

A Skinhead classic in the tradition of the great Richard Allen novels, and the first book written by Simon Wellington.

The Youth

Fighter, lover, musician; 18-year old Mark Heaney walks the skinhead path and faces trouble head on. He'll rumble if you cross him, he'll steal your girlfriend's heart if you're not careful, and as the lead singer of a ska/oi band known as the Juice Monkey's, he'll set your nightclub on fire with some great energy!

It all changes however, when Mark's father loses his job, and he has no choice but to join the army to help support his family. He leaves high school in the final year and is trained as a medic within the Canadian army. Later as his service time increases, Mark finds himself Para qualified and is attached to the Canadian Airborne Regiment. He sees action on battlefields and in bedrooms around the world until, six years later, he becomes a man in all senses of the word.

The Man

With his father dying after a tragic work site accident, Mark decides to return home to his home turf in order to assist his mother in raising the rest of the family. Working as an ambulance paramedic in Vancouver's skid row opens his eyes even further to life on the street. It helps to pay the bills to some degree but it's usually only a part time job that is incredibly stressful and thankless. The only consolation is meeting Terri Battle who is one of the pretty waitresses at his favourite venue and drinking spot - the Skavoovee Tavern. It's not long before Mark is working there himself as an assistant manager.

Skavoovee

It's the place where Terri works. It's where Mark's band got its first start. It's home to so many of the cities subcultures - including skinhead's, punk rocker's, and a host of other people that identify with the vibe of the place. Mark is proud to call it his second home.

But one night when a bunch of American Skinhead wannabe's try to cause trouble in the tavern, Mark makes a point to voice his displeasure and sends several of them to hospital.

In retaliation, the boneheads from down south make it a priority to get back at Mark by kidnapping his younger sister. The war has started. Will he and his commando friends survive?